MW01600444

Charlie's ANGLE

BY

JOHN PAUL MCKINNEY

This book is a work of fiction. Names, characters, places and incidents are products of the author's imagination or are used fictitiously. Any resemblance to actual events or locales or persons, living or dead, is entirely coincidental.

Copyright © 2013 John Paul McKinney
All rights reserved.
ISBN: 1491091894
ISBN-13: 9781491091890

Library of Congress Control Number: 2013914035
CreateSpace Independent Publishing Platform
North Charleston, South Carolina

DEDICATION

For Kathy,
My Ideal Reader;
in fact, My Ideal Everything.

Acknowledgments

A number of people have helped me in a variety of ways as I wrote this first novel. I wish to acknowledge their help here and to thank them. I apologize if I have forgotten someone.

- Etta Abrahams, professor emerita, American Thought and Language, Michigan State University, who first suggested years ago, when I was teaching psychology at MSU, that I write a novel and has since reviewed my work and encouraged me along the way
- Rosie Anderson, who really understands teaching high school
- Erin Cookman, who wrote a several page "book report" for me; thank you, Erin
- Gael Cookman, who read the story before Erin
- Cindy Geib, a retired principal who reviewed and commented on the entire manuscript
- Henry Gubler, a high-school classmate, who read and commented on an early draft
- Kristi Hickman, a harp teacher, who found time to critically review this story

- Dorean Koenig, Ph.B, J.D., an attorney and friend who clarified several legal issues for me
- Marty Loy, Dean of the College of Professional Studies, University of Wisconsin-Stevens Point, a former college wrestling champion and coach, who understands Charlie from multiple perspectives
- Kathy McKinney, my "IR," to whom this work is dedicated
- Mike Olkowski, who read the story from the perspective of a police officer
- Jim Waun, M.D., who read an early version and made many suggestions about medical issues
- Michael Winters, who read and commented on a very early version of this story
- Marie-Pier Winters-McKinney, who read the manuscript and made several suggestions
- John Paul Zawacki, who can read more in a day than most people do in a month

Others read sections, encouraged me in other ways, or explained things I didn't fully understand:
- Amanda Adams, who with an encyclopedic knowledge of infant heart syndromes encouraged me to get it right
- Jim Colbert, who knows wrestling and the language surrounding it
- Kerrie Flanagan and colleagues at Northern Colorado Writers, who know and support writing
- Teresa Funke, who is a superb writing coach
- Carol McKinney, RN, who told me with precision what a hospital room might look and smell like
- Tim Northburg, who introduced me to Create Space
- Lisa Péré, copy editor, who is way more than a copy editor
- Fran Wilson, Colorado State University bookstore, who believed in this from the beginning

- Sandra Zygarlicke, House Director at Ronald McDonald House of Marshfield, WI, who helped me understand the wonderful service they provide and described the facility to me

Finally, more than 130 people read the first chapter when it was posted online as part of a contest and kindly voted for my submission.

To all of you, THANK YOU. I hope you find this book worthy of your help, support, and encouragement. I take full responsibility for its flaws.

Pax et bonum

CHAPTER 1

The noise in the casino became louder and more raucous. Charlie Brannigan set his coffee down and looked up through the double doors that led to the black jack tables and slot machines. A scuffle had broken out. From the corner table in the restaurant of the Chippewa Nation of Wisconsin's White Deer Casino, he could just make out what appeared to be two employees wrestling someone to the floor.

Charlie and his wife, Katie, were finishing their strawberry cheesecake when their waiter—a young Native American in a white shirt, black vest, and bow tie—placed their check on the table. "Mr. Brannigan," the young man suggested, "if you're not gaming tonight, you may want to take our side door to the parking lot. We apologize but there's been a slight altercation in the casino."

The couple paid the bill, thanked the young waiter, and headed for the side door. As they were leaving the building, a loud crash, like a falling chandelier or an overturned cart full of glasses, came from the main room. The parking lot attendant was a student Charlie knew from the high school. From him, Charlie learned that the assailant in the casino was a regular who came in two or three times a week. Lately, he'd been overdrinking and becoming belligerent.

***

On Monday morning, as Charlie swung into the space marked "Principal" in the parking lot of Waumeka High School, he noticed a car pulling away from the front of the building. He'd seen the same car, a gold Thunderbird Super Coupe, just about every morning during the past week. At seven o'clock, it was too early for a parent to be dropping off a student.

Despite the early hour, he found the office manager, Tricia Cameron, already busy at her desk and on the telephone when he entered the outer office. She looked up, one hand over the mouthpiece of the phone, and said, "It's for you." When Charlie wrinkled his forehead in a questioning grimace, she whispered, "Mrs. Newsome."

"Lord, help us. What would the school board do without Catherine Newsome," he mumbled, shaking his head and rolling his eyes. He grabbed the mail off Tricia's desk, opened the door to his office, and dropped his book bag on the empty couch and the mail on the corner of his large oak desk. He threw an imaginary tennis ball into the air with his right hand and swatted it with the imaginary racket in his left before lowering his six-and-a-half-foot frame into his desk chair. A large window behind him allowed the morning sun to pour into the room and provided a view of Heckney Woods. Later, when the leaves fell, he would be able to see Bear Creek through the trees.

Charlie enjoyed his comfortable, albeit a bit disheveled, office. Books and papers stood piled on the credenza beneath the window sill behind him, and a wooden coat rack by the door held a sweater, an umbrella, and his winter hat. The faint smell of dusty books lent the room an aged but inviting atmosphere. The brown leather couch with a coffee table to one side and the large conference table in front of his desk suggested that this was a place for both quiet conversation and serious business.

Bookshelves lined the other side of the room. Texts on academic administration, educational psychology, and physical education were stacked horizontally on top of books with worn spines, yellowed pages, and titles such as Tacitus, Madame Bovary, A Tale of Two Cities, Ulysses, and Latin I, II, III, and IV.

Taking a deep breath, Charlie picked up the telephone, waited a second, and then spoke in a clear, deep voice:

"Good morning, Catherine."

"Good morning to you, Charles. Now, have you seen the morning's paper? The headline on page two? Have you seen it?"

"I'm afraid I..." Charlie grabbed the morning's *Waumeka Gazette* from the top of the mail pile.

"It sounds as though you haven't read the article yet. Well, I think it's vitally important that you have someone look into that matter. Yes, and I would suggest that you let the board know—perhaps at our next monthly meeting—how you intend to handle it. I don't like to bother you so early in the morning, but I knew you would want a heads up."

Only half listening to Catherine Newsome's babbling, Charlie swung in his chair and stared out the window. He looked out across the parking lot toward Heckney Woods. The oaks and maples were just starting to turn from green to orange and red. Perhaps he would take his lunch down to the creek later, and sit with his back against a huge willow, the way he and his classmates had done twenty years earlier. *Bear Creek,* he mused, *a tributary of the mighty Mississippi. Locally renamed "Bare Creek" after legendary midnight adolescent escapades.*

Pulling himself from his daydreaming, he turned back toward the desk and glanced across the room at his file cabinets. On one of the drawers, the lock stuck out, not pushed in like the others. He hadn't left it that way.

Catherine Newsome had finished talking.

"Thank you for the call, Catherine. I agree it's something we should look into," he said, trying to keep the insincerity out of his voice. One had to keep the Newsomes happy. Tom Newsome, after all, owned Newsome Ford, one of the largest car dealerships in the northwest part of the state. He'd been on the school board for four years, and had twice run (unsuccessfully) for city council. The Newsomes' teenage son and daughter were by no means stellar students, any more than the son who had graduated two years before. Tom and Catherine Newsome, however, knew how to get their way.

Charlie put down the receiver, took a deep sigh, and read the article on the second page of the *Gazette.* Next to a large picture of the White Deer Casino, the article recounted the altercation that Charlie and his wife had witnessed two nights before. Two items in the article caught his attention: "The unidentified assailant fled in a blue late-model pickup before police arrived. According to two witnesses, a high school staff parking permit hung from the inside mirror." And the final sentence: "Chief of Police Aaron Kohlberg was unavailable for comment, as was Charles Brannigan, principal of the high school."

"Unavailable for comment?" Charlie grumbled. "When the hell did anyone try to call me?" Why was it that every time he talked to Catherine Newsome, Charlie felt as though he was being pinned in a wrestling match? He recalled his college wrestling days and the constant potential for a wrestler's angle: a grudge between wrestlers that could last for years.

He stood up, hung his sport coat on the coat rack, loosened his tie, and rolled up his sleeves. He swatted another phantom tennis ball across his desk before checking the file cabinet.

The keys to the cabinet hung where they belonged, in the top-right drawer of his desk, but the one drawer marked "Personnel Files" had been left unlocked. One of the hanging files, that of Ann Shelby, was pulled slightly up and askew. He didn't remember reading her file recently, nor leaving the drawer unlocked. In any case, it reminded him to schedule a developmental review session with one of his favorite teachers.

He recalled how he had hired Ann three years earlier to teach math and to help coach the girls' soccer team. As it turned out, she did an excellent job in the classroom. She created sample problems on the board, had students work with one another in small groups to solve them, and then went from table to table, helping and encouraging as needed. Of course, she endured the usual problems that all young teachers experience: handling students who were goofing off at the back of the room, combining understanding with firmness, and attempting to deal with a wide diversity of both talent and motivation among the students.

Charlie arranged monthly meetings with teachers in their first four years, a probationary period as he called it. During these developmental review sessions, he could provide the novices with support, feedback, and a safe place to vent. Any teacher who wanted his guidance after that could ask for a

4

conference at any time, but he insisted on meeting regularly with the new faculty. When faculty neophytes conferred with one another in the teachers' lounge and the chatter centered on their regular review sessions, the consensus was one of appreciation and feeling supported. The young teachers who were in the classroom for the first time reported that they found it comforting that someone had their backs.

He opened his door and called out to his office manager to schedule an appointment with Ann Shelby—just a general review session, but one he would look forward to.

***

Catherine Newsome hung up the phone and pulled down the newspaper that her husband was reading across the breakfast table.

"This time I think we may have him right where we want him," she hissed.

Chapter 2

"How do you like that? It looks as if my luck will never run out." Charlie slapped his full house, three kings and two queens, face up on the table in front of him, cupped his hands behind his neck, threw back his head and laughed. The other three men began to laugh with him and shake their heads.

"Holy shit, Charlie. You know what? You've got to be one of the luckiest men I know. You don't deserve it. You know that, don't you, Brannigan?" commented Cliff Smalley, a doctor at St. Luke's as well as Charlie's next-door neighbor and closest friend.

Charlie scooped up the pile of coins from the center of the table and looked over at Frank Feuermann, who was beginning to shuffle the cards. "The evening's still young, Frank. Your luck's bound to change," Charlie encouraged his friend.

For eight years now, the four men—Charlie, Cliff, Frank, and Marty O'Brien—had met just about every Wednesday night to play poker. They had started out playing for pennies and nickels; now it was dimes and quarters, and an occasional fifty-cent piece. A player could win—or lose, for that matter—fifteen or twenty dollars in an evening if he wasn't careful.

"Who wants another beer? Anybody?" Charlie got up from the card table in his family room and went over to the fireplace. With fists the size of large grapefruits, he opened the screen with one hand, grabbing a large log and tossing in onto the fire with the other hand. After closing the fire screen, he went into the kitchen to wash his hands and get more refreshments.

"Hey, Charlie, you did one hell of a job on this cherry paneling," Frank yelled as he dealt the cards.

"Thanks. It took me long enough. I still wish I could get the stuff from you guys at Fleet Farm. Don't you think you could get me a deal on it?"

"We just wouldn't be able to compete with the big lumber yards, Charlie. It's all about volume."

Bringing two beers back to the table Charlie asked, "Cliff, you want another soda?"

Examining the cards in his hand, Marty commented, "Speaking of luck, Charlie, it looks as if one of your teachers made a narrow escape last night. Did you see this morning's paper?"

"Yeah, I saw it. One of my overbearing board members brought it to my attention first thing this morning. I'm not at all sure it was one of the teachers, though. I don't know anybody with a late-model Ford. Anyway, the two witnesses who supposedly saw a staff parking permit could be almost anyone." Charlie handed Cliff a soda and then sat down and examined the cards that Frank had dealt him.

"Like who?" Marty asked.

"Like someone who doesn't like the school. A kid with a gripe, or a lying parent with an axe to grind. Anyway, the cops were in this morning. They're not sure about that story either. But they're following up on every lead. I still need to call Kohlberg to see what he's got to say."

"I'll bet a dime on this pile of junk," Cliff offered, folding his cards down on the table and throwing a dime in the middle of the table. "I'll bet I know who your overbearing board member was, Charlie." He grinned. "You mean you don't appreciate Mrs. Newsome's input?"

"See your dime and raise you one." Charlie put twenty cents in the pot. "Tell you one thing: I'm getting pretty tired of the board trying to run the place themselves. Every time a teacher steps out of line by a hair, they're sticking their noses into it. Not that I'd like to be quoted, thank you very much."

"Why's that?" Cliff laughed.

"Catherine Newsome and her old man have a bit too much clout with the board and also at City Hall, for that matter. She would just love to chair that board."

"Maybe she wants your job," Cliff kidded him.

"Not for herself, but I wouldn't be surprised if she has somebody in mind to be my successor," Charlie replied.

"Hey, weren't you sweet on her when you were in high school?" Marty O'Brien asked with a smile.

"Give me a break. We were in the same class. That's about it."

"I thought you two used have lunch together down by the creek," Marty persisted.

"Well, maybe we did once or twice. What of it? Just friends, as the students would say now, just friends," Charlie said, laughing.

The betting continued around the table until both Frank and Marty folded and Cliff called Charlie's twenty-cent bet. This time Charlie had been bluffing, and Cliff laughed as he swept in the coins.

"She wasn't bad looking in those days—a little heavy, maybe. Didn't she try out for the cheerleading squad?" Marty noted as he dealt the next hand.

"Yes, but didn't make it. And then she wanted me to help her win the election for class president. When she lost that, she blamed the rest of us on the student council for not supporting her enough. Does that sound like we were an item?"

"Maybe she was more interested in you than you were in her, Charlie. At least, that's how I remember it."

Charlie looked again at the cards in his hand. "I'll see you and raise you a quarter, Frank," he said, changing the subject. Charlie was on a tear and indeed did quite well at cards that night, winning about $17 by the time the game began to wind down.

"Guess it's time for me to call it a night," Marty announced. "Looks like I'm finishing just about even. Maryann should be happy with that." They all laughed.

"Same here," Cliff announced. "I've got surgery tomorrow. Gotta give these hands a rest."

Although he didn't say anything, Charlie figured that if Cliff and Marty had both finished even, Frank's luck hadn't changed after all.

***

The Brannigan house was a large colonial at the center of a tree-lined cul-de-sac that included four other homes, two on either side of the Brannigans. Charlie and Katie had done a lot to make it their own. Katie had planted rhododendrons by the front porch and put a sugar maple, whose leaves turned bright red in the fall, in the front yard. She used to say, "That's the baby's tree, whenever she comes." She would describe the whole thing to Charlie: a swing hanging from a lower branch, and pushing a one- or two-year-old, whose long red hair—just like her mother's—would blow in the wind as she giggled and said her first word, "Higher.".

After ten years and no baby, Katie had all but given up those fantasies. God knows they had tried. Her obstetrician couldn't find a cause for their inability to conceive, but at age thirty-four, her chances of conceiving were diminishing and infertility treatments had been useless.

"Even if we just knew why," Katie used to say, sometimes mournfully and sometimes bitterly, "maybe we could accept it." Katie's hopes for a large family were replaced with a serious effort to fill up her life with regular activities. She worked hard at being an up-to-date nurse, caring for elderly patients, teaching her subordinates, and becoming charge nurse in three years. She became active in the community, taking meals to shut-ins once every two weeks for Meals on Wheels and attending regular evening meetings of the Altar Society at Our Lady of Sorrows Catholic Church.

After his friends left, Charlie picked up glasses and put them in the dishwasher. He folded the card table and chairs and put them in the hall closet.

Katie would be home any minute—she tried to schedule meetings with the nursing staff on those evenings when Charlie had a card game at the house—so he climbed the stairs to get ready for bed. She came home shortly afterwards and came into the bedroom with a glass of milk and a string cheese.

"How was your meeting, sweetheart?" Charlie inquired.

"Oh, the usual. Some of the staff had to go on and on about the fact that the new rotations are never scheduled until the last minute. Then we had to decide whether or not we wanted to take on undergraduate trainees from Central."

"What'd they decide?"

Charlie sat on the edge of the bed in his under-shorts and t-shirt and watched as his wife unbuttoned her blouse, took it off and hung it up. She unzipped and pulled down her trousers.

"We'll try it for a year and see how it goes."

She stood in her blue bikini panties and thin brassiere.

"It could create a nice liaison with the university, couldn't it?" he asked. He loved watching his wife undress. As she unlatched her brassiere, he thought, as he always did, of how round and firm her breasts still were, and wondered, as he always did, if they would always stay that way.

"I only hope we're not taking on too much." Katie finished undressing, took the clasp out of the back of her hair and shook her head so that her long red hair flowed down over her shoulders. Grabbing a towel from the linen closet, she went into the bathroom and closed the door. She yelled back to her husband, "Don't worry, honey, I can hear you from in here. I just wanted to take a shower before we go to bed."

After Katie showered, Charlie could smell the sweet fragrance of her Ralph Lauren perfume coming from the bathroom. She ordinarily didn't use cologne until the morning, but he always looked forward to those nights when she put some on before they went to bed. Nor was he to be disappointed on this particular night. It always seemed better to Charlie when sex was as much Katie's idea as his own. Cliff Smalley, he thought, was right. He was, indeed, a lucky man. He tried to put the events of the day and his troubles at school out of his mind, at least for the time being.

CHAPTER 3

"Bye, darling. Have a good day." Charlie kissed Katie and grabbed his backpack from the chair by the front door, hoisting it up onto his back and shoving his arms through the straps.

"Aren't you taking the car?" Katie asked.

"No. It's a beautiful day for walking. You never know how many more of these we'll get. See you."

Charlie stepped out onto the sidewalk and threw his imaginary tennis ball into the air, raising his left arm as high as his cumbersome backpack would allow before swinging it down quickly. "Damn," he muttered, "I love this game." A wrestler in college, Charlie hadn't done much in the past few years to keep himself fit. At thirty-eight, he knew he wasn't being a good role model for the students, and Cliff Smalley had been urging him to take up a sport. "Like tennis," Cliff recommended. "Just meet us at the court some Saturday morning." For the past four weeks Charlie had been learning the game from Cliff and three of his friends from the hospital.

It was a bright, sunny morning, cool enough for a jacket, excellent for walking, as he had told Katie, and the school was less than a mile from home. A gentle breeze blew through the valley, but it came from the west. On some mornings, when the breeze blew in from the north, a walk through town could be a decidedly unpleasant experience unless you were born and raised in Waumeka or the surrounding area. The acrid smell from the paper mills just ten miles to the north would make any but a true native feel like retching. The natives would tell newcomers, "You just get used to it in time." Most Waumeka residents didn't even use the word odor; they called it an "aroma" or, at the very worst, a "scent." Some said it was the smell of money. As the primary industry and the largest employer in the county, paper was king. Newcomers, who retained greater olfactory sensitivity, would describe the sulfurous smell as a mixture of rotten eggs and cabbage. They suggested that over the years, evolution had produced a race of Waumekans with inadequate nasal equipment, making them insensitive to strong odors and giving them a decidedly pallid skin tone caused by inhaling the polluted air from the mills, which contained traces of the bleach used in the production of paper.

A frequent boast among a certain segment of the high school boys was the ability to camouflage their adolescent flatulence on a date if the wind was just right.

As Charlie walked down Wheaton Street, he decided not to turn left on Appleton to go directly to the high school. Instead he walked five blocks further south to Pine Street, where he took a left and headed towards North Main, a walk that took him through the center of town. As he walked by Sorenson's Jewelry, he automatically checked his watch against the large clock that stood on the sidewalk in front of the jewelry store.

"The Clock," standing atop a black twenty-foot fluted iron post, boasted three-feet-wide faces, in all four directions, and Roman numerals. Above each clock face was an inscription, "Town of Waumeka, est. 1869," on a bronze nameplate surrounded by decorative scrollwork. On the faces themselves, in smaller print, a simple black caption read, "Sorenson's Jewelry - Diamonds and Antiques." A well known landmark in Waumeka, residents set their watches by the Clock and often used it as a familiar meeting place. Many a tentative first date began with the uncertain question, "Meet you at the Clock?"

It was five minutes to seven, just a few minutes before Charlie generally arrived at school. Still, he thought, he had time to stop at John's Bakery at the next corner and get a box of doughnuts for the staff lounge.

Charlie came out of the bakery, warm doughnut box in hand, and continued down North Main when suddenly a car pulled out of an auto lot on his left, crossed the sidewalk right in front of him, and turned left toward Appleton Street. The driver obviously hadn't seen him or he would have slowed down and not sped out of the lot and onto North Main as fast as he did. The car, a gold Thunderbird coupe, had dark auto glass on all the windows, so Charlie couldn't see who was driving. It must have been a young driver. The auto lot belonged to Newsome Ford, whose agency showroom sat across the street.

Charlie watched as the Thunderbird turned left onto Appleton, heading in the direction of the high school. When he got to that intersection himself and began walking down Appleton Street, he noticed the car parked in front of the high school.

That's where I've seen that car, the mysterious Thunderbird that's been parked every morning in front of the school lately. Before he got to the school, Charlie decided to go around to the back of the building, avoiding the front altogether. He wanted to avoid whoever was in the car.

Charlie took his keys out of his jacket pocket and unlocked the back door, which otherwise could be opened only from the inside. He walked down the long corridor to the front office, stopping on the way at the faculty lounge, where he deposited the box of still-warm donuts, which filled the room with a faint but distinct and welcoming aroma. When he got to his office, he swung his backpack off his back and onto the couch. He hung his jacket and cap on the coat rack and returned through his office manager's office, down the hall to the window facing the front of the building. From there, he could see the Thunderbird still parked in front. It faced the driveway into the parking lot.

Charlie walked back into his office and came out again about five minutes later. He saw that the car was still there. After he came out a third time, Tricia asked, "Is there something I can do?"

"No, I'm just ... Yes, Tricia, there is something. Could you check every now and then and let me know when that gold-colored car leaves?"

"Yes, of course. Is something wrong?" she asked with a soft voice.

"No, I'm just curious."

The office manager seemed satisfied with his answer, and promised to let him know as soon as the car pulled away, which was about twenty minutes later, at 7:40. Charlie was about to ask her to get Aaron Kohlberg, the chief of police, on the telephone for him, but decided to make the call for himself.

"Good morning, Aaron. Hey, you missed a good game last night."

The police chief asked him how much he had won.

"Oh, about fifteen bucks. Have you learned any more about the scuffle at the casino last week? Supposedly someone from the high school, but I can't figure out who."

"Nothing new," Aaron answered. He explained that the casino had decided not to press charges so even if his investigators did find out who it was, Charlie shouldn't have to worry about it.

"Thanks," Charlie answered. "Still I'd like to find out if it was one of our staff. It could be someone who needs help with a gambling problem. I'm going to keep my eyes open around here for a blue late-model pickup."

"Probably a good idea, but I wouldn't worry about it too much if you never find out," Kohlberg replied.

"Thanks, Aaron. But there's something else I wanted to ask you about. It's got me puzzled." He told his friend about the gold Thunderbird that had been parked in front of the school building, facing the parking lot every morning for the past several days.

"It's there every day about seven o'clock when I pull in. They drive off just after I show up. Today I walked to school and came in around the back and they didn't leave until just a few minutes ago. Like I said, it may be nothing, but it seems suspicious to me." He asked Kohlberg if one of his policemen could check on it the next day and find out whose car it was.

"Sure," the chief answered. "I'll switch you back to the front desk. File a report, and I can take it from there. I'll have someone in an unmarked car in the lot across the street from the school, keeping an eye out tomorrow morning."

"Thanks, Aaron. Oh, by the way, I saw that Thunderbird pulling out of Newsome's lot this morning when I was walking down Main. That doesn't tell you much but it does seem strange."

"We'll check it out, Charlie. Talk to you later. I'll let you know what we find out."

***

Just before the first-period bell, Charlie Brannigan stepped out into the hall of Waumeka High School with the sleeves of his freshly pressed blue shirt rolled up to his elbows, the top button opened, and his tie loosened. The hall was crowded and noisy with students banging lockers, laughing, and running to their classes.

"No running in the halls, ladies and gentlemen. No running." The pace slowed slightly but the laughter continued. Charlie smiled and raised his right arm high into the air. Standing six-and-a-half feet tall, he struck an impressive pose as he raised his phantom racket and came down with a swish so hard and fast that anyone watching would have sworn they heard the ball fly through the air.

"Net ball, Mr. Brannigan," announced a voice from behind him—a spontaneously self-appointed tenth-grade referee.

"Are you kidding me? That was an ace if I ever saw one," the principal laughed. "Anyway, how would you know? You were standing behind me. Besides, there goes the bell. You'd better get yourself into class in a hurry, or I'll write you up for being tardy."

"Yes, sir," the young referee replied with mock seriousness and dashed down the hall to the second doorway on his right and into his math class. Charlie slammed closed a few lockers that had been left open. Suddenly the math student/tennis referee stuck his head back out of the class and called down the hall, "Wait a minute, Mr. B. I thought you were left-handed."

"Ah, ha," Charlie laughed. "Got ya. Very good obstetrical skills, young man. Actually I'm ambivalent."

"Don't you mean observational skills?"

"Oh, yes, observational skills. Now get back into class."

"And isn't the word 'ambidextrous'?"

"Oh, yes, that's right. Ambidextrous. Now go."

"Yes, sir." The giggling head pulled itself back into the classroom as the principal continued down the hall, closing lockers.

Charlie smiled, looked up at the ceiling, and mumbled, "Thank you, Lord, for bright and engaging students. Thank you."

When he got to locker number fifty-two, Charlie spotted a pack of Marlboro cigarettes sticking out of a jacket pocket. He took them from the jacket, shoved them into his own shirt pocket, and continued closing lockers and walking down the hall. When he came to the math classroom, he peered in to see Ann Shelby handing out papers. He didn't want to startle her, as she appeared engrossed in what she was doing. A few students helped him get her attention by coughing and signaling with their eyes and then gazing toward the door. When he did catch her eye, he thought she appeared slightly embarrassed, her face lightly flushed, to see the principal standing in the doorway.

"Eleven?" he asked.

Smiling, she nodded. "Yes."

Charlie continued his rounds down the hall, bent to pick up a crumpled piece of paper, and opened a few of the windows as he went, turning their handles down and pulling the panes toward him to let in the cool autumn air. He could hear a pair of cardinals singing in the tree near the sidewalk leading up to the building.

As it was still early in the school year, the marble floors gleamed from their recent scrubbing and waxing. The whole corridor, especially that section near the supply room, had the faint clean scent of lemon detergent, mixed with the fresh smell of school supplies, new books, school paste, and Sharpie markers. He took a deep breath and realized that it would not be long before the Wisconsin winter snows would mean lockers full of wet coats and hats and corridors with a very different odor. He opened two more windows and headed back to his office.

"Tricia, would you see who has locker number fifty-two for me? By the way, why do you think a student would leave their locker open with a pack of cigarettes exposed in a jacket pocket?"

***

"Come in, Ann." Charlie opened his door wide as the young math teacher, carrying a small stack of papers, a daily planner, and a grade book, came into his office. A tall, slender woman with blonde hair pulled back in a ponytail, she was dressed in a long, paisley pencil skirt and a cream-colored blouse, both of which appeared to Charlie to accentuate her youth. She sat on the couch across from Charlie's desk, smoothed her skirt, pulling it over her knees, and set the papers on the coffee table in front of her.

With large, dark-brown eyes, high cheek bones, and no make-up, her effortless smile suggested a quiet self-confidence. Everyone knew Ann Shelby was youthful and attractive. Charlie also knew she was a superior teacher. The better students, her honor students, liked her and openly expressed a high regard for her ability. In fact, in the short time since he had hired her, a mere three years, she had already prepared a handful of students to go off to prestigious colleges both in and out of state, to major in math.

Like all young teachers, however, her performance in the classroom was still a mixed bag. While the better students were willing to work hard in a course that was not intended to be easy, she had trouble reaching the less motivated students and sometimes struggled to maintain any sense of decorum in the classroom.

After asking her if he could get her a cup of coffee or a glass of water, Charlie sat down on a chair opposite the young woman.

"How's it going?" he began.

"Not bad, although I don't think this class is going to turn out as well as last year's."

He offered that it was still early in the year and asked if she had any grades on the students yet.

"Just homework assignments and one quiz."

"And?"

"Mediocre at best."

He asked if the students were paying attention, suggesting that it sometimes took a few weeks for even the good students to settle down.

"You know, that's the interesting thing. Most of them are paying attention," she answered. "But there's still that clique in the back of the room, four boys goofing off and talking. I'm afraid I'm not doing a great job of getting that under control."

Charlie leaned forward and listened carefully to this young teacher, who appeared both confident and frustrated at the same time. He suggested that she might try to identify the ring leader and put some pressure on him. "Ask the class a question when the four of them are talking and then call on the ring leader to answer the question."

Lifting her ponytail with the back of her hand and pushing it over her right shoulder, Anne Shelby responded that she knew who the ring leader was but didn't think he was easily embarrassed. "Not knowing the answer might actually be a mark of distinction among his buddies, something to laugh about," she added, shaking her head, and then gazing toward the window as if trying to picture the scene in the classroom.

"Who is this gem?" the principal asked.

"Tommy Newsome. His mother is on the school board. I'm not sure, but he may think that gives him some leverage."

"Ann, if it gets too bad, send him down to see me. You don't have to put up with that." Looking directly at the teacher, he spoke with firmness and conviction.

The two went on to discuss grades, lesson plans, goals for the class, and Ann's general satisfaction with her job. Charlie told her directly that he was pleased with her performance and not to let irritating, entitled students get her down. He was glad she was a teacher at Waumeka High School and told her so in so many words. In return, she expressed her appreciation for the fact that he had her back and said she felt encouraged to consult with him when needed.

As she left his office, Charlie wondered how he would handle young Mr. Newsome when the boy was sent to the principal's office, which was sure to happen. As he opened the door for Ann to leave, he asked Tricia if there were any messages.

"None," she replied, and then added, "Oh, by the way, locker fifty-two belongs to Tommy Newsome."

Before Charlie went to lunch he asked Tricia have Tommy Newsome in his office at eight thirty the next morning.

**

Charlie stuck his head out of his office door and looked across the office manager's desk and the counter toward the assistant principal's office. He could see that Chet Magnuson's door was open but, from where he stood, the office appeared empty. He walked around the counter and peered in, just to make sure.

"Tricia, do you know where Chet is?"

The office manager looked up from her computer. "Oh, he had to go down by the gym to break up a fracas. A couple of sophomore girls again."

"When he gets back, would you tell him I'd like to see him for a few minutes?"

Back in his office, Charlie stood looking out the large window overlooking the parking lot. He still wondered about the strange events at the White Deer Casino three nights earlier and how he would answer Catherine Newsome and the rest of the school board.

It was almost three o'clock. As the bell rang, Charlie watched the students pour out of the building and into the parking lot, some of them screeching tires as they spun out of the lot and into the street. The scene frustrated him. He had been unable to come up with a reasonable plan for controlling what he considered dangerous driving in the parking lot.

"Come on in, Chet," he yelled when he heard a knock on his door.

Chester Magnuson, a physics teacher, had been at Waumeka High for what seemed an eternity. He was twenty years older than Charlie, and as his assistant principal was a supportive older mentor. He was also admired by a majority of students and their parents, some of whom had also had Magnuson as a physics teacher when they had gone to Waumeka High. He was beginning to walk with a slight bend in his back. He was balding, and what hair he had left was grey. He never bothered to comb it over to hide his bald spots, the way some men his age did. Instead, he had the barber cut his hair the way he always had, so that now he appeared to have a tonsure right where a skull cap might go. Sam Cohen, the chemistry teacher, sometimes teased him, "Hey, Chet a yarmulke would cover that just right. Should I bring one in for you?"

"What's up, Chief?" Magnuson pulled a chair out from the work table across from Charlie's desk and sat down, leaning the chair back on two legs and propping his knees against the table.

Charlie sat down at his desk and grabbed a pencil from its holder. He began to twirl the pencil back and forth between his two palms. "Chet, the Board's on my case again."

"What is it this time? Don't tell me old lady Newsome is serving you up a dish of crap again." Magnuson laughed a deep laugh.

"Bingo." Charlie put the pencil back in its holder and leaned forward. "I got a call from her the other morning about that fight at the casino. The newspaper reported that the perpetrator drove off in a vehicle with a Waumeka High School parking permit."

"That's easy. Just have Tricia check the records for all the cars that have permits."

"That's the problem. She has, and there's no record of any 'blue late-model pick-up.'"

Magnuson suggested he talk to the police chief.

"Did that this morning," Charlie responded. "Kohlberg doesn't know any more than we do."

Just then Charlie heard another tire squeal in the parking lot. He swiveled around in his chair and watched as a red Camaro spun out of the lot and onto Bay Street.

"There's another problem we have to deal with, Chet. Some of these kids have no business driving at all. At least they should be safe on school grounds."

Before he turned back to face Magnuson, Charlie noticed the janitor, Orlando DiFabrio, leaving his truck and walking toward the school building.

"Darn it, there's DiFabrio ... half an hour late again." He muttered.

Charlie appreciated that Orlando DiFabrio was an excellent custodian, but lately he had been showing up late for work at least once or twice a week. When Charlie had confronted him about his tardiness, he noticed the custodian had become irritable and defensive. It just wasn't like DiFabrio.

"Wait a minute," Charlie said, looking at the truck, "Holy shit. So that's the 'late-model blue pick-up'."

"Great! Problem solved," Chet Magnuson said as he stretched himself up from his chair to leave. "Let me know whenever I can help you again," he laughed.

"But wait a minute. Why wouldn't Tricia have a record of DiFabrio's new truck?"

"He probably just transferred the tag from that old wreck of a Ford he had without even mentioning it to Tricia."

"Yes! Of course."

"Like I said, Chief, let me know whenever I can help," the older man quipped.

CHAPTER 4

———◆———

When Tommy Newsome knocked on the principal's door at eight thirty the following morning, and then pushed the door open before Charlie had time to say, "Come in," the pack of Marlboro cigarettes lay on the desk. Charlie suggested the boy take a seat.

"Do you know why I asked you to come in this morning, Tommy?"

"I have no idea," came the sullen reply.

"Do you have any idea whose cigarettes these are?" the principal asked.

"No. I'd say they're probably yours, except I've never seen you smoke. You don't smoke, do you?" the boy asked, every word dripping with sarcasm.

Charlie drew himself up straight in his chair and leaned forward toward the student. "These are not mine. I found them in your locker yesterday," he snapped.

"And what were you doing in my locker?" the student asked, raising his eyebrows in an expression of mock indignation. He had the self-confidence of a sword fighter parrying with his opponent.

"I beg your pardon. You're a junior. You know perfectly well we have keys to the lockers and inspect them whenever we have a good reason. However, in this case your locker was left open," Charlie explained, "and these were sticking out of your jacket pocket in plain view. Now, can you explain that?"

"No, those are not my cigarettes and I don't know how they got there. Can I go now?" the young man demanded as he began to rise from his seat. The sword fight was over.

"No, you may not go," Charlie replied. "We're not done here. Since the law's been broken, I need to inform your parents as well as the police. I'll tell them what you've told me—that these are not yours—and let them know that we've begun an investigation into the matter. That's what the law requires. Now, do you want to be here when I make those calls?"

"Not especially," the boy replied, mildly subdued but still sarcastic.

"Then you're free to leave. Miss Cameron will give you an excuse slip to give to your teacher."

The principal heaved a sigh and shook his head as he watched the young man stand up and walk out without saying another word, shutting the door behind him. Charlie did not look forward to the two calls he knew he had to make.

***

Charlie left the building and walked to the park to eat his lunch alone outside for a change. The sun was out, the air was warm, and the leaves were already beginning to change; he wanted to get away for an hour. He walked up Appleton Street to Sheldon Park, just past Main Street, and spotted an empty picnic table by the creek. The weeping willow trees along the creek had already turned a bright yellow, and the sugar maples throughout the park were beginning their annual show of dazzling reds and oranges. The trees in Heckney Woods would not be far behind. The colorful display reminded Charlie that he and Katie had talked about a weekend trip to the Northwoods to see the colors. *It better be soon,* he thought, *or we'll miss it. In another week or two it'll be all over.* He thought about a cabin on one of the lakes near Hayward, where the loons might not have migrated south yet and where they had spotted a bald eagle's nest on their last visit. The Northwoods was a great place to listen to the eerie tremolo of the loons gliding over the quiet waters of the autumn lake, or to spot a lone eagle overhead or a blue heron sitting at the end of a dock or at the water's edge, waiting for some unsuspecting bass to get too close to the surface. Once, when he and Katie had been sitting at the end of a dock with their feet dangling in the almost frigid water, they had been startled by a white-tailed doe and her two fawns, which had come out of the woods and down to the water for a drink. The deer had gone about their evening meal of water and willow leaves, unbothered by the couple sitting and quietly enjoying the sunset. It wasn't unusual to observe deer, and even an occasional black bear, crossing between the cabin and the lake.

When Charlie shook his head to clear it of his daydreams, he realized that he had eaten almost all his lunch. He had just enough time to finish his yogurt and get back to school.

He walked briskly down the corridor to the office and saw one of the school's customary yellow telephone messages stuck to his door: "Return call to A. Kohlberg." Charlie dialed the chief of police.

"Hi, Aaron. It looks as if you were reading my mind," Charlie began.

"No, actually I was just calling you back about the car that's been parking in front of the school every morning. The car is new so it hasn't been registered. The plate is a dealer plate, registered to the Newsome Ford agency." Kolhberg explained that the car was either a demo or a loaner and that everyone on the Ford sales staff had two plates they could use in that capacity, putting them on any car in the lot to lend to potential customers or to rent to someone whose car was in the repair shop. "A lot of times they just use those cars themselves," he added.

Charlie asked if the chief knew who drove that one.

"No, but I can find out if you like."

"I wouldn't bother just yet. I'll see if they keep showing up and let you know. Someone is keeping an eye on the school or on me. They leave as soon as I get here," Charlie commented.

Kohlberg encouraged the principal to call whenever he wanted help, and promised to get more information if Charlie requested it.

"Thanks," Charlie replied. "Actually I have another issue to report. I'll send in a formal report, but just to let you know—I found cigarettes in a locker yesterday."

"Whose locker?"

"Guess," Charlie replied. "It seems that there's a Newsome problem every time I turn around. It was Tommy, although he denies that they're his, of course. So does his old man. I called to let him know we'll be investigating. He just read me the riot act, 'How could you accuse our son,' etc. etc. You know the type."

***

Charlie walked down the hall to the janitor's closet, picking up scraps of paper from the floor and tossing two soda cans into a recycling bin as he went. If there was one task he didn't feel like tackling, it was confronting Orlando DiFabrio about the scuffle at the casino. DiFabrio was an excellent custodian whose only flaw was showing up late for work on occasion; even that had only recently become an issue.

DiFabrio offered the principal a stool to sit on, the only piece of furniture in the janitor's closet. DiFabrio himself turned an empty waste basket upside down and sat on it across from Charlie. They talked for about ten minutes.

Charlie spoke softly so that anybody walking down the hall would be unable to hear them. He spoke about his concern for Orlando's situation, and Orlando admitted the confrontation at the casino. After Charlie assured him that the casino manager had decided not to press charges, he asked the custodian about the possibility of his having a gambling addiction. DiFabrio acknowledged that he went to the casino more and more often and that he was beginning to worry about the money he was losing. Charlie put his hand on the janitor's shoulder, stood up, and promised to get him some help.

Then, remembering the unlocked file cabinet in his office, Charlie turned back and asked the custodian, who had also stood up, if he knew of anyone who might have had access to Charlie's office in the evenings.

"The only ones who ever go into the main office in the evenings would be the board members. When they have those meetings in the conference room, ever so often they needs to use the copy machine in the main office. I don't think they'd go into your room. Course I don't lock it 'til I'm done working. That's all I know."

That evening, after putting the car in the garage and before going into his house, Charlie stopped next door to talk to his neighbor, Cliff Smalley. He knew the doctor would have a good idea about where he could find help for his custodian. Cliff met him at the door, invited him in and offered him a soda.

"No, no thanks, Cliff," Charlie answered. "I just need a bit of advice. This is confidential. Is that all right?"

"Yes, certainly. What is it? You're all right, I hope."

"No, no. It's not me. I just need some information for one of our employees. Does Ministry Health Care have counselors for gambling addiction?"

"Not specifically. Why? I'm guessing you've identified the teacher who got in trouble at the casino last week."

Charlie would say only that it was one of his staff and that he had confronted the person and spoken with them in confidence and that the person wanted help. He had promised to try to get it for them without mentioning their name. He told Cliff that as far as he was concerned, he would be satisfied if the person just took the help that was offered. And since the casino wasn't pressing charges, that would be the end of the story ... unless, of course, Catherine Newsome continued to make an issue of it. He asked Cliff again if he could think of any resources.

"Sure. The university at Eau Claire has an excellent counseling center and they offer addiction counseling. Besides that, there is a chapter of Gamblers Anonymous in Eau Claire. I know it's a bit of a drive, but I think it would be worth it. If it's anything like Alcoholics Anonymous, I know it would be worth it."

"Great. Do you know where they meet?"

"I'm pretty sure it's at First Methodist Church. You could call over there and find out the times they meet."

Charlie thanked his neighbor, saying he knew Cliff would be the one to ask. He then asked if Cliff planned to come over for the Wednesday night card game.

"I'll be there. So get your wallet out," Charlie's neighbor laughed.

***

The card game started with only three players that evening: Charlie, Cliff, and Marty O'Brien. Frank Feuermann came an hour late, explaining that he had been too busy at Fleet Farm to leave work on time. As usual, Frank ended up on the losing end of the card game, though not by much, Charlie calculated.

CHAPTER 5

———◆———

"Who the hell was working late last night? Cartwright, was this yours?" Frank snatched a Jim Beam bottle from behind a pile of two by fours as he yelled at the other three men in the shed.

"I know. I know…" Lou Cartwright replied.

"What do you mean, 'I know, I know'? You don't know anything. Wouldn't that make nice headlines? We could all of us take a pay cut—or worse. You're out of work for a week, asshole. Now get out of here."

"Frank, I need—"

"Don't 'Frank' me. Get the hell out of here. And don't let me see your face for another week, or you'll lose your job altogether. If you're not careful, you're going to end up a drunken alki sot like your old man."

Lou snatched his coat off a hook next to shelves of lumber that stretched all the way to the high ceiling.

"You just wait," he hissed under his breath, passing two co-workers on his way out the door. "That son-of-a-bitch'll get his. You just wait and see." He put his middle finger in the air with one hand as he pushed the door open with the other.

***

Lou Cartwright flicked on the television in the living room of his trailer home and dropped into an overstuffed, mustard-yellow chair. He swung his feet up onto a torn ottoman of the same color.

His wife, Amber, in a blue terrycloth bathrobe and with her hair up in curlers, came out of the bedroom and asked why he was home so early.

"Because I'm off work for a week. That's it. That's all. Don't wanna hear any more about it." He threw the newspaper down on the floor.

Amber lowered herself onto the torn olive-green couch, one of the few other pieces of furniture in the room, besides the TV and a couple of floor lamps. The arms and edges of the couch were frayed where the cat had scratched them.

"But you won't get paid," she persisted. Her face was full of fear and her voice full of anxiety.

"Now how was you able to figure that out?" Lou asked with a condescending sneer.

"Don't you go being sarcastic with me, Louis Cartwright. Were you drinking again? Tell me that." As Amber let go of the fear and anxiety, her voice began to rise in anger.

"Hey, it was cold as a whore's heart out there last night."

"And booze is supposed to keep you warm. Is that it?"

"Why do ya always have to take their side? Ya always assume it's my fault whenever anything bad happens."

"You haven't answered my question. Now there goes Rainbow. You've woken her up again." The baby began to cry in the bedroom.

"That's what I mean. So I'm the one who woke her up. Like I'm not supposed to talk. It's always my fault."

Amber went to the baby's room and stopped the crying. After changing Rainbow's diaper and laying her back down in the crib, she came back to Lou, who had opened a can of beer and sat on the couch in front of the television.

"Honey," she asked in a more conciliatory tone, "what is it with that Frank Feuermann? Can't you two get along?"

"I dunno. Sometimes he's smooth as silk, nothin' seems to ruffle him. Then suddenly he blows. I don't get it."

"Look, honey, I know how we could make some money."

He got up to adjust the bent rabbit ears on top of the TV. "Forget it, Amber."

"But how are we going to pay for groceries? And the medicine? The pharmacy ain't going to let the bill go forever."

"We'll figure it out."

"And us with a new baby, and Christmas coming up, and all."

"I said we'll figure it out!" he shouted.

Lou Cartwright had been in worse situations before and always seemed to find a way out. Sometimes he'd get his mother to bail him out, and once or twice he had gone to his older brother, James. He hated to do that, though. James always made him feel like a loser. Amber's parents lived in Minneapolis, and he kept them out of his business as much as he could. They never paid much attention to him when they visited and ignored him whenever he and Amber and the baby went to Minneapolis. If they called on the telephone and he answered, they would ask for Amber without so much as saying "Hello" to Lou. He figured they never liked that their daughter had married him.

***

As a light snow began to fall late that evening, announcing an early beginning of winter in Waumeka, Lou drove his beat up '84 Ford Bronco to his brother's place on the other side of town, a small brick bungalow in a quiet neighborhood near the high school. James Cartwright and his wife, Agnes, had bought the home three years earlier on a GI loan. The assistant basketball coach at the high school, James took classes at the local community college and planned to apply to the education program at UW-Eau Claire, so that one day he would be able to apply for a regular teaching job. He wanted to teach history and coach the basketball team or the girls' soccer team.

Lou let himself in without knocking. "Anyone home?" he yelled.

Agnes looked out from the kitchen to see who was calling. She wiped her hands on a towel and folded it twice before hanging it on the oven door. She had just finished cleaning the dishes, and the smell of chili and cornbread lingered in the room.

"Lou. Hi. Your brother's back in the garage, tinkering with his new toy. Why don't you go out and see what he's doing?"

Lou let himself out the back door and walked through the snow, down the driveway to the garage. The large door was closed, so he walked around to the small door on the side of the building. He was about to make a sarcastic remark about the driveway not being shoveled, when he remembered why he had come over to see his brother.

James bent under the hood of a '55 Hudson V8 that he had bought from a used car dealer who didn't know what he was selling, or so James thought. He had gotten the antique for $500 and figured it was worth maybe ten times that.

"Hey, Lou, what brings you here? Say, how do you like her? Like the way the chrome on the grill polished up? Look, this baby still has the original V8 engine. You know '55 was the first year they put a V8 into this Hornet." He lifted the hood the way one might open a jewelry box to display the crown jewels. "Still has the brass nuts that held the mount in place. They don't make 'em like that anymore."

James poured some polish from a can onto his clean rag and began working it around the chrome and steel parts under the hood, starting with the air filter.

"You got yourself a sweet bargain, brother Jim. How much did you say you paid?"

"Five hundred big ones. That's it."

After a few seconds of silence, Lou spoke up. "Speaking of money ..."

"Uh-oh. Here it comes. Wondered what brought you out on a cold night like this. By the way, how come you're not at Fleet Farm tonight? You're not working days now, are you?" James put his rag down on the workbench, leaned back and looked his brother straight in the eye.

Lou looked away, toward the antique car they had just been inspecting. He explained without looking up why he had come to see his brother and that he wasn't working either nights or days since his fight with Feuermann.

"Off for a week? Since when can Fleet Farm afford to let workers off for a week one month before Christmas? How come they didn't shift you into hardware if they didn't need you out in the yard, especially during their busiest season? Why don't you tell me the whole story?"

"Never mind, Jim. If I'm going to have to go through the third degree every time I ask for a little favor ..."

"A little favor? So what is it this time? Did you get fired?" James wiped his hands on an old rag and began to pick up his tools and cans of polish, cloths, and steel wool. He put each can and tool in its place on the shelves over his workbench or in their proper drawer below it.

"No, Feuermann got pissed and told me to take a week off—without pay, of course."

Lou's brother wasn't satisfied and asked him what he had done to piss off Feuermann.

"He found a bottle in the back of one of the shelves. I was just trying to keep warm on Wednesday night, I swear. I don't know why, but Feuermann came in there looking for trouble. He usually don't even come in the back. He usually stays in his little office. He's really been pissy lately."

"So you got caught drinking on the job again. This isn't the first time." James put the rag down. "I swear to God, you're getting to be just like the old man."

James and Louis Cartwright had grown up on the west end of town, not far from the trailer park where Lou and Amber now lived. Their parents had owned a run-down three-bedroom frame home about a mile from the paper mill where their father had worked, when there was work, and when he hadn't been laid off for drinking. Amos Cartwright was known around town not only for his drinking, which was legendary, but also for his fondness for other men's wives. He would meet them at Mulligan's bar, where younger men hung out and played pool. Amos would just sit at the bar until one of the women sat down beside him and waited for him to buy them a drink or two or three, and later take them to a motel.

"Don't you go comparing me to Dad. He had his problems and maybe I got mine, but they ain't the same."

"Can't you remember how it was in high school, the other kids snickering behind our backs all the time? I hated him for that. And the stuff we had to wear, that stuff from Goodwill. I always wondered when some kid was going to recognize some old jacket he had thrown out, or some shirt he'd hated. And all the games, and proms, and class trips. How many dances did you go to when you were in high school, Lou? Answer me that?"

"At least you had the basketball team," Lou snapped back. "You weren't even home on Friday nights. Don't worry. I know what you're talking about, but it wasn't as bad as you make it out. And I got nowhere near the problems he had, and I ain't sneaking around on Amber, either. Anyway, you going to help me, or not? I mean if you're not, just say so, and I'll leave you alone."

"I'll have to ask Agnes. How much do you need?"

"Just enough to tide us over. I'll be back to work in a week."

"I'll talk to Agnes in the morning and let you know tomorrow. You know how I feel about this." James looked directly at his younger brother, trying to make eye contact. Lou avoided his gaze.

"I know, and I'll make it up to you. I promise I will."

"It's not the money, Lou. You know that."

***

"Lou needs our help again." James poured coffee into their cups and put the pot back on the stove, then sat down across from his wife. She had gotten up early and fixed pancakes, bacon, and orange juice, Jim's favorite breakfast.

"I'm not surprised. How much this time?"

"I guess a couple hundred bucks should carry him over the week."

"Jim, we've got six weeks until Christmas. Can we afford it?" Agnes asked.

"He's my brother. What can I do?"

"You can tell him 'No.' That's what you can do. You know your father had the same problem and look how he ended up. We should be helping Lou—I mean seeing that he gets help—not just bailing him out every time."

"It's been almost six months." James put his fork into the last piece of pancake on his plate and wiped up the remaining syrup with it before putting it into his mouth. He wiped his lips with the paper napkin.

Agnes set her coffee cup down. As she finished the toast she had buttered, she sighed. "It's up to you, James. I just hate to see us dragged down into this. I think if we're going to do this, though, he needs to pay us back."

"I've already told him that," James assured her.

"I wonder if it would help if we invited them over for Christmas dinner with your mother. It might help them out—and it would give you two a chance to talk."

"Not with mother here," he cautioned.

"No, but after we take her home."

***

After he got home from the community college that afternoon and put his book bag down, James made the call to his brother.

"Lou? I talked to Agnes this morning. Yes. We can lend you $200, but you'll need to get it back to us this time. We're really sort of pinched ourselves … You're welcome. By the way, we'd like you and Amber to come over for dinner on Christmas. We can make plans later, but ask Amber and let us know. You and I need to talk … I said you're welcome. Stop by and I'll give you a check."

James felt guilty as he hung up the telephone. Here he had just paid $500 for an antique car, nothing but a toy really, and now he had second thoughts about giving his little brother less than half that to get him out of a jam. And Lou was right; Friday nights at home had been a drunken mess with their father, and Lou had had to stay there and put up with it while James, at least, could go off to his basketball games. His little brother really had nothing, although their parents, especially their mother, had always seemed to favor Lou, buying him things whenever she had a little extra money. Maybe that's why Lou didn't get out of the house, he thought, and do stuff on his own unless it was to get into trouble. James knew he couldn't be his brother's counselor, but he badly wanted Lou to get help. James promised himself that he would see to it that Lou did.

***

"Seven card hi-lo this time, boys." Charlie Brannigan began to deal the cards all around. As he reached Aaron Kohlberg, he said, without slowing down, "So, Aaron. Glad they gave you the night off. It's been too long since I've been able to take some of your money." The men all laughed, including Aaron.

"Yeah, get it back to the taxpayer is what I say," added Frank Feuermann.

"Anybody wants my job, they're welcome to it," Aaron joked.

"Come on, Aaron. Make sure your boys get their quota of tickets every month, knock a few skulls. Sounds like a snap to me," Cliff Smalley teased.

"Easy? What about you, Brannigan? Work for nine months, leave every afternoon at three o'clock, then take three months off. Now there's a cushy job."

"Three o'clock? When the hell did anyone see me home before six or seven lately? And even then I have to go back for some stupid school-board meeting."

"Twenty-five cents? I'll raise you a dime, Frankie boy." Cliff was bluffing, and probably only Charlie suspected.

"I'll see that," Kohlberg betted.

"So will I. In fact, double that." Charlie called Cliff's bluff.

Marty O'Brien declared that he was out and threw his cards face down onto the center of the table. He leaned back in his chair, smiling, and took a swallow from the bottle of beer in front of him, then wiped his mouth with the cuff of his shirt sleeve.

Frank was next to fold his cards up and set them in a pile in front of him.

Finally, Kohlberg admitted that he didn't have the cards to warrant his staying in the hand either. He leaned over to Cliff and pointed out that he was the only one left to call Charlie.

"You're damn right, I will. Call you and add a dime," Cliff countered.

Both men threw a dime in the pot, and Charlie turned up a pair of kings. Cliff laughed as he turned his five cards over. A pair of nines!

As Charlie took his winnings, Frank took up his cards again, as if he couldn't believe that he had really folded with three aces. "Damn," he muttered, as the other men laughed, and Marty poked him in the arm.

"Hey, Frank. I hear you went and fired Lou Cartwright. What's he doing? Getting into the sauce like his old man?" Marty asked.

"No, I didn't fire him. He's got one week unpaid vacation," Frank snapped back.

"Geez, Frank. Just before Christmas, when he probably needs the money," Charlie said. The Cartwrights were known to be poor, after all, and it did seem unfortunate. Still, Charlie's tone was not accusatory, but rather questioning.

"I can't help it. If I let that go, all my people would be screwing off on the job," Frank said, more quietly this time.

"Who's going to take his place?" Charlie asked, figuring that it might be difficult to hire an extra worker just for the Christmas trade.

"I asked two of the others if they could help out and work a little overtime. When you've got a small boat like mine, everyone's got to take extra turns at the oars now and then, right? Besides, I don't have a school board looking over my shoulder."

"No, you've just got a union," Charlie retorted.

"Don't worry," Frank assured him. "Cartwright didn't even bother to hide the evidence. The union won't be able to help him."

"You know, I remember that kid when we were both in middle school. Sort of a loner," Charlie recalled. "There was only one time he got sent down to the principal's office for goofing off. Otherwise, nobody noticed him." He gazed off toward the fire, recalling the old days.

"I don't know," Marty added, "I knew his older brother, Jim. He was a year behind me in high school. That was before your time, Aaron. Kids made a lot of fun of him, the way he dressed and all."

"Yeah, but wasn't he on the basketball team?" Aaron asked.

"Yes, and that's the only thing that saved him. Basketball was king in those days," Marty noted.

"Still is," Cliff added. "Just ask Coach Justice, or just about anybody on the school board. You can cut funding for art and music, but you better not touch the athletic program."

"Still, I think those guys had it rough when they were in school. Their old man was always out of work ..." Marty said.

"... or getting drunk," added Kohlberg.

"... or sleeping around," said Frank, smiling.

Like Marty, Charlie was born and raised in Waumeka, and Frank had lived there since he was five. They'd all gone to the same schools, ridden their bikes out on the old State Trunk highway on Saturdays, fished in the creek together ... and they all knew the history of most of the characters that had lived there for the past thirty-five years. Cliff had moved up from Madison to open his first medical practice right out of his residency, and bought the house next door to Brannigan's. Aaron Kohlberg had moved from the Twin Cities area ten years earlier to take over as assistant police chief. Three years later he was appointed chief.

"I'm surprised none of those guys at the mill ever shot old Amos Cartwright, the way people say he slept around," Kohlberg wondered.

"I'll take three cards," Frank told Cliff, who was dealing.

"Down and dirty," Cliff replied, as he passed the cards to Frank.

Once again, the three cards didn't help him. Frank folded his cards before the betting even started.

CHAPTER 6

———◆———

"**M**r. Newsome? Hi." Ann Shelby checked the schedule on her desk and then stood to shake Tom Newsome's hand as he came in the classroom door and proceeded to one of the two chairs she had set up in front of her desk. "Thanks for coming tonight. I've talked to Tommy several times about his grades in my class, but nothing seems to help, so I'm glad you came."

She reached out to shake the unwilling hand of the large, obviously confident man who stood in front of her, a bit too close for her comfort. As he appeared to be scanning her from head to toes, she was glad she had chosen to wear a simple, modest white blouse and a long paisley skirt. She knew that some of the older boys called her a "hottie" behind her back, so she was careful to dress in a plain, unassuming style, though it was admittedly hard to hide her youthful shape.

Having taught math at the high school for only three years, this was the first contact she had had with either of Tommy's parents. Even before he was in her class, she knew Tommy by his reputation as something of a troublemaker. She also knew his younger sister, who was a freshman. She knew that Tommy's mother was on the school board, but Ann tried to stay away from the politics of the district. She had talked with some of her colleagues in the teachers' lounge that morning about how they got through parent-teacher conferences, especially with difficult parents.

"A good bottle of bourbon," one of the older math teachers had told her, "but only after you get home. There's nothin' you can do to prepare, 'cause you never know what to expect."

Newsome leaned forward in his chair, and looked at the young woman, as if inspecting her clothes. She checked to make sure that her skirt fell well below her knees. He glanced around the room before commenting, "Well, his mother usually comes to these things, but she had a board meeting tonight. Something about one of your colleagues, I believe. Maybe you know about it." He turned back to look at the teacher over the rim of his glasses, which he had let slide down his nose.

Newsome was a big man and looked awkward sitting in the chair across from his son's algebra teacher. He had graduated from this high school twenty-five years earlier, mainly on the strength of his skill as a track and field athlete; he was district champion in three events in his senior year. He'd graduated from Stevens Point four years later with much the same record. He moved back to town after college and set up a used car lot across from the old Ford agency. When the Ford dealership began to struggle and the owner began looking for a way out, Newsome bought him out for a fraction of what the business was worth. Newsome turned it into a huge enterprise, hiring some of his old track and field buddies as salesmen and luring a top mechanic away from the town's GM dealership with the promise of making him the head of the service department.

"It's not that I think Tommy can't understand the material," Ann explained.

"Of course he can understand it," Newsome interrupted, sitting up straight. "Of course he can. And I'm sure he's trying his best."

Ann Shelby was not to be dismissed. "But too often I catch him goofing around in class. He sits in the back whispering and laughing with his friends. It's distracting for the others," the young woman said, becoming more direct.

"Oh, well, you know how boys that age can be. I'm sure I don't have to tell you." She couldn't tell whether his smile was more condescending or flirtatious. In either case, she insisted on making her point.

"I'm afraid if his grades don't improve—"

"I'll have a talk with him, Mrs. Uh … Shelby, is it?" he said, looking at her nametag. "I'm sure he'll come around. You're doing a fine job. Keep it up. And thank you. I know Tommy enjoys your class." Newsome got up to leave. Anne took a small stack of papers from her desktop and handed the top three to Tommy Newsome's father. "You might want to look at these," she said as she handed them to him and then reached to shake his hand.

Newsome folded the papers and put them in the front pocket of his sport coat. Leaving the room, he checked the schedule his wife had given him, and found each of the other classrooms where he had appointments with his son's teachers. As he left the building that night, he reached into his coat pocket to get his car keys. Pulling out the math papers, he looked at the top page, and then threw the papers into the trash can at the front door.

***

"Dad, didja go to the parent-teacher things last night?"

"Yeah, I went. Your mother had a board meeting."

"Didja meet Shelby?"

"Your math teacher? Yes, I met her. Hot little number, isn't she? I would have guessed she just got out of teachers' college."

"What did she say—about me, I mean?"

"Oh, you're doing fine. Should pay a little more attention, probably. Otherwise, you're doing fine."

Tommy Newsome smiled and finished his toast, gulped down a glass of orange juice, and got up to leave for school.

"Dad, I'm gonna take the Mustang. Is that OK?"

"Does your mother need it?" his father asked without looking up from his newspaper.

"No, I don't think so. I'll ask her."

Tommy raced up the stairs and yelled to his mother through the bathroom door. "Dad said I can take the Mustang if it's OK with you. It's OK with you, isn't it?"

"Come home right after school, hear me?" his mother replied.

"Yeah, yeah, I hear ya." Tommy dashed down the stairs, took the keys from the rack next to the side door, and grabbed the book bag that he had left on the floor the night before. "See ya," he yelled back to his father, who still sat at the kitchen table, finishing his breakfast and reading the paper.

***

"Catherine, we're going to have to give that boy his own car one of these days."

"I guess you're right. He can't keep using the Mustang," Catherine replied. She suggested they get him a used car, a trade-in from the lot.

"No, we should get him a new car and let him pick it out, himself. He'd like that," his father insisted.

Catherine agreed. As she began stacking dishes in the dishwasher, she asked casually how the parent-teacher conferences had gone.

"Just fine. He's doing a good job," her husband answered.

She pressed him further, her questions becoming more pointed, asking specifically about his math class. Newsome replied that math, like the other courses, was going well.

Finally she got to the point. "Did you meet his math teacher?"

Sensing her exasperation, Newsome put down the paper he was reading. "Oooh, yes. Quite a little number."

"I swear, you men are all alike," Catherine said, drying her hands. "What did she say about Tommy?"

"Like I said, he's doing fine. She says he talks to his friends in class now and then, but what does she expect? He's popular, got a lot of friends. Of course they want to talk to him." Then Newsome abruptly changed the topic. "How did your board meeting go?" he asked.

"Like I said, I think we have Brannigan where we want him," his wife replied with a smirk.

"I hope you have a plan," he cautioned.

"Oh, I do, believe me," she replied.

CHAPTER 7

———————

As Charlie Brannigan climbed into bed, he leaned over, kissed his wife and whispered, "Happy anniversary."

Katie smiled and reminded him that their anniversary wasn't until the next day. When he said he knew that but just didn't want to be late again, she grabbed his arm.

"That only happened once, Charlie Brannigan, and it was years ago. I love you."

He asked if they could go out to dinner the next day, unless she already had something planned for them at home.

"No, going out sounds great. Can we plan it tomorrow?"

"Mmm, yes. Good night."

***

The next day went by quickly for Charlie. He stopped by the gym mid-morning to watch Chet Magnuson work with the wrestling team. One wrestler straddled his opponent in an illegal starting position. The straddled wrestler turned red. With an angry, almost vicious look, he responded with a cross-face, slapping his forearm into his opponent's face. Magnuson blew his whistle.

"May I?" Charlie asked as he stepped toward the coach.

"Be my guest, boss."

"Gentlemen, it's been a few years since I wrestled in college. But I can assure you that straddling is an illegal starting position. Don't do it. As for that cross-face—well, sometimes it's allowed, but don't ever use it in revenge. Remember, we're men of character first." Turning to Chet Magnuson, he added, "Thanks, coach."

"Thank *you*."

Charlie walked back to his office, fondly recalling his own wrestling days at UW. He had just borrowed a phrase from Coach Hudson's play-book: "We're men of character first." Would Chet's wrestlers remember that admonition later in life, as Charlie had? Would it serve them as well as it had him?

After going over the budget for the next semester, reviewing a list of potential substitute teachers, and conferring with teachers about their schedules, he looked out the window across the parking lot toward Heckney Woods and thought about Katie and their fifteen years together. Not having children had been a disappointment for her, and he worried that she worked hard, perhaps too hard, to keep busy and cover that disappointment. He stopped at Swensen's florist on his way home. He got to the house before Katie and put a tall, Waterford crystal vase with fifteen long-stem red roses and a note that read, "I do. Love, C" on the kitchen table.

"Oh, Charlie, would you look at those roses—and that gorgeous vase! I love it! But I only have something little for you." Katie handed her husband of fifteen years a small white envelope. He opened the envelope, read the card, and laughed. "I'm glad we got married," it said; on the inside, "Now when your parents come over, I don't have to hide you. Happy anniversary!" Inside the card was a coupon for a three-year subscription to *Field and Stream* and a gift certificate to Trout Central Sporting Goods Store.

"Yes!" He thanked her. "Now I don't have to wait until I go to the barbershop to read this every month."

"Are we still on for dinner?" she asked.

"Yeah, I was thinking we could go to The York. How does that sound?"

"The York sounds great. Are you sure we can afford it?"

"Hey, it's our fifteenth anniversary. And tomorrow is Saturday, which means you don't work." Charlie nuzzled his wife's neck below her ear as she smiled and backed away.

***

Charlie let his wife off at the door of the restaurant and went behind the building to park the car himself, rather than let the attendant park for him. The York, an old Victorian manor on the outskirts of town, had been remodeled and converted into a restaurant.

Katie stood at the front door, waiting for him. He took her coat and handed it, along with his own, over the counter to the hatcheck clerk. As Katie walked up to the maître d' Charlie noticed that two young men at a nearby table had both turned to take a quick glance at her. In fact, she was easy to look at, he thought. Her long red hair was pulled back with a silver clasp, and hung down her back over a black dress that opened at the back. She wore the pearls that her mother had given her on her wedding day, and a pair of matching pearl earrings. She was tall and slender; "stunning" was the best word to describe her. He was pleased that, even after fifteen years, he still saw her that way.

The restaurant was more crowded than usual, even for a Friday night, and they hadn't remembered to make a reservation. "Thirty minutes?" Charlie repeated when the maître d' told him they would have a wait. "Sure, we can do that," he said, looking toward his wife, who gave him a nod. "We'll be at the bar."

Charlie put his hand on the small of Katie's back and led her through double oak doors to the bar, a smaller room lined with hot pink–and–brown flocked wallpaper. Charlie thought it might have looked more appropriate in the waiting room of a nineteenth century bordello in the Wild West.

"Tonight I want to get drunk and make mad, passionate love," he whispered to Katie.

"Charlie!"

"Just kidding. Just kidding—about the getting drunk part, that is."

"It doesn't seem to me as though you've ever needed the drink, Charles Brannigan," she said, affecting her favorite Scottish accent.

They sat on stools at the bar, and Charlie ordered a glass of single malt Scotch for each of them. "In fact, make those doubles," he told the bartender, "We have a long wait. Now that I think of it, I see you have Oban up there on the third shelf. That's what we'd like." He pointed to the rows of whisky that were lined up in front of a mirror behind the bar. It was the one alcoholic drink they could agree on, something for which they had both acquired a taste on their honeymoon in the highlands of Scotland.

"Do you remember Shieldaig?" Charlie asked.

"How could I forget," she smiled back. They had rented a car in Scotland and driven into the highlands as far as Ullapool, then down the winding roads toward the Isle of Skye, dodging sheep on the open range for much of the way. The first night, they had stayed at a bed and breakfast in Shieldaig, a coastal village approached only by a narrow highland road that dipped down toward the coast in fits and starts. The steep road had been difficult enough, but driving on the "wrong"—namely the left—side of the road had made it downright treacherous for Charlie. Luckily, few cars had passed him either way.

Once in Shieldaig, they had found Mrs. MacPherson's B&B on the main road, which had turned out to be the only road stretching along the shore of the loch. They hadn't realized how late it had become; that far north, the daylight in early July stretched well past ten o'clock. Still, Charlie had apologized to Mrs. MacPherson for their late arrival. She had accepted his apology and brought out tea and biscuits on a silver tray.

It had been another hour before they had left Mrs. McPherson in her comfortable living room and fireplace to go up, tired and satisfied, to their own room, with its four-poster, queen-sized bed and drapes covering an entire wall. Before falling asleep, however, Charlie had uncorked the bottle of single malt Scotch that they had bought in Oban earlier that day.

In the morning, the couple had opened the huge drapes that covered the windows at the front of their room and saw Loch Torridon across the road. The sun had already begun to play on the waves, fishermen either repairing nets on the shore or cleaning their boats moored a few yards from the shore, and a few children running along the sand and skipping stones into the loch. A knock on the door; Mrs. MacPherson had brought tea and scones to their room. Charlie had accepted the tray with a smile and thanks and set it on the large oak dresser. In no hurry to get up and spoil the magic of this romantic awakening, Charlie and Katie had stayed in bed and made love for the second time. It had been almost noon before they were downstairs with their bags, saying goodbye to their hostess.

***

Charlie reached down and pulled his barstool closer to Katie. "Is this as good as the Oban we had in Shieldaig?" Charlie asked after he toasted his wife and their fifteen years together.

"It really gets better every year, Charlie. I mean it. And you never needed to get drunk, never once." She leaned over and kissed her husband on the cheek.

Charlie turned to his wife, apologized for changing the subject, and asked, "Speaking of getting drunk, do you remember Amber and Lou Cartwright? They were at the high school a few years after we graduated. She was Amber Pulte then. You might remember his older brother, James? He was on the basketball team. Helps out as assistant coach now."

"Oh, Lord, yes. Wasn't the boys' dad Amos Cartwright, boozer extraordinaire?" Katie asked

"That's the one."

"Good God, I'll never forget the night they brought Amber into the emergency room a couple years back."

"What was that for?" He swiveled in his barstool to look at his wife, who just shook her head.

"Somebody had beaten her up. Pretty bad, too. I think it was somebody where she worked. I know it wasn't her husband."

"Well, anyway, it seems that Lou got in trouble at Fleet Farm. Frank Feuermann laid him off for a week."

"Just before Christmas? Sounds like your friend Feuermann's being a prick."

"Well, I don't know. Cartwright was drinking on the job, but you may be right about Frank. I don't think he's a happy man, either. But Cartwright was drinking."

"Maybe he takes after his old man."

"That's what I'm afraid of. And I always liked those guys. Everybody made fun of them in school, but you know, they were nice guys once you got to know them. James was on the JV basketball team when I was on the varsity team. He was a couple of years behind me. His little brother was in middle school then, but he always came out to watch us practice. Never came to the games. I think he was too embarrassed or self-conscious."

"Why don't you give him a call and see if there's something you can do. Do you know him well enough?" Katie asked

"I've been thinking about that. I'll have to be careful. They're sensitive. You know, and with that new baby and everything—damn, seems like a shame."

Katie didn't answer. They were both finishing their drinks when the maître d' called their name over the loudspeaker: "Brannigan for two. Brannigan." Neither of them spoke much after that. Charlie ordered a steak and a glass of merlot, and Katie got fresh walleye and a glass of Chardonnay. He tried a few times to start a new conversation, but it never seemed to go anywhere. Katie would answer him in a few words, and then there would be another long silence until he tried again. The evening that had started out with such promise seemed to peter out. They both agreed that their dinners were good, and the wine was excellent. Still, Charlie couldn't help but notice that something was missing. Lately, it more often happened that way when they went out to dinner.

CHAPTER 8

Lou Cartwright sat on the front steps of his brother's house, waiting for James to get home, when the car pulled into the driveway.

"Hey, Lou, what are you doing?" James called as he got out of the car.

"Just waiting for you to get home. Thought maybe you'd have your checkbook handy. I hate to ask you for this."

"No, we agreed." James asked his brother to try his best to get the money back to him as soon as he could, since the holidays were coming up and he and Agnes would need the money. Then he added, "Oh, by the way, what did Amber say? Are you two coming over for Christmas?"

"Oh, shit. I forgot to ask her. I'll ask her tonight. But I'm sure it's gonna be fine."

James took his wallet from a back pocket and took a check out of his wallet. "Here, I wrote this out for you this morning. I hope that's going to be enough." The check was for $250.

"That'll be plenty. I'm gonna be back to work on Friday."

On his way back home, Lou began thinking about the casino on the Chippewa Reservation. He hadn't been there in two years. The casino was only about forty miles from home, but how could he get there without having to explain himself to Amber? He decided on a strategy that night while they were having dinner.

"You know, your parents haven't seen Rainbow in over a month. Why don't you take the truck tomorrow and drive down there?"

"Are you sure? I'd have to stay overnight."

"So, what's wrong with that?"

"But what about you?"

He explained that he would be fine, that he had gotten a little money from Lou that morning, so maybe he could give her $30, so she could go shopping with her mom. Maybe do a little Christmas shopping.

"You didn't go and ask your brother for money again. How much did he give you?"

"Uh, hundred and fifty."

Amber insisted that they would have to pay Lou's brother back as soon as they could.

"I know. I told him we would."

The next morning, he helped Amber pack a small suitcase with Rainbow's clothes, diapers, and bottles, and then put her own overnight things in a large plastic bag. He threw the suitcase and bag in the back of the covered truck and fixed the baby seat on the passenger's side. It would take about two hours to get to the Twin Cities, so Amber fed Rainbow just before they left.

***

The casino was more crowded than Lou Cartwright ever remembered it. The parking lot, which held over a thousand cars, was completely full. A Native American boy who was directing traffic asked him to roll down his window and then suggested that he park in the new parking lot across the street. Even that second parking lot was almost full. Lou had to park in the last row, in a dark corner near some woods. Beyond the woods, about a hundred feet away, was the river.

Inside, the casino was just as he remembered it: the sound of coins splashing into the trays of the slot machines, bells going off when somebody hit the jackpot, and the loud music on the PA system all made his heart beat faster. It was smokier than he remembered, though, and there were a lot more people. And it seemed darker, not so that you couldn't see where you were going, but just darker than it used to be.

He went to the line in front of the cashier's window and waited his turn. When he got to the window he asked for $50 worth of quarters. *That should be enough to get me started*, he thought, *that there's my seed money. That's all I'll need to take out of my wallet.*

He went back to the corner, where the 25-cent slot machines were. It was hard to get through the aisles with his bucket of quarters. There were people on both sides on every aisle, sitting on stools playing the slots. Some people played two machines at a time, reaching over the stool next to them, which they sometimes pushed back into the aisle. Finding an empty stool, he put his bucket on the counter next to the slot machine and undid one of the rolls of quarters, pouring them into the bucket. He started with two quarters. "Damn, rotten …" Three quarters. "Still nothing." Back to two quarters. "Geez, by now …"

After Lou had spent about $20 dollars, his luck began to change. He put two quarters in the machine and $15 in quarters poured down into the tray, making a loud clanking noise. The woman to his right looked over and smiled. He bet four quarters on the next set. Again, quarters clanged into the tray—$25 worth. The woman looked over again, not smiling this time, just looking.

A hostess with a tight blouse and a short skirt came over to Lou with her tray and order pad. She asked what he would like to drink. He hesitated. "Don't worry, honey, it's on the house," she said.

Lou kept playing the same machine, drinking his Canadian whiskey, winning some and losing some, until he hit a losing streak. He calculated that he was ahead only about $10 at that point. He started to get up to go to another machine, when the hostess came over again. His glass had been empty for about 10 minutes. "Like another, sweetheart? It's $2.50." Lou ordered another drink and moved to a stool across the aisle.

Once again the quarters started to fill up the tray and the bells began to ring. It was another lucky streak and time for another drink. After finishing his third rye and water, he got up to go to the men's room, taking his bucket of coins with him. When he returned he went to the blackjack table. He didn't do well there. He couldn't seem to remember the rules and the other players began to get annoyed with him.

"Why don't you go back and play the slots?" the man on his right snapped, "You're pissing me off."

"Better yet, why don't you go sober up," snickered a younger man with a black turtleneck sweater, a gold chain around his neck, and a watch with a large gold wristband. The others at the table laughed.

"Yeah, well fuck you all," Lou slurred. "I made me a lot of money over there." He went back to the slot machines and continued to win, scooping the quarters into his bucket until it was almost full. When he went to order another drink from the hostess, she called a large Native American man over to talk to him.

"You've had a good time tonight. Maybe it's time to go home now and sleep it off."

Lou began to protest when the guard took him by the elbow and escorted him to the cashier's window. The cashier poured his bucket of quarters into the counting machine. "That's $184 dollars and 50 cents." She counted out the bills on the counter and handed him the change.

"Whoa, I won bi-ig tonight," Lou stammered and waved his bills as he went by the blackjack table. Never before had he left the casino a winner. In fact, whenever he had gone to the casino in the past, he ended up leaving with no money at all.

He found his way to the door. The night air hit his face like a cold washcloth. He straightened up, put his winnings into his large overcoat pocket, grabbed the railing, and walked down the steps.

"Can I help you find your car?" a young man, probably a parking attendant, asked.

"No, it's right over there," he answered, pointing to the lot across the street.

"Have a good night, then."

"Yeah, you too, do have a good night, too," he slurred.

As Lou walked toward the road he sensed other patrons behind him, probably also going to the second parking lot. He turned to see if anyone was right behind him. Nobody was there.

He crossed the street and headed toward the dark corner of the lot where his car was parked. Again he thought he heard somebody—feet shuffling. He turned to look but didn't see anyone. He went down the row of cars, looking for his green Chevy. Not finding it at first, he began to go back in the other direction when he felt something pull on his arm.

"Hey, punk." The next thing Lou felt was a thud on the back of his neck. He fell to the ground, and felt someone kick him in the chest. He thought his insides would come out through his mouth. He began to gag when he felt another foot smash down on his face. He tried to look up, but blood poured out of his mouth and down from his forehead into his eyes. He saw a large gold watchband... then his world started to spin and go black. He heard nothing.

After a while he began to hear sounds again. He tried to open his eyes, but everything was a dark, bloody blur. Blood had dried on his face and eyes. He began to shiver. His hands and feet were numb from the cold. He wondered how long he had been there and realized that he couldn't move. He thought he heard people laughing, "You're a drunken alki sot, just like your old man." It was getting lighter out. He heard a siren and saw a red and blue flashing light, on and off and on and off.

CHAPTER 9

———

Clearing her desk, putting note pads in a plastic desk organizer, pencils in their holder, and a stack of papers in a three-tier tray, Tricia Cameron was getting ready to leave for the day when Charlie Brannigan came out of his office, locking the door behind him. He thanked his office manager for all the extra effort she was putting in. She looked up with a puzzled smile, but accepted his gratitude.

"Any time," she said laughing.

Charlie thought about how grateful he was to have a mature, competent staff. He had met with several of the teachers in the lounge between classes and again at lunchtime and had gotten a good sense of how they coped with parent-teacher conferences. Even his young math teacher, Ann Shelby, had survived the ordeal unscathed. They had both laughed when she told him of her encounter with Tom Newsome.

When Charlie got home, he hung up his coat and hat on the pegs beside the back door and walked up the step leading to the kitchen. He smelled a roast cooking. He looked through the kitchen into the dining room and saw a tablecloth, candles, and flowers on the table.

He yelled upstairs to his wife. "Darling, what's up here? Are we expecting company?"

"No, no. I'll be right down."

Katie was freshly showered and dressed in a red dress that she had bought for the Sturdevant Memorial dinner dance, a fancy annual fund-raising party that always called for new clothes, at the hospital the year before. Her hair was pulled back and she wore small gold earrings.

Charlie sounded his approval with a soft "mmm," smiled, and met her at the bottom of the stairs. Taking her in his arms, he kissed her on the neck and then on the lips.

"What's going on here? Do I need to dress up? Did I forget a birthday?"

"No, no, no," she laughed. "I knew we would finally have the evening to ourselves, so I thought I'd make it special. Besides, I didn't have to work this afternoon, so I had time to cook a roast and bake a pie."

"And I notice you got some painting done." An easel in the family room held an oil painting of a country scene in spring, an abandoned farmhouse, barn, and outbuildings surrounded with flowering bushes and wildflowers.

"I had some fun with my oils, remembering an old farm near Hazelton when I was a kid. Let's eat."

Katie went to the kitchen to get the food. She took the roast, potatoes, carrots, and onions from the roasting pan in the oven and put them on a platter, which she brought to the table and set in front of Charlie. After the two of them said grace, Charlie began to cut the roast. He asked his wife about the painting.

"It's going fine. I just wish I could find more time for it," she answered. "But tell me about your day."

"Well, I talked with a bunch of the teachers in the lounge this afternoon—sort of a post mortem on the parent-teacher conferences. Ann Shelby got to meet Tom Newsome. Lucky her."

"That must have been some conference. How did it go?" Katie asked.

"Apparently all right. She let him know his kid isn't pulling his weight in class."

"How did Mr. Newsome like hearing that?" she asked, with a touch of sarcasm.

"Well, Ann said she thought he couldn't be less interested. She thinks the kid's a replica of the old man. At least she didn't have to meet Mrs. Newsome."

"Good grief. That woman's a menace. How did she get on the school board, anyway?"

"Politics, my dear."

"Well, I'm not sure that—"

"You know what," he interrupted, smiling, "I'd rather talk about the painting. Better yet, why don't you tell me about your day?"

"Well, now that you mention it, there was one other thing, besides the painting and cooking, that I did today." He looked over at his wife and realized by the coy smile that this special dinner was not just to celebrate the fact that she had the afternoon off or that he got home early.

"Yes? Yes? So?" he asked.

"I missed my period this month." Tears began to fill Katie's eyes. Charlie stood up and went over to her, kissed her forehead.

"Did you ask Cliff?" He knew that their neighbor would be the first doctor that Katie would consult.

"Yes, he wants me to see the OB specialist, but he did test me." She was crying now.

"Are you serious? Is this it?"

She just nodded as he stood next to her, drawing her head to his chest. He kissed her on the top of her head and went back to his seat, then stood up again. "Wait a minute. Where is that '85 Chateau Pavie we've been saving?" He went into the kitchen and came back with a bottle of Bordeaux and two wine glasses.

"St. Emilion, 1985. Grand cru classe. I guess this is the occasion this bottle has been waiting for. I love you—both of you." He put the glasses on the table, kissed his wife again, and went back for the corkscrew.

"Charlie," she objected, "I'm pregnant. Do you really think wine…?"

"Oh, crap. Of course, you're right. OK. Soda it is. But as soon as that baby is born…." Charlie set the wine back in the kitchen, returned with two glasses of ginger ale, and kissed his wife a third time.

CHAPTER 10

—◆—

Police chief Aaron Kohlberg was about fifteen minutes late getting to the station. He put his lunch in the workroom refrigerator, went into his office and hung his coat up behind the door. He had just sat down when George Akishembie, one of his deputies, knocked on the open door.

"Did you see last night's log, Chief?" George Akishembie was the only Native American on the force. The other officers often asked him to ride along when there was trouble at the reservation or the casino. He knew his own people and spoke their language. He also knew that they occasionally got framed by unscrupulous white authorities. Plenty of people in Pinecone County had no love for the Chippewa population. He often told about having overheard a gas-station attendant saying, "Why don't they go back where they came from?" Furthermore, people on the reservation respected him. The son of a chieftain who had gotten an education off the reservation, George had married a white woman, but nobody held that against him. Sylvia Akishembie was a teacher's assistant in the public school and for years had treated the Native Americans with respect. She always went out of her way to tutor the Chippewa children who were having trouble with their school work. She was also known and respected by the white community with whom she had grown up.

Chief Kohlberg looked up from the papers on his desk. "No, I haven't seen the log. Could you bring it in, George? And tell Jimmy to get me a cup of coffee—please."

"Jimmy, the chief wants a cup of black coffee—please." Officer Akishembie returned with a clip board with a log of the previous night's activities: two traffic citations, one for speeding and another for DUI, two domestic arguments, and an apparent assault and battery at the White Deer Casino. The deputy went back to the counter in the outer office.

Kohlberg sat at his desk and read the report, paying closest attention to the apparent assault. A few minutes later, a younger deputy, Jimmy Ashblane, brought him his coffee.

"Jimmy, you were on this morning. This assault at the casino... It says, 'Victim: L. Cartwright.' Is that Lou Cartwright?"

"Yes, sir, I believe it is. Lives with his wife in a trailer over there—what we used to call the flats, you know, over on the west side, past the river."

"Damn it anyway." He slammed the clipboard down on his desk, picked up his coffee and blew across the top of the cup. "How bad was it? Was he drinking? Who did it?" He began to look down at the report. "'Assailant: Unknown.' What the hell is this?"

"Dunno. We didn't get there until way after it was over. Must have happened about one or two o'clock. We didn't get a call until five this morning. We'd just come on duty."

"It's a damn surprise he didn't freeze to death if he was out there that long."

"I think parts of him were frozen; and he was pretty bloody. We called the ambulance and got him over to the hospital."

"And then what?"

"We were going to talk to him, but he was too far gone."

"You didn't get a statement? Did someone take him home?"

"No, the doc in the ER wanted to admit him. Said he wasn't fit to go anywhere. Said it was a good thing we weren't having a real Wisconsin winter yet. He would've frozen. He was afraid of hypothermia ... especially with all the alcohol in him."

"Was Akishembie with you?"

"Yes."

Kohlberg looked up. "Thanks, that's all." He reached for his telephone as Deputy Ashblane left his office, closing the door behind him.

After fifteen minutes, Kohlberg came out of his office and went over to Akishembie at the counter.

"George, what do you think happened this morning at the casino?"

George Akishembie told the chief is was pretty hard to tell what had happened, that the guy had been drinking and nobody knew if he had been alone or with somebody else. But he had been drinking pretty hard, that was sure. Blood alcohol level in the ER was nearly .20.

The chief wondered if the victim had anything on him, such as money or a gun.

"If he had any money, it was gone; probably a robbery. His wallet was lying there next to him … but no money. He wasn't too coherent when we left him," Akishembie said.

"Who was on the desk?"

"Stevens, but he left at eight, when Louise came in."

"Any idea who might have done it?"

"Negative. Like I said, we didn't get there 'til it was all over." Akishembie stood up to go to the men's room. As Kohlberg turned to go back into his office, Deputy Olson, a thirty-year veteran who had overheard the conversation spoke up. "You damn well know what I think it was. One of those Indian kids got too much firewater in his belly and decided to roll someone for a few bucks. That's what I think."

"What makes you say that?"

"Bad enough they get a tax break on that money machine of a casino. Damn cash cow. That's what it is; you know that, don't you?" He hadn't seen Akishembie come out of the men's room. "Jesus, George. Sorry, I was just thinking—"

"I know what you think," Akishembie said. "You don't need to worry."

***

Kohlberg drove an unmarked car to St. Luke's Hospital and went directly to the surgical ward on the third floor. Stepping out of the elevator, he encountered the faint but distinct smell of antiseptic cleaner and assumed that the gleaming floors had been recently mopped. As he proceeded down the corridor toward the nurses' station, his suspicions about the odor were confirmed. Next to the men's room, a yellow bucket full of dirty, soapy water stood with a mop still sticking from it.

"Good morning. I'm Chief Kohlberg. I'm here to see Louis Cartwright. He was admitted last night from emergency."

Kohlberg thought the nurse looked young and frightened as she picked up a clipboard chart from a rack behind her. She flipped the chart open and kept turning the pages until her eyes finally settled on one sheet. "I'm not sure I can let you see him yet, Chief. I'll have to ask the doctor." She set her clipboard down and reached for the telephone. Her voice squeaked over the loudspeaker, "Dr. Philbert, eight, two, three, please. Dr. Philbert." She set the telephone down and reassured Kohlberg, "He'll call us right back. I know he's here this morning."

The telephone at the desk rang three minutes later. "Surgery. Margaret speaking—oh, yes, Dr. Philbert, I did call. It's about Louis Cartwright ... No, no, he's stable. It's just that Chief Kohlberg is here from the police department and would like to see him. Yes, I'll have him wait." She hung up the phone and turned to Kohlberg. "Chief, Dr. Philbert would like you to wait. He would like to talk to you before you see Mr. Cartwright."

"Is he awake?" the chief asked.

"Well, yes, he's awake, but he came in pretty badly hurt last night. Dr. Philbert will only be a few minutes. Would you like a cup of coffee while you wait?"

"No, thank you, I'm fine. I'll just wait over here." Kohlberg went to a lounge across from the nursing station. He flipped through the magazines on a coffee table until he found a *US News and World Report* and sat down to read.

The nurse was right. Within five minutes, the doctor arrived. "Hi, Chief. Stan Philbert. I understand you're here to see Louis Cartwright." The physician was short, middle-aged, heavy set, with a graying beard. He wore a white lab coat that opened completely down the front. His dark-blue trousers were held up with wide suspenders over a checkered shirt.

"Yes, we need to figure out what happened last night. My men didn't get to him until almost five this morning. They tell me it was a gruesome scene."

"That's true. I can let you see him, but I should warn you, he's still in pretty bad shape."

"Is he coherent?"

"Only some of the time." Philbert sat down on the couch next to the police chief. "Do you have any idea what happened to him? The report from ER was pretty sketchy."

"No, other than what my officers told me. They said he seemed to have been mugged, and somebody had rifled through his wallet. What's the prognosis?" Kohlberg asked.

The doctor explained that he might have to operate. One foot was pretty badly frostbitten, but his main fear when Lou was admitted was hypothermia. He was out of the woods on that score, but he still had the frostbitten foot, two cracked ribs, and a broken jaw to deal with. The doctor had grabbed the chart from the desk and went through the pages as he spoke. "He's scheduled for another CAT scan this afternoon. Didn't find anything more than that last night, but we'll need to be sure."

"How long do you think he was out there?"

"Probably two or three hours. He's lucky it wasn't worse, given the cold snap we had last night. Good thing it wasn't a real Wisconsin December night."

"When you say 'operate'..."

"He may lose his right foot."

"Have you told him that?"

"No, not yet. Not until we know for sure. It may take a few days to see if we can get enough circulation to the toes."

"And his wife. Have you talked to her?" Kohlberg asked.

"No, it's strange. We haven't been able to reach her. We keep calling but there's no answer. He doesn't seem to know why she wouldn't be home. Says they have a baby girl, too."

Kohlberg walked with the doctor down the hall to room 348. A red sign on the door cautioned "RESTRICTED ACCESS. See nurse before entering." Another sign hanging from the door knob stated, "Oxygen in use." Only one bed in the double room was occupied, and the curtain between the beds was pulled back. The smell of urine replaced the antiseptic odor. Kohlberg noticed the almost full bag that was clipped to the bed. Lou Cartwright lay with his left leg, fully wrapped in an ace bandage, propped up on two pillows. Where his foot stuck out of the bandage, his toes were black and dark blue. A tube from his nose extended up to a plastic container on the wall above his head.

"What's that for?" Kohlberg inquired.

"That's an NG tube, nasogastric; it sucks the contents out of his stomach. Periodically you'll see the vacuum pump operate." Kohlberg had already noticed green fluid slowly oozing up the tube and into the bag above the patient's head.

"Probably quite a bit of Jim Beam in that bag," Kolhberg said. Mildly inappropriate, but the joke seemed to make it easier to tolerate the sights and smells that permeated the room.

Cartwright moved his head from side to side occasionally, as if trying to dislodge the thick ugly tube that was taped to his face where it emerged from his nose. Other than those movements and an occasional groan, he appeared to be unconscious.

"I think you'll need to come back, Chief. It looks as though you won't be able to get much from him today," Dr. Philbert advised.

"Guess you're right," Kohlberg said as the two men exited the room and headed down the hall toward the elevator.

CHAPTER 11

Charlie was surprised to find that the house was quiet when he walked through the side door and into the kitchen. He looked around the kitchen door and called to his wife. He and Katie had planned to have an early supper and then go Christmas shopping.

After hanging up his coat and hat, Charlie noticed two pork chops on a plate on the kitchen counter. Figuring Katie must have put them there to thaw out for their supper, he went out to the garage to put some charcoal in the Weber grill. Even though there was a little snow on the ground, he pulled the grill out into the driveway and poured charcoal into it, but didn't light the coals. He came back into the house and settled down in the family room with a beer and the newspaper. Within ten minutes, Katie drove up the driveway and came in through the side door.

"Charles, are you insane?" his wife laughed as she opened the door.

"Hey, sweetie."

"It's snowing out there, and you have the grill going."

"I know. Just thought those pork chops deserved grilling. So what if the grill gets a little snow on it. It still works. Anyhow, it's not snowing hard. How was your day?" he asked.

"Exhausting." Katie put her coat and hat in the front closet, looked in the mirror, and pulled her hair back off the sides of her face, neck, and shoulders as if to make a ponytail. Smiling, she came into the family room and kissed Charlie.

"Did you see the potatoes I put in the oven? They're all ready to bake," she said.

"No, I didn't see them. How long will they take?"

"Forty minutes. No more than that."

"Good, I didn't start the grill yet, so we'll have plenty of time to sit here and have a beer together. Then after dinner we go to Sears, Kohl's, Penny's, and wherever else and find presents for your brother and sister, your parents ..."

"A beer sounds good, but it'll have to be soda for me. Remember?" She smiled.

Katie came back from the kitchen with a can of soda with a glass on top in one hand and a plate of crackers and cheese in the other. She put the plate and soda on the coffee table and sat down in the large leather chair next to Charlie, who sat on the sofa.

"If we weren't going out tonight, I'd have you make a fire in the fireplace and just eat here in the family room."

"I agree. But there'll be plenty of nights like this over the holidays. Anyway, it'll be good to get a little of the shopping out of the way," he answered. "By the way, what took you so long to get home?" He leaned over and kissed the hair on the side of her face.

"I stayed late because I had taken time out to see Dr. Berkside, the new OB-GYN. I really like her. Just plain down to earth."

"What'd she say? Everything OK?"

"I'm about six weeks. Everything looks good to her. She wants me to have an ultrasound in about a month." Katie got up from her chair and sat down next to Charlie on the sofa. He put his arm around her.

"Why is that?" he asked.

"Just my age, I guess. And the fact that we weren't able to conceive for so long," she answered.

"Six weeks," Charlie calculated. "Let's see. That means the baby will be coming about mid-August. Hope next summer's not too hot."

"I'll be just fine. Let's not tell anybody right away. Is that OK?" she asked

"Sure, but what about Cliff? He knows."

"He's a doctor. He wouldn't say a word—not even to Sally—unless I said he could."

"Cool. We'll keep it to ourselves for now."

"By the way, do you remember that Cartwright fellow you were talking about the other night at the restaurant—Lou Cartwright?" Katie asked

"Yeah, what about him?" Charlie took his arm from around his wife and reached over to the coffee table to get a cracker and some cheese.

"He's in the hospital."

"Really? What for?"

"I shouldn't even be telling you, but there was already a small piece in the *Gazette* this morning. He was out in the cold most of the night Wednesday. Over by the casino. Apparently he got mugged, and they just left him there in the cold."

"How bad is he?"

"Pretty bad. Dr. Philbert is taking care of him. They thought he might lose his foot. Got pretty frostbitten. A bunch of broken ribs and a banged-up face. I stopped in to see him. Looks pretty bad, but he was able to talk a little bit. When he was in elementary and middle school, he remembered you being in high school, said he knew you'd be the principal some day. He said you were one of the few people who were nice to him when he and his brother were there."

"Holy shit. So Feuermann was right. He's probably been drinking again."

"I would guess so. I told him you'd stop by to see him before he left the hospital. Hope that's alright with you. He really seems to respect you."

Charlie grabbed the morning *Gazette* from the coffee table and began to thumb through the second section, looking for any information on the assault. Not finding anything, he asked Katie if the doctors knew who'd beat up Cartwright.

"No, that's the weird thing," she answered. "It was almost sun-up when someone found him lying next to his car in the parking lot. They figure he must have been there for at least two or three hours."

Charlie promised that he would stop by the next day after work and mentioned again how difficult life in Waumeka had been for the Cartwright boys. He didn't want to excuse Lou before he even knew what had happened, but he was just commenting on their life circumstances.

Katie asked if the two of them could do anything to help the Cartwrights.

Charlie had an idea. "Remember how the usher's club always tries to help a few families every Christmas? Well, we've already picked three families to help out this year, but I could call around and see if we could add another. In fact, now that I think of it, we meet this Sunday after Mass. I'll bring it up then."

***

Charlie wasn't sure how many of the men at Our Lady of Sorrows would know the Cartwright brothers, but he knew it was always their intention to help as much as they could at Christmas time.

"Look, you guys. This fellow Cartwright was out of work for a week; then he got beat up over at the casino. They're pretty sure he'll be out before Christmas, but they don't have much money. My wife tells me she saw his wife and baby at the hospital the other day. They could use our help."

"Sure, we can add a family," one of the men spoke up. We'll need to get a food basket, enough for Christmas dinner, and a few gifts. Do you know clothes sizes, and that stuff, Charlie?"

"No, but Katie can get it for us," Charlie replied.

One of the older ushers asked if those weren't Amos Cartwright's sons, and remembered the old man as "quite a boozer" who couldn't keep a job. He felt that the apples hadn't fallen very far from the tree.

"You got that right," another added, "I was in high school with Lou. He was into the sauce even then. Don't think he's stopped since."

Charlie countered that while that might all be true, he didn't think that was their concern at the moment.

"Charlie, you're damn right," another interrupted, "but if you find out that he does have a problem that way, you know, well, just let me know. You guys all know that I go regular to AA. Gone every week for eight years now. If Cartwright needs us, we can help out. You can't force a guy, of course, but he ought to know we're there."

Charlie promised that if there was an opportunity to bring up that topic, he would do so and would be happy to put the two men in touch with one another. The men then voted unanimously to put the Cartwright family on their Christmas list and to try to raise some money as well as a Christmas dinner.

"They'll need that even more than the dinner," Charlie told them. "Whatever we can do to help."

CHAPTER 12

A aron Kohlberg left his office and drove a police car over to the hospital for the second time in three days. By now Lou Cartwright should be awake and able to give him some idea of what had happened the night he was mugged at the casino. Two days earlier, Kohlberg had sent one of his officers, Deputy James Ashblane, to Lou's house to inform his wife, who had come home from her parent's place in the Twin Cities, about the attack at the casino.

Once again, Kohlberg stopped at the nurses' station to get permission to enter the "Restricted Access" room 348. This time the nurse simply nodded and said, "Go right ahead, Chief." He asked how the patient was doing and learned that Lou was still not out of the woods—and that an argument had erupted in Lou's room when Amber came to visit. Amber had threatened to leave Lou when she learned that the money from his brother had been squandered, according to her, at the casino. Lou had been able to quiet her down when he explained that he had actually won that night, but that after winning he was the victim of a robbery.

The nurse told Kohlberg that Lou was recovering from the frostbite and internal injuries. His ribs were healing, and the lacerations on his face and neck had been stitched. There was still some question about how much movement he would ever get from his right ankle and foot, but the doctors were pretty sure that there would be no need to amputate. The emergency room staff and the nurses on surgery had treated the foot aggressively the night he came in, and it looked as if they might have saved it.

The police chief left the nurses' station and walked down the hallway to room 348. He hesitated when he saw the "RESTRICTED ACCESS" sign on the door, until the nurse called down to him from the nurses' station, "It's alright, Chief. You can go right in." He knocked on the door before entering.

The room was much the way he recalled it from three days earlier. Lou still lay in the second bed, with nobody occupying the first. The smell of urine, while not as strong, was still present. The NG tube still stuck out of Lou's nose, although there was only a small amount of ugly green liquid in the bag on the wall above his head. On an erasable white board on the wall next to the door someone had written:

PATIENT: Louis Cartwright

PHYSICIAN: Dr. Philbert

YOUR NURSE TODAY IS: Jamie

YOUR NURSING ASSISTANT IS: Sylvia

A call button was pinned to Lou's nightshirt, and a tray table was pushed away from the bed. His leg was still elevated, and his toes, although still black and blue, were not so dark.

"Lou, hi. I'm Chief Kohlberg." Kohlberg took off his hat and put it on the foot of the bed. He grabbed a chair from against the wall, turned it around next to the bed and straddled it, resting his arms up on the back. "I came to talk to you about last Wednesday night."

"I didn't do nothin', Chief. I swear. I may have had a few too many, but that's it. Played the slots and had a few drinks." It was clearly difficult for Lou to talk, as he winced periodically when he tried to speak.

"I know, but you got beaten up. Do you have any idea who did it? Did you meet anybody you knew that night?" Kohlberg asked.

"No."

Kohlberg pressed the patient on whether he saw his attackers, or had any arguments earlier at the casino that might explain the assault. Cartwright denied that he had seen anybody approach him or had any altercations.

"Why don't you tell me just what happened?" Kohlberg suggested.

"I played the slots for a while and then when I wasn't doin' too well, I went over to the blackjack table. I did pretty good, and then I went back to the slots. I had maybe five, maybe six drinks. Guess maybe I was pretty hammered. I don't remember too much."

"Did you win any money that night?"

Cartwright explained that he started with $220 that he had gotten from his brother, Jim, after giving $30 to Amber. He remembered getting $250, so figured he had $220 left in his pocket.

"Your wife said you had $120, that you had gotten $150 from Jim."

"Oh, is that what she said? She must have been mistaken."

"Did you lose that money playing the slots or at the blackjack table?"

"No, I won," Lou insisted. "I don't know how much, but I know I won. I told those assholes—sorry—at the blackjack table. They were laughin' at me. Maybe I had too much to drink. But I told them. Told them I had won. They were still sittin' there probably losing their shirts when I left."

"OK. So you went there with $220 and you made some money at the slots. But when my men found you in the parking lot, your wallet was there on the ground next to you and there was no money in it."

"Yeah, I know, someone rolled me … bastards—sorry."

Kohlberg asked the patient what he remembered after being hit.

"I got hit from behind. Then I blacked out. It was cold. I came in and out a few times but mostly I was out."

"Did you hear anything, see anybody?"

"The guy that hit me called me a punk. Then I don't remember nothing until a lot later. I woke up a little. I was bleedin' pretty bad. Some guys were walkin' by and one of 'em yelled at me, called me 'a drunken alki sot.' Said I was just like my old man. Then I blacked out again. You know, somebody else called my dad that same thing ... drunken alki sot. Can't remember who it was. But someone else used those same words. Pissed me off. That's why I remember. My old man had his problems, awright, but I don't like nobody calling him names."

Kohlberg instructed him to call if he could remember who had called his father those names. He took a card out of his wallet and told Cartwright to call the station if he remembered anything else about that evening. He put his business card down on the nightstand next to the bed. Just then, a nurse walked into the room.

Cartwright picked up the card and examined it front and back, then laid it back on the nightstand. He told the chief that he understood and promised to call if he could remember anything new, and he expressed the hope that he would be out of the hospital soon.

From the other side of the bed, the nurse said, "You can stay, Officer. I just have to take Mr. Cartwright's blood pressure here." She put the cuff on Cartwright's arm and began pumping up the bladder.

"No, it's OK," Kohlberg replied. "I was just about to leave. We're all done here. You take care of yourself, Lou. I'll look in on you again."

"Thanks, Chief."

Kohlberg stood up, turned his chair around, put it back against the wall, and left with a quick thank you to the nurse as he stepped around her.

***

When Lou Cartwright was going on his second week in the hospital, he began to grow impatient. His leg wasn't healing as fast as the doctors had hoped, although there was no more talk of amputation. It would just take more time, they kept telling him. In the meantime, a physical therapist came twice a day to help him exercise both legs and to teach him to use first a walker, then crutches.

Amber and Rainbow came to the hospital to see Lou every afternoon, about three o'clock. At first, their visits were taken up with arguments about money and about Lou's wasting his brother's loan at the casino. He had a hard time convincing his wife that he hadn't lost money at the slot machines or the blackjack table, but that he had been robbed going to his car. In time she began to forgive him, saying things like, "I'm sorry, honey. I'm sorry I didn't believe you," and "I wish this hadn't happened to you. I do love you."

Lou looked up at the clock. Two forty-five, almost time for Amber and Rainbow to show up. As he lay on his bed, his thoughts drifted back to the early days of their marriage and all the great plans they had made. Now here he was, a complete failure, swallowed up in debt, and needing help just to take a piss. He wanted to ease her mind about their financial state but didn't know how he was going to accomplish that. He had wanted them to have a good Christmas, and now there was nothing. He was only laid off for a week, but now it might be a month or two before he could go back to his lousy job. At least the little medical insurance he had from Fleet Farm would cover the hospital and doctor bills. He remembered that Jim and Agnes had asked them over for Christmas dinner. He wondered if he had forgotten to mention that to Amber. Shit, what a fuck-up. Anyway, he would tell her today. She liked spending time with his family and they could have a nice Christmas dinner. Maybe that would cheer her up.

"Hi, sweetie." Amber wore her long grey winter coat and a floppy light blue ski cap. She carried her purse in one hand and a bag in the other. "I brought you some oranges. I didn't know if they were giving you enough fruit in here, and anyway, these were on sale at Pick 'n Save." She kissed her husband and sat down on the easy chair next to the bed, after setting the fruit on the night stand.

"Where's Rainbow?" he asked.

"Oh, I left her with Sharon next door. She said she'd mind her for a few hours while I came to see you. When do you think they're going to let you out?" Amber looked around the room.

"I dunno. My leg's gettin' better. Fact, I walked down the hall today with that walker. Hate that damn thing. Maybe I'll get me some crutches in a few days."

"Did the doctor say how long it would be?" she asked as she picked a bit of lint out of his hair.

"Nah. They don't know nothin'," he complained.

"Did you ask them?"

"No, I'll ask the nurse when she comes in. Or else, when I see the doctor in the mornin'."

"Well, I sure hope you're gonna be out of here by Christmas." She looked up at the NG tube as it gurgled some fluid into the tank above Lou's head.

"Oh, hell yes. By the way, Jim and Agnes want us to come over for Christmas dinner. What do you think?"

"Nice, if you're able to get around. Even so, I'll have to fix something for us to take."

"Sure, we can make somethin'—maybe some cookies or somethin' like that."

"Lou, we're really low on food. And there's no more money in the grocery box. I went to Social Services yesterday and they said I should see the lady at Catholic Charities. I hope you don't mind."

"I hate for us to be askin' for a handout."

"I know, I know, but we ain't got a choice. I'm thinking of going back to work. Casey said they're looking for dancers, and Sharon said she could watch Rainbow, if I could pay her a little from what I make. You know, right before Christmas, tips are gonna be good."

"Jesus, Amber, you're not goin' back to that place. I thought we settled that."

"I know, but that was then and this is now. Besides, it's been six months since I had the baby. I'm getting my shape back. I think I could do it—just like the old days."

"Amber, it ain't the old days and your shape's just fine. What if one of the neighbors saw you in a place like that?"

"It's in Marshfield, over fifty miles from here. Nobody around here even has to know. Sharon don't even ask."

"Shit, Amber, takin' your clothes off in front of a bunch of drunken old bastards—it just ain't right."

His wife smiled. "You didn't think that way when you first met me over there, now did you? Fact, you were a regular."

"That was different. I was young and stupid."

She looked at him and shook her head. "All right, I'll think of something."

Lou settled back on his pillow. He felt guiltier than ever. And all the taunts of his classmates over the years kept coming back to him. He remembered the tattered clothes he wore as a child and the other students whispering behind his back, snickering about his father.

"Sweetie, could you close that door?" Lou asked. His wife got up to close the door and then sat down on the bed next to him. He leaned over and lowered his voice. "Remember, I told you about all the stuff the police chief asked me when he came in here?"

She asked whether the police had come back to see him and why he was lowering his voice. He said they hadn't come again, but he was being quiet because he wasn't sure of what he was about to say and wanted to tell her first before he talked to anybody else.

He told her that he remembered more about the night of the attack, that he had heard voices while he lay on the ground, but that he was going in and out of consciousness. He was sure it was some time after the attack, but was afraid he might have been partly dreaming.

When she insisted on knowing exactly what he heard, he said he heard somebody say, "You're a drunken alki sot just like your old man."

"Were they the guys who robbed you?" she asked.

"No, no, this was later. I was all bloody and couldn't open my eyes very well. I think it was gettin' light out. I was really cold and shaky."

"Let me see if I got this straight. You mean you got mugged when you left the place. Then you're just lying there for a while and some other guys come by, see you there, and don't do anything—just leave you there and call your old man names? What the hell?"

He acknowledged that it was weird, but he was pretty sure that's what he had heard ... even though part of it might have been a dream.

"Who do you think it was?" she asked.

He asked her to come closer. "That's the weird part. I don't want to say nothin', but it was exactly the same words that Feuermann used the day before, when he laid me off. 'Drunken alki sot.' That's just what he said, just like that."

She asked him to call the police and tell them. He was afraid that if he did call the police, it might backfire so that he'd get in even more trouble and lose his job for good. He reminded Amber that his mind wasn't very clear that night, that he had been drinking, and that he was attacked and hit on his head. "Anyone could say that I was just dreaming, even though I know what I heard."

Amber insisted. "Sweetie, I think you should tell the police anyway. Let them decide if you're making it up. I never trusted that Feuermann, anyway. One day you come home saying what a good boss he is, and then the next day you tell me he treats you like a piece of shit."

Lou knew that was just the way Feuermann was. You never knew what to expect from the bastard.

Amber stood up and said, "Honey, I gotta go. I told Sharon I'd be back by four fifteen. Promise me you're gonna talk to the police chief when he comes in."

He promised her he'd think about it and told her he loved her.

.

CHAPTER 13

C harlie Brannigan checked the teaching schedule on the bulletin board in the main office and then walked down the corridor to the gym, where the girls' basketball team was practicing.

James Cartwright, the assistant basketball coach who usually helped out with the girls' teams, blew his whistle. The girls on the court stopped in their tracks.

"That was good boxing out, Erika," James yelled. "Helen, you might have been called for an offensive foul that time. I like the way you drive to the basket, but be careful. Pass the ball when you're in heavy traffic. Jamie was open." The girls nodded. James was just about to blow the whistle again to resume the scrimmage when he noticed the principal standing in the doorway.

"Practice your drills," he shouted and went over to the door where Charlie stood.

"Mr. Brannigan, what's up?"

"Hi, James, looks like we'll have an awesome women's team this year," the principal observed.

"I hope so. We got the raw talent. It's just going to take a lot of dedication, and I think this bunch has it. What I really like is they're mostly sophomores and juniors. If I can keep their attention, we'll be unbeatable in a year or two."

"I guess they do get competing interests," Charlie laughed. "Actually, I wanted to ask you about your brother. I heard from my wife that he's in the hospital. I don't know if you know my wife. She's a nurse at St. Luke's. She couldn't say much, but it was in the paper so she told me Lou was pretty banged up."

"Well, sir, he is, but I think he's coming around OK. They've been able to save his foot. He should be home by this Friday, in fact."

"That's good news, James. Do you think it would be OK with them if I stopped by on Saturday or Sunday?"

"Sir, I'd give him a call if I was you, but I'll bet anything he'd really appreciate a visit. Do you remember him? He was three years behind me in high school, so you probably don't remember. You were already a senior when I was a freshman."

Charlie didn't quite know what to say. "It's a small town, James. I knew you guys as athletes. You know, after I went away to college, I knew you'd soon be coming up to take my place as guard on the basketball team," he lied. He knew the Cartwrights the same way everybody else in town knew them, as sons of a poor and drunken father. "I was always curious to see who was keeping that team together after we graduated, so whenever I was home, I'd come to watch the games. I always knew you had a brother—didn't know him well, of course. But if there's something Katie and I can do, we want to help out."

"Like I said, sir, I know he'd appreciate it."

***

On Friday night, Charlie called the Cartwrights to ask whether he could stop by on Saturday or Sunday. They agreed that Sunday might be the best time, so after church Charlie dropped Katie off at home and drove to the south side of town, to Lou and Amber Cartwright's house.

The Cartwrights lived down a dirt road in a doublewide trailer with a little picket fence around its base. There were two other trailers and a small house on the dead-end street. Charlie walked up the three steps leading to the front door and pressed the doorbell. The small bulb in the center of it was broken. He didn't hear the bell ring and nobody answered, so he knocked on the loose storm door. Amber came to the door.

"Hi, Mrs. Cartwright? I'm Charlie Brannigan."

"Come on right in, Mr. Brannigan. Now don't you worry none about your shoes. You just come on right in. Lou's going to be happy you came to see him." She took him through the cramped living room to an even smaller bedroom. He could hear a baby in another room. "Lou, this here is Mr. Brannigan from the high school. Like I told you, he came over to see you."

Lou Cartwright sat up in his bed as Charlie looked around for a chair. There was none.

"Honey, can we just go in the livin' room? If you give me those crutches, I'll grab me a bathrobe," Cartwright said.

"Sure," she replied and ushered Charlie back into the living room, where she took his coat and hung it on a hook behind the door to the kitchen. "Would you like to sit here?" She opened her palm and gestured toward the overstuffed, mustard-yellow chair next to a torn, olive-green, corduroy davenport. She turned off the TV, and Lou followed them on crutches. He made his way toward the davenport, dropped his crutches on the floor, leaned against the arm, and lowered himself onto the cushion, disturbing years of dust that had collected there. Amber pulled a straight back chair away from the dining table and sat down with them. "Can I get you some coffee, or somethin'?" she asked.

"Coffee would be fine. But please, don't go to any trouble. I just wanted to see how you were both doing and see if there was anything we could do to help out."

"Well, that sure is nice of you. Plus, we can use all the help we can get, as you can see." Amber sighed and waved her open hand across the room. Charlie Brannigan wasn't sure whether she was making a comment about their meager furnishings, their bare existence, or both. In any case, it was a gesture of resignation.

"Amber!" Lou whined.

"Well, it's true. And, doggone it; I just think it's nice when folks are willing to help out. But, let me put the coffee on." She got up and went over to the kitchen at the end of the living room.

"Lou," Charlie started, looking at Lou, "I'm on the usher's club at Our Lady of Sorrows. Every year at Christmas, we try to help a few families who are down on their luck. When my wife, Katie, said she had seen you in the hospital, I asked the group to put you on this year's Christmas list. I hope that was OK with you."

"Geez, I guess so. We never expected nobody to help. We got family. Fact, since James works over at the high school with you, he kinda helps us."

"I know James really well, and I know he can be a lot of help. We were just thinking your neighbors could step up to the plate this time, too. We were figuring on coming by the day before Christmas with enough food for a Christmas dinner and a few small gifts, something for the baby, that sort of thing. Would that be OK?"

Amber put a kettle on the stove and came back to sit down. "That would be great, Mr. Brannigan," she interjected. "We're supposed to go to Lou's brother's place for dinner, but we could take some of the stuff with us, or leave it in the fridge until the next day; sorta two Christmases, if we could do that. Could we do that?"

"Sure, have you got a freezer? I'll try to bring things you could freeze if you want to save them until later."

"We could do that," Lou said.

Amber got up. Through the kitchen doorway, Charlie could see her take the kettle from the stove and pour boiling water into three mismatched mugs. She brought the mugs and instant coffee to the two men, keeping the chipped mug, a souvenir from the Wisconsin Dells, for herself. She apologized that she didn't have any cookies to go with it as she gave them sugar and cream and then sat down, blowing across the top of her own mug.

The three of them talked for another ten minutes, about Waumeka High's basketball team, about the days when James was on the team, and about Lou's recovery and his prospects for going back to work after the first of the year.

"I got a call from my boss, Frank Feuermann, yesterday. He's sorry I ain't there at Fleet Farm to help out during this Christmas rush, but he just said I should take all the time I need to get better and he'll see me after New Year's."

"Nice," Amber added, "but good wishes don't put food on the table, now, do they?"

"Amber," Lou said.

Before they could say any more about Frank Feuermann, Charlie got up to excuse himself. Just as he did, Rainbow began to cry in the next room.

"Wouldn't you know it," Amber said. "Least she waited until we was almost done."

"Well, I guess that's my cue," Charlie said, "I told my wife I wouldn't be long. We still have some things to do for Christmas."

"It was sure nice of you to stop by, Mr. Brannigan," Amber said.

"Yes," Lou muttered.

"I better go fetch our little Rainbow. We'll see you on Friday then, is that right?" Amber asked.

"My gosh, yes, Friday is the day before Christmas. Should I come by about six o'clock?"

"Geez, any time would be fine with us. We ain't goin' nowhere," Lou said.

"Then let's make it Friday at six. And thanks for the coffee."

Charlie took his coat from the hook on the door and let himself out as Lou stretched his leg and Amber went to check on the baby.

Lou was still stretched on the davenport when Amber came back into the living room with Rainbow.

"My god, Lou, you could've at least thanked the man."

"Jesus, Amber, we're not some sort of a charity case."

"I know that. But he was being nice and he didn't mean to make us feel like that."

"Maybe not, but I felt that way, anyhow, all right? And here you go making out like we don't have anything, pointing to our lousy furniture. It works, don't it?"

CHAPTER 14

———————

That evening after dinner, Katie stayed in the kitchen making Christmas cookies while Charlie lit a fire in the fireplace, turned on the radio, and changed stations until he found some classical music. The aroma of fresh-baked cookies and fruitcake flooded the kitchen and family room.

"Hey, shall I get the ornaments?" he asked. They'd agreed to put up the Christmas tree that night.

"Sure, I'll be done here in ten minutes. So far, we have four fruitcakes and about five dozen cookies ... peanut butter, oatmeal, pecan sandies, you name it."

They had gotten a large Frazer fir tree from a local tree farm and, after cutting it down themselves, brought it home on the top of their Ford Explorer. Charlie had brought it in through the sliding glass doors leading to the back yard. It stood at the end of the room opposite the fireplace, where it could easily be seen by anyone coming in the front door. The tree was about nine feet tall. As it stretched up toward the cathedral ceiling, it dominated the family room, both with its size and with the aroma of fresh-cut fir.

Charlie brought a stepladder from the basement and strung three sets of lights around the tree. "OK," he yelled to Katie in the kitchen, "time for the artistic part." He had brought four cardboard boxes full of ornaments from the attic over the garage into the family room. He set the boxes next to the tree, ready to be opened in the annual ritual that Katie so looked forward to. They were home together, their last Christmas as a couple without children.

Katie put the last of the cookies into a tin and washed off the last two cookie trays. She washed her hands in the sink and dried them on the towel that hung on the oven, before coming into the family room. Charlie had already turned on the Christmas tree lights.

"Whoa," she said, smiling, "It's going to be beautiful. Let's get started." She went to the boxes and opened each before taking out any of the ornaments.

"Let's start with the little ones at the top and work our way down," he suggested. "I'll get on the ladder, and you hand me the ornaments and tell me where you want them."

"Oh, my God," she exclaimed, "do you remember when we got this one?" She took a small, wooden, painted church out of the box.

"Yes, I remember." He pursed his lips in an airborne kiss as he began to climb the ladder. "It was our first Christmas together in this house."

"Oh, and look at this star. My Lord, that's still the one we had at home when I was a little girl."

"Sweetie, if we go through the history of each one of these, we'll never get done. Let's watch some Christmas specials when we get done with the tree," Charlie suggested.

"Cool," was all she answered. One by one she handed him the ornaments, as if each one were a treasure beyond reckoning. Occasionally she would comment on the ornament as she gave it to him, or he would remember where they got it and remind her.

The tree was finished in an hour. They placed one nativity set at its base and another smaller set on the mantle over the fireplace. Charlie loved to take out all the animals that went with the smaller set. The traditional two cows and three sheep were joined by animals that he'd added over the years: a blue heron, some ducks, and some small wooden animal figurines from Africa ... rhinoceros, lion, tiger, elephant. When their nephews and nieces came over, right away they wanted to see if all the animals were in their place and if the three wise men were there in the middle of it all.

Charlie chuckled as he thought about the fun his sisters' children would have and then thought about the fact that they would have their own child at this time next year. He turned to Katie. "This is our last Christmas as just a twosome, do you realize that?"

"Funny, I was just thinking the same thing," she replied.

"How 'bout a B&B for me and—what would you like?" Charlie asked.

"You haven't made one of those in a long time. Do you think you still know how?" Katie laughed. "I better just have a ginger ale with a lot of ice."

"No sweat." In a few minutes, Charlie came out of the kitchen with the two drinks and sat down on the couch next to his wife. "Andy Williams? Whoa, now there's an oldie. Isn't there something better? All right, all right."

"How did it go at the Cartwrights' this afternoon?" Katie asked.

"Fine. I told them I'd stop by on Christmas Eve with a dinner and some gifts. You were right. It was a little tough at first; they're really sensitive. Do you want to come with me?"

"Sure. Can we do it after dinner? We're not going to midnight Mass, are we?"

"No, I'm supposed to usher at the ten o'clock," he replied.

"Then let's go right after dinner. I don't suppose you had a chance to ask him about his drinking?"

"No, I'll have to wait until after the holidays, or else I'll mention it to James and have him bring it up. If he's drinking again, I'm going to suggest AA," Charlie replied.

"Will James follow through on that?" she asked.

"Oh, yeah. I get the idea he's disgusted with his little brother, but he'd do anything to help him." Charlie leaned forward and grabbed a cookie from the plate Katie had put on the coffee table.

"Well, if we go to the Cartwrights on Christmas Eve and go to the ten o'clock Mass on Christmas day, it still gives us plenty of time to come home, have breakfast, open presents, and then go over to Mother and Dad's for dinner." Katie sounded exhausted. Her parents were in their seventies and lived across town, in the same house where she had grown up. She went over to see them whenever she could, especially now that her father was retired from the gas company where he had worked all his life. She was grateful they were in good health and enjoyed life together.

"We'll do what we can," Charlie suggested. "I don't want you getting worn out."

"I know. It's the only part of Christmas I don't like—all the rushing around."

"Oh, that reminds me," Charlie remembered, "I told Cliff we'd come over for a few minutes before we go to your parents. I thought we could bring him and Sally some of your cookies, or a fruitcake or something. It doesn't have to be a big deal. Is that OK?"

"Yeah, sure. You guys aren't planning on cards this Wednesday, are you?" she asked.

"No, we cancelled our game until after New Year's now. Just too much going on," he replied.

***

The week seemed to go by quickly for both Charlie and Katie, and before they knew it, Christmas Eve was upon them. It seemed perfect. The Christmas cards were sent and all the baking was done. It was snowing, the churches were all decked out, and Main Street and some of the side streets were decorated with lights and red bows on the street lamps. The shops had stayed open late every night and carolers, dressed in eighteenth-century English clothes and top hats, had gone from store to store, entertaining the customers. A huge nativity scene had been erected in front of the library. As they drove by on their way to Lou and Amber Cartwright's house, Charlie said that he thought the ACLU was going to have a problem with the Christian scene on public property. It had been brought up the year before, but the issue was never resolved.

They stopped at Our Lady of Sorrows rectory, a nineteenth-century stone building next to the church. Katie waited in the car while Charlie went up the steps to the door and rang the bell. The housekeeper let him in and showed him about twenty shopping bags lined up along the wall of the dark foyer. As she pointed out the bags that were meant for the Cartwright family, Father Dan O'Shaunessy, the assistant pastor, came out of an office and into the foyer. His collar was off and his shirt was opened at the top.

"Well, for heaven's sake, Merry Christmas. What brings you out this early? Mass doesn't start until midnight."

"Hi, Father," Charlie replied, "No, we're just here to pick up the bags that the Ushers Club prepared for the Cartwright family."

"Oh, right you are. Carolyn, aren't those the bags?"

"Yes, I was just giving them to him, Father."

"There's also a check here. We combined all the donations and divided the total by the five families and wrote one check for each family." The priest handed Charlie an envelope with a check for $195. "I thought the parishioners were especially generous this year," he added.

"Thanks, Father. Thanks, Carolyn. Merry Christmas. We'd better be getting on our way. They'll be expecting us."

"Let me help you with those," the priest said as he picked up two of the grocery bags and followed Charlie to the car." After saying hello to Katie, he put his arms across his chest, shivering, and ran back up the steps and into the rectory.

Charlie could see that the three bags held enough groceries for a week. There was a ham, several cans of Libby's vegetables and fruit, a bag of red apples, cookies, a pie, two bottles of Tropicana orange juice, and assorted cans of Spam and Bush's baked beans. In addition, three gifts, wrapped in Santa Claus Christmas paper and green and red ribbons, had been placed in a cardboard box.

Charlie and Katie made two trips with the bags from their car to the Cartwright's front steps before they knocked on the door. Amber, holding Rainbow, came to the door.

"Merry Christmas, Amber," they both said at once. Charlie explained that the packages were from Our Lady of Sorrows Parish. As they helped Amber place the bags and box inside, Charlie noticed a small Christmas tree at one end of the room.

Lou came out on crutches from the bedroom. "Hi, Mr. Brannigan. Hello."

Charlie introduced Katie, "You know my wife, Lou. Amber, this is my wife, Katie. Lou would know her from the hospital."

"Nice to meet you both." Katie reached out to shake hands with Lou and then to touch the baby in Amber's arms. "You have a beautiful daughter. How old is she?"

"This here's our Rainbow. She'll be just six months the day before New Year's. Would you like to hold her?" Amber handed the baby to Katie, who still stood by the door. As Katie hugged the child to her breast, Rainbow looked up and stared at her long hair. "Won't you two come in and sit down, and have something to warm you up? Maybe some hot chocolate?" Amber asked.

"We'd better not," Katie replied, "you'll be busy with Rainbow, and we still have some last minute chores, too. But we'd love to come back another time." She handed the child back to Amber, smiling, and then quickly wiped her eyes with the back of her hand.

"Well, then, do."

"Yes," Lou added. He looked down at the bags. "My gosh, is that all for us? Geez, thanks. I mean, you got us a lot."

"It's from the parish," Charlie explained, "Our Lady of Sorrows. Oh, my gosh, I almost forgot this." He reached in his coat pocket and took out the envelope and handed it to Lou. "It's just something to help out until you're back on your feet."

"Geez, if there's some way I can pay it back ..."

"Don't even mention it. When it's your turn," Charlie said, "you'll be helping somebody else, Lou. Now we better be on our way."

***

When they got back home, Charlie turned the Christmas tree lights on and began to light a fire in the fireplace. Katie wrapped the last of her presents and put them under the tree with the others. Charlie had gotten his old electric train out of the basement and put it at the base of the tree around the nativity scene. Two of the presents that Katie put under the tree were wrapped with Winnie the Pooh paper and were addressed to "The angel."

CHAPTER 15

———

A silvery frost glistened in the bright sunlight and clung to the trees on Christmas morning; a dusting of snow on the ground made the sunlight doubly intense. Katie could see her breath in the cold December air, so she pulled her scarf up around her face as she and Charlie walked up the steps to Our Lady of Sorrows for the ten o'clock Mass. Father O'Shaunessy said the Mass and gave the sermon. He took the opportunity to thank the congregation for their generosity during the past year and then spoke about the meaning of God's being born to a poor family. "Jesus could have come as a great prince," he said, "but preferred to be born in poverty. He later told us, 'Blessed are the poor, for they shall inherit the earth.' As we open our gifts today, let us recall all the other gifts that God has given us, starting with the gift of His Son."

Charlie was seated at the back of the church with Katie, waiting to take up the collection. As he listened to the priest, he began to think of all of his own blessings over the past year: Katie, the child to be, his teachers and staff, his card-playing buddies, his health …

After breakfast, Charlie and Katie opened presents. She had bought him a pair of waders for fishing in the streams—something he had been looking at in the Fleet Farm catalogue for a long time. "Yes!" he exclaimed as he opened the box. He then handed Katie a small, long present. She unwrapped it slowly, as if not to destroy any of the wrapping paper. When she finally opened the long slender box, her eyes began to well up. The box contained a gold chain, with a gold pendant that had a small diamond in the center.

"The jeweler at Sorenson's designed it for you," Charlie said as he took the necklace out of the box and put it around her neck. Katie stood up, went to the mirror and whispered, "It's gorgeous," as she turned and kissed Charlie.

"Let's open the baby's presents," Charlie suggested. Katie had bought two presents for their child-to-be: a musical mobile to hang over the crib and a soft, yellow one-piece pajama outfit.

They spent the rest of the morning having coffee, reading the paper, and listening to Dylan Thomas recite "A Child's Christmas in Wales." It had become a tradition for them. Since PBS always aired it on Christmas noon, right after "Nine Lessons and Carols" from the Kings Chapel choir in Cambridge, it was something Charlie had come to look forward to. He loved to hear Thomas reminisce about the presents a child in his day in Wales could always expect to receive. As he listened again, Charlie knew them almost by heart:

"There were the Useful Presents: engulfing mufflers of the old coach days, and mittens made for giant sloths ..."

"Get on to the Useless Presents."

"Bags of moist and many-colored jelly babies and a folded flag and a false nose ..."

When the program ended, Charlie got up to turn off the radio, leaned over to kiss Katie, and said, "You know what? Let's make sure our new angel always gets a few useless presents on Christmas."

"Fine with me. They were always my favorites," she answered.

"What do you say? Shall we call Cliff and Sally and stop by for a few minutes before we go to your parents?"

"Sure, we can take the book over, and I'll put a fruitcake and some cookies on a plate." Cliff and Sally were looking forward to a two-week trip to Italy the following summer, so the Brannigans had gotten them a coffee-table book on Venice as a Christmas gift.

It began to snow as Charlie and Katie walked over to their neighbors' house. Cliff met them at the door.

"Welcome. Merry Christmas, you two." He took their coats and hung them in the front closet as Sally came from the kitchen, wiping her hands on her apron. The house smelled of cinnamon, cookies or brownies baking, and a roast turkey. Holding her hands out so as not to get flour on her guests, Sally leaned over and kissed Katie on the cheek, took the plate of cookies and fruitcake from her, and thanked her.

"Come into the living room," Cliff said. Sally had gone back to the kitchen, presumably to set the cookies down, take off her apron, and wash her hands. When she returned, the four of them sat in front of an enormous Christmas tree in the living room.

Charlie handed the wrapped book to Cliff. "This is for both of you. We hope you have a great New Year, and especially a great trip to Italy."

After exchanging gifts, and during a break in the conversation, Katie smiled at Sally and said, "Speaking of a great New Year, we Brannigans have a surprise."

"No!" Sally screamed. "Are you serious?" She looked at Katie's stomach.

"Well, you can't see it yet, but, yes, Dr. Berkside says it's there." Katie answered.

Sally jumped up and went over and hugged Katie. "We're not terribly religious you know, but I have been praying for this one." Like the Brannigans, Sally and Cliff were childless. As a teenager, Sally had been in a bicycle accident that had left her incapable of bearing children. Sally's delight for Katie was genuine—she cared deeply for her neighbor and good friend—but it was also bittersweet.

"This calls for a drink," Cliff suggested. "How about a glass of wine?" Everyone agreed.

"It'll have to be ginger ale for me, though." Katie said.

A few minutes later, Cliff came back from the kitchen with two glasses of Chardonnay, juice for himself, and ginger ale for Katie.

"Here's to the newest Brannigan. He ... or she ... shall be well loved." Cliff said as he raised his glass.

"Here, here," the others answered.

"We're not saying anything yet," Katie cautioned. "I'm glad you two know. But we're not even going to tell my parents until after I have my ultrasound and we're sure everything is OK."

"We won't say a word. But I'm glad you're sharing this with us. It's the best Christmas present ever," Sally said.

"Speaking of Christmas presents, Charlie, come with me. I want to show you my newest toy." The men went to the garage, where Cliff had a new Delta ten-inch table saw set up in a workstation at the rear. They talked for a few minutes about tools, and then Cliff asked, "Charlie, did you see the Cartwrights yesterday? You said you were going over."

"Yeah, Katie and I both went. They're in rough shape. The church helped out a little bit, but I think it's going to take more than that. I'm going to talk to James. I want to see if he's willing to encourage Lou to go to AA. I really think his drinking is a big part of the problem. What do you think about that idea?"

"I think it's fine. You know, though, that people have to want it for themselves. You can't force it on someone. It won't work."

"I know. But I think Lou may be ready."

As the two men walked back into the house, Cliff changed the topic. "By the way, we'd like the two of you to come over for New Year's Eve. We thought it would be fun to get the poker crowd together with their wives, so we've asked Aaron and Anita, and Marty and Maryann. I tried to call Frank, but there hasn't been any answer. Anyway, what do you think?"

"Geez, yes, I'd love to. Let me ask Katie."

The two women were still sitting on the sofa when Cliff and Charlie walked into the living room.

"Honey, Charlie's invited us for New Year's Eve. We don't have any other plans, do we?"

"Nope, none that I know of. That would be great. What can we bring?"

"Nothing at all," Sally answered. "Just yourselves. But I should warn you, we ladies are going to have to put up with those poker players for the night. We've invited the Kolhbergs and the O'Briens, too."

"But no card game that night, right?" Katie laughed.

"No, just a few drinks. And be prepared to sing in the New Year," Cliff answered.

"Well, thanks." Katie turned to her husband, "Honey, we'd better go. We promised my mother we'd be there by three o'clock."

As they got into the car to drive to her parents' house, Katie turned to Charlie and asked, "Honey, after dinner, could we leave Mom and Dad's early tonight?"

"Sure, if you don't think they'll mind. Are you OK?"

"Well, I was sick again this morning and I'd like to get to bed early. I think it's just morning sickness. Berkside warned me it might happen."

"We're not going to tell your parents yet, are we?"

"No, I'll just say I'm tired and think I'm coming down with something."

CHAPTER 16

———

The week after Christmas was relaxing for the Brannigans. Charlie was able to catch up on a lot of administrative details and still get home from school early almost every afternoon. Katie's morning sickness began to subside, although she still complained about feeling queasy.

"Do you think you're up for going to the Smalleys' party tonight?" Charlie asked Katie on the morning of New Year's Eve.

"Sure. I've been looking forward to it. I'll rest up this afternoon."

***

They walked down the shoveled sidewalk over to the Smalleys' around seven o'clock and found that a number of people had already arrived: several of Charlie's card-playing buddies, some of the neighbors, and Nellie Fromager, a colleague of Katie's from the hospital.

"Are the Kohlbergs coming?" Charlie asked Cliff.

"Oh, they're coming. Aaron said they'd be a little late. The only one I couldn't reach was Frank Feuermann and his wife. They must have left town for the holidays."

"I know. He wasn't at the last Rotary meeting either," Marty O'Brien said.

The Christmas tree, which rose almost to the top of the ceiling in the living room, still glittered with tinsel, and two Christmas stockings still hung from the mantel. The baby grand piano that usually sat in front of the bay window had been moved closer to the entrance to the foyer to make room for the Christmas tree. Sally had arranged candy and nuts on the coffee table and on both end tables near the sofa. In the dining room, she had placed party plates and napkins at one end of the table, and had a large tray with an ice sculpture surrounded with shrimp in the center. At the other end were a cheesecake, brownies, assorted cookies, and small pieces of fruitcake. In the kitchen, Cliff had beer bottles and soda cans sitting on ice cubes in one side of the sink. On the kitchen table, he'd arranged glasses and several bottles of wine, whiskey, and soda.

"Please come in and help yourselves," Cliff said as he escorted the O'Briens toward the kitchen. Maryann stopped to talk to Katie and Sally in the dining room. Marty followed Cliff into the kitchen, where Charlie was pouring himself a drink. "As usual, your wife looks stunning, Charlie Brannigan," Marty greeted his old friend. "You don't deserve her. You know that, don't you?" he kidded.

Charlie laughed and wondered how long it would be before he would be able to tell his friends that Katie was expecting. Tonight she wore a long, sleek red dress that showed her still-statuesque form to its full advantage. Her dark coppery red hair was combed back and held together with a large silver barrette. Several inches shorter than Charlie, she still stood almost six feet tall. "Thanks, Marty. Now get yourself a drink before you get yourself into trouble."

After Marty left to join the others in the living room, Charlie and Cliff were alone in the kitchen. Charlie looked around at all the alcohol. "Cliff, how do you do it? Don't you ever get tempted with all this booze in the house?"

"Not after sixteen years. In the beginning it was hard, but then I didn't keep the stuff around."

"I suppose going to your AA meetings helps."

"Twice a week. You bet. In fact, I'll celebrate my seventeenth anniversary next month. By the way, Lou Cartwright showed up on Tuesday. I've got his permission to tell you that. It can't go any further, of course. He told me you had urged him to go and I'm glad you did. Wants me to be his sponsor."

"Nice going. He didn't feel pressured, did he?"

"No. I don't think so. Have you had any of Sally's party mix?" Cliff changed the topic when Sally and Maryann and Katie came into the kitchen. "Sally, after everyone has a drink in their hands, how 'bout some music?"

"Only if everyone agrees to sing," she answered.

Sally stood in front of the baby grand piano and turned around to open up the top of the bench behind her. It was filled with sheet music. After sorting through it for a few seconds, she pulled out an old well-worn and somewhat tattered red book: *Songs all America Sings*.

"Shall we start with some Christmas music?" She sat down to play "Adeste Fideles," "Jingle Bells," and then "The First Noel." By the third song, everyone got into the act. Even the elderly Chickerings sang along. Just as they were ending the chorus of "The First Noel," the door bell rang. It was the Kohlbergs.

Cliff left the living room to open the door. "Aaron, Anita, come in, come in. We're just getting warmed up with a little holiday music."

As he took off his coat and gave it to Cliff, Aaron stuck his head into the living room. "Hi, everybody. Sorry we're late. Had to stop at Anita's mom's place on the way."

"Come back this way first," Cliff suggested, "and get yourself a drink and some goodies."

"Looks like your whole poker club is here, Cliff," Aaron Kohlberg said as he poured a glass of wine and gave it to his wife.

"All but Frank Feuermann," Cliff answered. "I couldn't reach him."

Kohlberg poured himself a drink of the same red wine. "I know. We've been trying to reach him, too."

Cliff walked with Aaron and Anita into the living room, where the others had wandered away from the piano. Sally was in the dining room, serving cookies and cutting the cheesecake. Cliff seemed pleased that people seemed to be helping themselves to the food and drinks. "Before too long, maybe we should go downstairs and turn the television on, so we don't miss the stroke of midnight in Times Square. That'll be eleven o'clock here."

Just before eleven the crowd wandered downstairs, where Cliff and Sally had a large-screen TV at one end of their recreation room. Overstuffed chairs, a comfortable sofa, and four large floor pillows made the room a pleasant place to watch movies or football games on Saturday nights.

Cliff gave everyone a champagne glass and poured a small amount in each glass from a magnum of Moet and Chandon, having already prepared himself a flute of ginger ale.

"That little sip won't hurt you," he urged Katie.

Sally gave everyone a paper hat and either a party whistle or a clicker. These were novelties that Cliff had resisted, but had finally agreed to when they were planning the party. As the TV announcer counted down the seconds and the ball on Times Square fell, announcing the stroke of midnight in New York, Cliff and Sally raised their glasses to wish everyone a happy New Year. "Here's to your trip abroad—finally," Marty shouted. As his guests tooted their horns, blew their whistles, clicked their clickers, and looked appropriately silly in their New Year's hats, kissing their own and others' wives and husbands, Cliff leaned over to Katie and whispered, "And here's to the newest Brannigan." Guy Lombardo's Band played "Auld Lang Syne."

An hour later, the stroke of midnight—Waumeka time—called for another round of champagne, toasts, kisses, and horn tooting. Sally served cake and coffee, and gradually the guests began to leave, thanking Cliff and Sally for the party and wishing them a good New Year and a great trip to Italy.

Charlie and Katie, along with Aaron and Anita Kohlberg, were the last to leave. After the four of them had helped Sally and Cliff pick up dirty dishes and put away the leftover food, Cliff turned to his guests. "Anybody like a cup of coffee?" The Kohlbergs said they would take a pass, but Charlie accepted the offer. When Sally left the room with Anita and Katie, talking about the plans for their upcoming trip, Aaron turned to Charlie and Cliff.

"Cliff, you mentioned that you couldn't get a hold of Feuermann. Well, I'm afraid he's under investigation. We can't find him either. There's nobody at his house, and he apparently quit his job at Fleet Farm—quit out of the blue, right after he picked up his paycheck. That was just before Christmas. Now there's evidence of some pilfering in his department. Nobody wants to accuse Frank, but it looks pretty suspicious. Besides that, Lou Cartwright thinks Frank was at the casino the night he got rolled. I hate to think Frank was involved, but we have to get to the bottom of it. If you hear anything, would you give me a call at the station?"

"I wonder if Marty could help you," Charlie suggested. "He knew Frank from Rotary. Actually the only contact I've ever had with Frank was when Marty started bringing him to our card games. Seemed like a nice enough guy."

"Holy shit. I hope he's hasn't gone off the deep end. You know, he did seem a little edgy at times, but you hate to think …" Cliff interrupted himself in mid-sentence when he heard Sally call from the living room, "Why don't you guys come out here and sit down?"

"We'd better be heading out," Aaron said, "It's getting awfully late, and the babysitter's charging double tonight."

Cliff and Anita said goodnight to their guests and saw them all to the door.

As the Brannigans headed down the sidewalk to their house and the Kohlbergs went to their car, Charlie called out, "Aaron, I'll be phoning you." Katie pulled her collar up and her coat closed. The temperature had dropped. A light snow began to fall.

CHAPTER 17

N ew Year's Day dawned bright and clear in Waumeka. It had snowed several inches before dawn, and by noon the sun shone bright on a blanket of new fallen snow. Sunlight streamed through the bay window into the Newsomes' kitchen. At the stove, Catherine fixed bacon and eggs for her husband who, sitting in pajamas and a bath robe, nursed a mild hangover from the previous night's festivities.

"Are you going to be ready for the crowd this afternoon?" Catherine asked in a somewhat demanding tone.

"Yeah, yeah. I got the booze and all I need to do is pick up the party trays from Pick 'n Save. What's to worry?"

"And don't forget paper plates and plastic utensils," she demanded. Tom shook his head and blew across his cup of hot coffee. It was a tradition in the Newsome household to invite Tom's employees from the auto agency, about forty including family members, to a Rose Bowl party at their house. What had started out years before as a simple gathering of a few friends had grown to be one of the town's largest parties of the holiday season.

"By the way," Catherine continued, "I've invited Harold and his wife to come over from Wausau if the weather isn't too bad. He wasn't sure, but I think they'll be here."

"Fine," Tom mumbled. "Be good to see your brother."

"He's looking to get out of the Wausau school district, so I told him there'll possibly be an opening here next year."

"But he's the assistant principal at Wausau High." Tom was beginning to wake up.

"I know," she said, "but it's time for him to think of a principal's job. He's ready for that."

"What makes you think there's going to be an opening for a principal here next year?"

"I'm on the board, Thomas. Remember? Charlie Brannigan's days are numbered. Just you wait and see."

"I don't think you learned much from having one of my staff check out the school building every morning last fall, sitting in front of the school waiting for him."

"I just wanted to make sure he was getting there on time and wasn't stopping to pick up that little chippie of a math teacher on his way to work."

"What?" Tom was puzzled, still half asleep.

"You know who I'm talking about. That Shelby woman, Tommy's math teacher. You met her at the parent-teacher conference. 'Hot little number,' you called her."

"Yeah, what about her?"

"Well, Tommy's been complaining about her teaching all year, and I just happen to have in my possession her complete personnel file."

"How in the hell did you get that?"

"Let's just say I acquired a copy. It's not the original, of course. But it makes rather interesting reading, Thomas. It's no wonder Tommy's been complaining. She has no class-management skills. Brannigan has even made notes about it after his monthly meetings with her. *Monthly* meetings."

"Oh, Jesus, Catherine."

CHAPTER 18

———

"Don't forget, we're going to see Dr. Berkside this afternoon," Katie yelled from the bathroom as Charlie dressed in the bedroom. "Oh, that's right. I put it on my calendar at the office. Should I pick you up here, or will you still be at the hospital?"

"No, I think I'll come home and shower. The appointment isn't until four o'clock, so you can just pick me up here."

Charlie stood at the window looking out over the backyard as a pair of cardinals tried to keep a blue jay out of the bird feeder. The crocuses were already up along the edge of the patio. The tulips and hyacinths were next, he thought, as he surveyed the yard. Winter was not making a serious effort to hang on. A little snow lingered back in the woods, but for the most part the days were now sunny and warm. With Easter in only two weeks, spring was clearly on its way. It was hard to believe that it had already been four months since Katie announced that they were going to have a baby—four months, and time already for the first ultrasound.

They had started to get the house ready for the new arrival. Katie had brought home a few books on pregnancy and birth from the hospital library and put them on the coffee table in the family room: *The Pregnant Body Book*, *Pregnancy and Childbirth*, and Charlie had gotten a book on naming babies from Flanagan's Bookstore. On her nightstand Katie kept a book her mother had given her, *My Pregnancy Journal*. She tried to make at least a brief entry every evening: *Dec. 13, YES! It's true; told Charlie. Dec. 20, Feeling a little nauseous in the A.M. Jan. 4, First time I've ever felt happy about getting fat.*

In the wood working shop in his garage, Katie's father had made a cherry-and-maple crib on rockers that Charlie put in the living room with the baby quilt Katie had used when she was a baby. The yellow-and-blue quilt with a bright star pattern had been made by her mother's mother. Katie's mother was busy knitting baby boots and sweaters. This would be their first grandchild.

Charlie finished dressing and went down to the kitchen to put coffee on and set the table for breakfast. Katie joined him a few minutes later. She was ready for work, dressed in a pair of grey slacks and a loose-fitting blue blouse.

Charlie put his arms around his wife and hugged her.

"Hey, mother," he teased her as he kissed her cheek. "You are one sweet Mama." Katie sat down without saying anything. He noticed that she kept adjusting her belt and pulling at her pants, trying to make them fit. Although she didn't complain, it was clear that she was uncomfortable.

"I can't seem to fit into anything ... didn't think that I'd already be showing this much at four months," she complained.

"You look good to me," he countered.

"Oh, can it, Charlie. You'd think I was carrying twins. Nothing fits and I'm only four months."

"At least you've stopped throwing up every morning."

"Yes, but my stomach is still queasy. I need to ask Berkside about that this afternoon."

***

Katie sat on the edge of the vinyl-covered examining table in nothing but the gown that the nurse had given her and a sheet over her legs.

"It's chilly in here."

"Of course," Charlie replied, "You don't have anything on. I'll ask the nurse for a blanket."

"Don't bother. Berkside will be here any minute. She's really prompt—especially for an OB."

A few minutes later the doctor arrived. She was a short woman with large horn-rim glasses and dark brown hair cut very short, like a man's standard haircut.

"Good afternoon, Mrs. Brannigan." The doctor then turned to Charlie. "I don't think we've met. I'm Janet Berkside."

"Hi. Charlie Brannigan. Katie's told me about you. She's glad you're her doctor."

"Good. Let's get started, then. Katie, how have you been feeling?"

Katie mentioned the nausea, the uncomfortable feelings, and the fact that she was surprised at how much weight she was gaining. After a brief conversation, the doctor stood up and, putting the stethoscope to her ears, began her examination. She listened to Katie's back and then reached under the gown at the top to listen to Katie's chest. She asked Katie to lie down and then raised the sheet and gown and listened to sounds coming from her slightly enlarged belly. Standing at the other side of the examining table, Charlie could clearly see the swelling. He wiped away the tears that had begun to rise in his eyes.

"Let me listen again. Huh. That's something. Well, we'll know more once we do the ultrasound," the doctor said.

"What is it?" Katie asked, sounding concerned.

"I thought for a moment that I heard two heart beats, but at this stage it's awfully hard to tell what you're hearing. I'll be able to see things in a few moments. In the meantime, put your feet up here in the stirrups and let me have a look."

Dr. Berkside went to the equipment table and put on a pair of rubber gloves; standing at the end of the table, she examined Katie's pelvis. She stood at Katie's feet and pressed her legs further apart so that she had easy access to her abdomen and genitalia. She pressed down slightly on Katie's abdomen. Katie winced.

"Does that hurt?" the doctor asked.

"No, I just wasn't ready."

"We're just about done here. Everything looks good."

With the physical exam over, Dr. Berkside began the ultrasound. Charlie heard the gurgling and sloshing sounds of a four-month fetus, and on the television monitor beside the bed he saw the tiny blob moving about in his wife's belly. Finally the doctor took the stethoscope from her ears.

"Look here." She pointed to the television monitor. "Here's the baby, probably a little girl, though we can't be absolutely certain at this age. See, here's the head—two arms right here, and there are the legs. This large dark spot is her heart. Now the interesting part is over here." Moving her pencil across the screen, she pointed to another large mass similar to the first. "I do believe—in fact, I am absolutely certain—you have two babies here." Katie leaned up on her elbows to see the monitor better.

Both Katie and Charlie began to well up with tears as Katie leaned back onto the examining table, her legs still in the stirrups.

"Can you tell if they're both girls? Or is there one boy and one girl?" Katie asked.

"It's really too early to tell. The first one looked like a girl, but I wouldn't put any money on it. What I can say is that you've got two little ones growing in there. Congratulations."

The doctor went over to the desk, opened up a chart that lay there, and wrote her notes. She then returned to the table, lowered Katie's legs and covered her with the gown she wore. Putting her hand on Katie's shoulder, the doctor congratulated her again and told her to be back in a month, and to call if there was any problem at all.

"Wow. Wow. Wow." Charlie hugged his wife as she put her coat on. "Not one, but two. Nice going, Mom." Katie smiled. They decided to have dinner out to celebrate.

"Let's just go to the Olympic," Katie suggested. "It doesn't cost much and we always get a good meal. Besides, you can get a glass of wine—and I can take a sip."

"I'll do that if you'll go to the basketball game with me afterwards. It's the WIAA regionals."

"Really? I know they've had a good season, but I didn't realize they'd gotten to the regionals. Go Bumblebees! Is the game at the high school?"

**

The Olympic Restaurant was only four blocks from the high school, so Charlie and Katie decided to walk to the gym after dinner and got there just before the game started. A group of teachers sat high in the bleachers on the right side.

"Do you think you can walk up there?" Charlie asked.

"Sure. Grab my hand and just go slowly."

There was a huge turnout for the first game of the regional playoffs. The stands were packed, but the students moved out of the way to let their principal and his wife up into the bleachers.

As they walked up, a raucous group of Waumeka High seniors, surprised to see their principal at the game, yelled, "Hey, Mr. B.!" Then one of the bolder senior girls with a tight "WH" sweater asked, "Do we get a free day tomorrow, Mr. B?" as the others all laughed and pushed her.

"What's all the constipation over there?" Charlie yelled back.

The students hooted and hollered. Tight Sweater yelled back, "You mean 'consternation,' don't you, Mr. B?"

"Oh, right. Whatever." he laughed as he and Katie climbed further up the bleachers and the students continued to giggle and laugh.

"Must you, really, Charles?" Katie asked, laughing.

"Fun, aren't they?" he answered.

The teachers in the upper bleachers squeezed together to make room for them. Charlie introduced his wife to those who didn't know her and then sat down next to Chet Magnuson, who sat next to Ann Shelby. Patrick Filey sat on the other side of Ann.

"There's James Cartwright, sitting next to the coach. That's Lou's brother." Charlie told his wife. "He's a great assistant coach. He'll have Justice's job some day."

It was a close game, and just before the half there was an altercation on the court. One of the Waumeka Bumblebees banged with full force into the back of a Wausau player. The ref blew her whistle and called the player over to the side.

"That's Tommy Newsome," Charlie told Katie. "He's known for that sort of thing. The refs are on to him."

"Hey, ref, what the hell are you doing?" someone shouted from the stands.

"And I suppose that's Tommy's father," Katie laughed.

"Right you are. Happens every time."

Only this time, Tommy's father kept it up. "Asshole," he screamed at the ref. The referee walked slowly over to the sidelines where Tom Newsome sat and spoke to him. For the moment, Newsome was quiet and sat down.

After the half, Coach Justice sent five players onto the court. They did not include Tommy Newsome, who was a starter at guard. After a few minutes, Tom Newsome got up from his seat and pushed his way toward the bench where the coaches were sitting. It was easy to see from up in the bleachers that he was arguing with the coach.

"Does the coach always have to put up with this?" Katie asked.

"Not always," Charlie replied, "but often enough."

Toward the end of the game, after a lot of badgering, Justice put Tommy Newsome back in the game. Tommy hogged the ball, trying to make every shot by himself. The game ended in a tie and went into two overtimes before Waumeka finally won on an outside shot made by Tommy Newsome.

"What did I tell you!" his father yelled at the coach, so loud that the entire packed gym could hear him.

On the way back to their car, Katie asked Charlie about some of the teachers they had been sitting with. "Now which of those men is interested in Ann Shelby?" she asked.

"Actually, I think they both are. Although Chet Magnuson is probably close to twice her age, I think he still has an eye for her. It's funny; he hasn't shown any interest in anybody else, so far as I know, since his wife died ten years ago. But he does flirt with Ann, all right."

"So she has two admirers?"

"I think so."

"I can see why."

"Why do you say that?"

"Oh, for heaven's sake, Charles Brannigan, she's drop-dead gorgeous. And I don't think she wears that pretty blue sweater just to keep warm."

CHAPTER 19

C harlie went to the mailbox and retrieved the newspaper and a stack of mail. "Mostly bills," he told Katie as he laid the stack on the kitchen table, already full with dishes that had come out of the dishwasher and were ready to be put on shelves.

"Wait," Katie said, "here's a postcard. A picture of St. Peter's Square in Rome. Hey, it's from Cliff and Sally." She turned the card over and read it, then handed it to Cliff. "Sounds like they're having a great time."

"They really needed that vacation," Charlie said. "I worry about Cliff sometimes, with all the patients he sees. He never takes time for himself unless it's to go to his AA meetings. I keep thinking if he doesn't slow down he's going to get tempted again."

"I know. I'm glad they went," Katie said, acknowledging how hard Cliff worked at the hospital and his office and how much the hospital staff relied on him.

***

The very same day, a card in an envelope arrived at the mailbox in the trailer park down by the flats, addressed to Mr. Lou Cartwright, #102 Oak

Tree Park, Ashmore Lane, Waumeka, WI. Lou slit open the envelope with a kitchen knife, looked at the card with a picture of Michelangelo's David, and then opened it to read:

> Dear Lou,
> Hello, my friend. Just wanted to let you know that we're having a great time in Italy and hope you're doing well. Be sure to call Sam whenever you need to until I get back. Looking forward to seeing you. All the best to Amber and the little one. Best wishes in sobriety, Cliff.

***

The spring semester at Waumeka High was quickly drawing to a close. In many respects, it had been a good year. The drama department had put on what the Waumeka Gazette called "the school's best musical to date"—an adaptation of Cole Porter's "Kiss Me Kate." And the girls' fast pitch softball team was on its way to the regional playoffs. Charlie Brannigan now, at the end of the term, faced two stacks of paper on his desk: one small stack of potential schedules for the coming year and another larger stack of teacher evaluation files.

When he had first come to Waumeka High, Charlie had decided he would review the progress of each of his teachers, not just the novices, every spring—summary "developmental reviews," he called them. He would collect their teaching portfolios and lesson plans and schedule appointments with each of them in turn. It was a tiring job but one he enjoyed. As the appointments in his office lasted over an hour each, he could see only two teachers in an afternoon. He saw Chet Magnuson, the physics teacher, and then James Cartwright, the assistant basketball coach. Both felt that they were doing well. There had been no complaints about either. The girls' basketball team wasn't everything James had hoped it would be, but he was convinced that he would have some good players coming up from the junior varsity the following year. After closing James's file, Charlie took the opportunity to speak with him briefly about his brother, Lou.

"He's keeping up with his AA meetings," James confided, as he leaned back on the couch and set his notes down next to him. "I don't know anything about what they do there, but I think it's helping him. He's back working at Fleet Farm, and with the new boss I think he's doing a lot better. I know he appreciates what you did for him."

No sooner had James left Charlie's office than the telephone rang.

"Mr. Brannigan. It's Mr. Newsome on line one for you."

"Damn," Charlie mumbled. "Thanks, Tricia. Hello, this is Charlie Brannigan. What can I do for you, Tom? ... No, I'm afraid I haven't seen his grades ... Yes, sure, how's Friday afternoon? ... No, I'm sorry, Tom. I just don't have any time this afternoon ... Yes, I know you're a taxpayer and I appreciate all you do for the school. It's just that ... Well, if you're going to be away Friday, perhaps I could see you Monday. That'll be fine. See you then."

***

But Tom Newsome didn't bother to wait. At four thirty, Tricia buzzed Charlie, who was going over his files for the two teachers he was scheduled to see in the morning.

"What is it now, Tricia? By the way, how come you're still here? It's four thirty. You should be home cooking dinner for Clem. It's who? I thought I told him this morning that I'd see him either Friday afternoon or Monday morning. Better send him in."

Before the office manager had time to relay the message to Newsome, he had barged past her desk and pushed open Charlie's door.

Charlie stood up straight behind his desk. Standing six and a half feet tall, his fingers barely touched the desktop. "Tom. What the hell is this? Like I told you this morning, I don't really have time this afternoon."

"I know. I know. This won't take long," Newsome barked.

Charlie looked his opponent straight in the eye. He still remembered Newsome from the days when Tom was a high school track and field hero.

117

Charlie was still in elementary school at that time. *Nasty Newsome,* he recalled, *toughest track star in the Great Lakes region.* Tom was still taller than average, had broad shoulders and almost no neck. He was beginning to show his age. His curly hair was turning gray and his jowls shook when he talked. With the beer belly he had acquired, it was hard to recall that he had been a champion at the discus and hammer throw in his day.

"Sit down, Tom. I can give you five minutes." Charlie pointed to the chair across from his desk and then sat down.

"I believe you'll give me however long it takes. Now, what I'm here for is to find out what you intend to do about Shelby."

"What are you talking about?" Charlie straightened up in his chair.

"I'm talking about that little chippie who's trying to teach math to our Tommy. A sad excuse for a teacher, in my books. I saw the condition of her room when I was here for parent-teacher night. She's a disgrace and she can't teach worth a damn."

"Tom, if you've got a complaint you'll have to file it with the grievance committee." Charlie picked up a pencil on his desk and slammed it upright into a pencil holder.

"Hey, listen," Newsome jabbed a thick, accusing finger at the principal. "It's not just me. There's a whole bunch of us who think her attitude needs a little adjusting. Not only that, one of the kids saw her smooching in the hall with another teacher. Goddamn unprofessional, if you ask me."

Charlie wanted to say, "Nobody's asking you, you silly son of a bitch," but he squelched that response before it came out of his mouth. Instead, he shook his head in disbelief. "Well, as I said, get the group to file their grievance."

Newsome leaned closer, putting his hands on Charlie's desk. "In the meantime, what are you going to do about Tommy's grade?"

"There's nothing at all I can do about grades. Grades are entirely up to the discretion of the teacher."

"That little ... She knows damn well that if he don't pass math, he's not playing basketball next term. Now that's not gonna wash and you know it. Coach Justice can tell you that."

Waumeka High had won three district championships in a row and had just gone to the state tournament the previous year. Tommy Newsome, while not a star player, was a starter at guard. Some people questioned the coach's judgment, but it was Coach Justice's contention that he was important to the team. James Cartwright, the assistant coach, concurred in that decision.

Charlie looked his adversary straight in the eye. "Tom, let me get this straight. Are you asking me to change a grade because a student happens to be an athlete?"

"I'm not asking anything. I'm telling you that Tommy Newsome is going to play basketball for Waumeka High School next term and no simpering math grade is gonna stop him. And I'm saying you should see to that." Newsome pounded his fist on the desk.

Charlie Brannigan stood up again from behind his desk. He was a full five inches taller than the former track star who stood up across from him. Walking around the end of his desk toward Newsome, Charlie extended his hand. "Thanks for coming in, Tom. It's always good to hear from parents. It helps us keep track of how we're doing. Sort of a report card for us."

Newsome turned without taking the principal's hand. He opened the door and slammed it behind him.

***

Charlie sat back in his swivel chair and turned to stare out the window. It looked out across the parking lot and the girls' soccer field to the woods beyond. In the winter, when the leaves were gone, Charlie could see Bear Creek through the trees. A former dentist, Elmer Heckney whose home was just across Bear Creek from the school, had given Heckney Woods to the city. The students had renamed the woods "Hickey Woods," and the creek "Bare Creek," in honor of the late-night activities for which they were known.

Charlie loved the view from his office. He took a deep breath and looked across the field into the woods. He loosened his tie and then ripped it off and threw it on his desk. It was almost five o'clock and he still hadn't prepared for the board meeting scheduled for that evening. And now he had the issue of Tommy Newsome and Ann Shelby. With any luck, he could deal with it before the end of the week. As far as Tommy's grade was concerned, Ann could do whatever she wanted. And as for the "smooching in the hall," Charlie didn't believe it. He knew she had dated Patrick Filey, the social studies teacher, a few times but couldn't imagine any "PDAs," as the school board called public displays of affection. He turned back to his desk and reached for the telephone. Remembering that he had told the office manager it was getting late and she should leave for home, he replaced the receiver and opened his door to the outside office. Tricia was just putting her coat on to leave for the day.

"Trish, you still haven't left. Well, lucky for me, I guess. Do you know Ann Shelby's schedule for tomorrow?"

"Not off hand, but I can get it right quick."

"I don't want to keep you if—"

"It's no bother. The schedules are right here." She went to a file on her desk and flipped through the pages until she came to the one she wanted.

"Here it is. Ann Shelby. Thursdays. Let's see. She's got pre-calculus the first hour, and algebra the second. Then she's off third hour until lunch. She's helping—"

"That's fine. That's just great. Do you think you could leave yourself a note to let her know in the morning to come and see me during her break? Tell her to have her grade book with her. Let her know that I want to talk about Tommy Newsome."

The office manager wrote herself a note and taped it to the top of the telephone.

"Now, goodnight, Patricia! And thank you."

"You're welcome, boss."

Charlie knew he was blessed with a good staff. Tricia Cameron had been on the job for ten years and always did more than he had a right to expect. She had trained three assistants who had gone on, one to another district, and two to the elementary schools as head secretaries. He felt the same way about his teachers. *Loyalty* was the word that came to mind. Several had been there for years; many had grown up in the town, and some—like

Chet Magnuson—were teaching students whose parents he had taught years before.

"Old Man Magnuson," they would say, "Geez, my mother had him. I wouldn't doubt if my *grandfather* did, too." But they admired Magnuson and respected him. He taught physics, and the students knew that if they did well in his class they would be well prepared for college physics. Parents reinforced that view. Not all students could do well in Chester Magnuson's physics class. But even those who did poorly were never left feeling like failures, so long as they did their best. It was a gift he had and one that he had shared with the community for almost forty years.

Charlie ended his reminiscing and headed back into his office with a sense of urgency about the upcoming board meeting. At least he could put off any more concern about Tommy Newsome or Ann Shelby until the morning. Now he could concentrate on the budget and the library assistant position. He knew how the librarian relied on her assistant, Mrs. Finley, an older woman who had come to manage the entire audio-visual program. She dealt with the rental of films and scheduling of equipment, overhead projectors, and speakers. She also made sure to call General Services whenever equipment broke down, if she couldn't fix it herself. Charlie had heard that the board wanted to get rid of that position by the end of the year, but he didn't know how they would be able to get along without her. They were trying to downsize and were cutting costs wherever they could. Athletics seemed to be the only department that escaped their hatchet. The school had winning teams, both boys' and girls'—basketball, soccer, football—and nobody wanted to disturb that. But the elementary schools had already eliminated one secretarial position, two classroom assistants, and the after-school music program. The high school was next on their agenda, and Charlie Brannigan wanted to be prepared.

***

The meeting that evening went well. Charlie was able to convince the board that staff cutbacks, especially in the library, were not the best place to look for financial resources. If they really needed to reduce the budget by $50,000, they might start with library acquisitions, supplies, and the lunch program. He thought his teachers might be willing to help out so that additional hall monitors wouldn't be necessary. In fact, he had already discussed this move with his teachers, who were reluctant but would rather do a stint as hall monitor twice a month than lose their audio-visual aide. He said he also thought some of them might be willing to take on assistant-coaching duties that would free up the athletic budget from hiring outside help with football and soccer. Again, he came prepared, already having discussed this with two of the younger teachers who had expressed an interest in helping out in the athletic department.

Charlie's suggestions about using teachers as hall monitors and putting controls on the supply budget seemed to go over well, but when he offered his ideas about the athletic budget he felt a greater resistance from the board members, as if they were beginning to dig in their heels. It was a little bit like trying to reel in a walleye, he thought; just when you thought you had him well hooked, he would pull back on the line, threatening to snap it. Catherine Newsome, especially, had reservations about any "meddling" with the sports program.

"Waumeka High School, I might say, is known all over this state for its excellent athletic program. It's what makes us outstanding," she pontificated from the head of the large conference table. She conceded, however, when Charlie explained to her that the basketball coaches would not be involved. The school had, after all, produced winning basketball teams three years in a row, and they were counting on a state championship the following year.

CHAPTER 20

Sitting at his desk the following morning, Charlie felt confident about his presentation to the school board. He began to prepare a memo for the teachers:

> This is just a quick memo to let you all know what happened at the board meeting last night. I noticed that several of you were there, but for those who were unable to make it, I thought I'd bring you up to speed..."

Remember to thank them for their loyalty through this budget crunch, he thought. *Mention Shelby and Filey by name for their support of the athletic program and for stepping up to the plate and helping James Cartwright out as assistant coaches. Ask them all for their suggestions in case further cuts are called for.*

After he finished his memo, he asked Tricia to proofread it and then email it to each of the teachers.

As he approved the office manager's changes to his memo and turned to go back into his office, Charlie noticed Ann Shelby coming into the main office, a folder under her arm.

"You asked to see me this morning, Charlie?" she asked.

"Yes, hi Ann. C'mon in and close the door behind you. Do you want some coffee?"

Charlie motioned to the worktable across from his desk where they each took a chair. Ann Shelby set her papers on the table and pulled the chair up under her, smoothing her skirt under her as she sat down. Once again, Charlie couldn't help but notice that she was a gorgeous woman with incredible shapely legs. Ann put a folder of papers directly in front of her and a small grade record book to the left of the papers, a pen and pencil to the right. Charlie Brannigan smiled. She was lining up her ammunition.

"Ann, I saw Mr. Newsome yesterday afternoon. Tommy Newsome's father."

Ann suggested that she didn't think Newsome much cared about his son's school work one way or the other.

"Oh, I think he cares all right. Or at least you got his attention. And with his wife on the school board, it's hard to ignore him."

"What did he want? I met him at parent-teacher's conference and frankly, he gave me the creeps. If I had his attention that night, it wasn't about Tommy—and it wasn't the sort of attention I chose."

Charlie sat up straighter, leaned forward and waited for Ann to look up at him before asking what sort of attention she was talking about, and inquiring about what Newsome had done.

"I dunno. It's just the creepy way he stares, looks you up and down, and ogles … like he's trying to undress you in his head," she replied. She combed her hand through her hair, pushing it off her forehead and shoulder and behind her ear so that it fell down her back.

"Yes, I'm sure he knows how to do that. But now he wants to know about Tommy's grade."

She reached for the gray record book. Round one.

"Well, Tommy Newsome has passed just one of six tests this semester," she said, scanning a page. Turning to the next page, she added, "As for homework, eight of twelve lessons have been turned in, but only half of those were complete." She handed the principal the book.

"No, no, I believe you, Ann," he said handing the record book back to her.

She opened the folder in front of her. "Here are some of his homework assignments." He could see that she corrected errors with a blue pencil on most of the sheets she spread out.

"He took his final exam. How did he do on that?" Charlie asked.

She explained that he had gotten a D, which would not be enough to pull him out of the hole he had already dug.

"So he fails?" Charlie asked.

"I don't see anything else. Not if I'm going to be honest. And I don't think you're asking…"

"Don't even think it, Ms. Shelby. You're the math teacher here. You tell me who passes and who fails, not the other way around."

"Did his father think…?"

Charlie explained that Tom Newsome was more concerned about his son's high school basketball career than about his math grade. If Tommy didn't pass, he explained, he would not be able to play the following fall.

"Well, I've got one suggestion," Ann offered. She closed the record book and her file and set one on top of the other, arranging her pencil and pen on top.

"Let's have it. Anything," Charlie said.

"He could always make the course up by taking it in summer school—if he could pass it, that is."

Charlie wondered aloud what the boy's chances of passing would be. He leaned back in his chair and rubbed his hand over his chin.

"Pretty good, if he buckles down. I don't think the kid is dumb. He just doesn't apply himself. More interested in impressing the ladies and goofing around with his buddies," Ann explained.

Charlie suggested that maybe the boy wouldn't be so distracted in the summer, if his cronies weren't around. He was beginning to see the firm side of Ann Shelby. It was a characteristic he knew would develop and one which he admired.

"I'm glad I won't be teaching the course this summer. Shibilski has it this year," she said.

"Well, I'll get back to Tom Newsome and let him know what they can do. I'm not sure he's going to like it, but it will keep his Tommy on the basketball court. Frankly, just between you and me, I'd like to tell the son of a— I'd like to tell him he can stick his kid's grades where the sun doesn't shine. No quoting me, right?"

"Right," she agreed, laughing. "I'll be curious to know how he responds. Good luck with him." There was that stern side again. Charlie smiled.

"Ann, there's one other thing. It's, ah, more on a personal note, and I'm really reluctant to bring it up. It could wait until we have your developmental review, I suppose, but—"

"Let's have it, Charlie. After talking about Newsome, nothing will seem painful."

"Well, in a way it still is about Newsome. How are you and Filey doing?"

"What do you mean? Romantically? Oh, Pat and I have dated a few times. I like him, but nothing serious. We try to keep it to ourselves, being in the same building and all."

Charlie leaned back and turned to look out the window. "Well, that's what I wanted to ask you about. Newsome mentioned that some student had seen you 'smooching in the hall,' to use his term." Looking back at her, he added, "Ann, it's none of my business and I don't believe it, naturally, but I did think I should tell you that Newsome thinks he's got something on you."

Ann Shelby shook her head and then looked down at the papers in front of her. She put her hand up to push her long blond hair back again and finally spoke. "Oh, my God, Charlie. One time about a month ago, Pat kissed me on the cheek as I was going into my eleven o'clock. We didn't think anybody saw us; the kids were already in their seats. Still, I knew it was a mistake and we talked about it later. I can assure you that won't happen again. Good God. 'Smooching?' Newsome said that? That bastard. Sorry, Charlie."

Charlie laughed. "My sentiments exactly. Thanks for the information. That's all I needed. And, yes, I do trust you, you and Patrick, I mean, to deal with a situation like that yourselves." As they both stood up, Charlie noticed that he was at least a foot taller than his young math teacher. He went to open the door for her and added, "Ann, thanks for coming in this morning. You've been helpful, as always. You know how much we value your work, how much Waumeka High needs you—including the Newsomes of this world."

Ann thanked him and left.

***

Later that day, Charlie telephoned Newsome at his automobile agency to relay the gist of his conversation with Ann Shelby and her recommendation that Tommy make up his math course by going to summer school.

"You know that's impossible, Brannigan. We have a summer place up in Ashland. The kids go with their mother for the whole summer," Tom Newsome shouted over the telephone.

"Well, summer school starts in two weeks and it's over by the end of July, Tom. That's why they go for two hours every day, so they can pack it all into 6 weeks."

Newsome yelled that that was more than half the summer and that Shelby's suggestion just wouldn't wash, in his words.

"Tom, I'm afraid there's nothing I can do. I looked at his papers, and his test scores. He simply hasn't passed the material. He'll need to take it over. And, yes, if he wants to play basketball, the way the rules now stand—" Charlie cringed inwardly, realizing that comment might have been a mistake, opening the lid to a can of worms—"he won't be eligible unless he passes all his classes."

"And just what are we expected to do? Sit down here for the summer while he makes the damn course up? Why the hell couldn't she teach it to him during the year, the way she was supposed to?"

"Tom, Ann Shelby's an excellent teacher, one of our best. But Tommy will have a different teacher in the summer, if he decides to go that route. Just let us know. Registration starts next Monday."

"We'll see about this."

"Good-bye, Tom." Charlie hung up the telephone before Newsome could beat him to it.

CHAPTER 21

———

The Newsomes' home was a large brick Tudor-style mansion. It was situated on a hill overlooking the town, one of four homes, two on each side of a dead end street. Each lot was about five acres and all had manicured lawns and long sweeping drives. Newsome's drive ended in a circle in front of the house. From there, a walk led to a porch with four columns. Large oak trees grew along the drive and a weeping willow stood in the center of the circle in front of the house. Catherine Newsome had hired a professional landscape company from Eau Claire to maintain the gardens.

Three cars were already parked in the circle when Adele and Fred Anderson pulled up. "Looks like we're the last one's here," Adele said.

"Jesus, would you look at the size of this place," her husband commented. "Didn't know you could make this much money selling cars."

Catherine Newsome had called Adele earlier that day to an "*ad hoc*" meeting of concerned parents." Since Catherine was on the school board, Adele thought it best to attend, even though she wasn't sure she shared the views of the other parents. Catherine met them at the door.

"Hi, Catherine. Thanks for inviting us. I hope we're not too late," Adele apologized.

"Not in the least. We're just getting started."

Three other couples were seated at one end of the family room, talking and laughing. A table with cookies, small cakes, and a stack of dessert plates and eight cups and saucers were placed on a serving table at the other end of the room. Adele and Fred joined the group, taking two of the three empty chairs. Catherine Newsome came in right behind them.

"Does everybody know everybody else? Why don't we introduce ourselves just to be sure? Jill, how about it. Shall we start with you?"

A young blond woman across the room from the door looked at her hostess and then up at her husband, who spoke up. "We're Tom and Jill Helman. Our son, Eric, is in the ninth grade."

A short, heavy-set woman, sitting on the couch with her husband, was the next to speak. "I'm Emily Frankel, and this is my husband Seth. Our daughter is in the tenth grade with Tommy."

Two people were sitting on large pillows on the floor in front of the fireplace. The woman introduced herself, "We're the Abramsons; I'm Terri and this is my husband, Al. Our son, Jerry, is also in the tenth grade and our daughter, Anne, graduated last year."

Finally it was Adele's turn. She had met all the others before, either at parent-teacher conferences, band and orchestra parents' meetings, or just at some of the activity nights at the high school. She was glad to hear their names again. "Hi. I'm Adele Anderson."

"And I'm Fred. Our son, Eddie, is in the ninth grade, and our daughter, Aubrey, is in the eleventh."

Catherine Newsome took the last empty seat, a straight backed chair nearest the door to the kitchen. "I'm glad you all could come. Tom wanted to be here tonight but he had another meeting at the Rotary. I know it was short notice but I thought that, under the circumstances, we'd better call a meeting quickly. I guess you could call it an emergency meeting of concerned parents."

Adele Anderson looked around the room, assessing the agreement among the other parents. "I guess I'm still not sure what the main concern is. Is it one that we all share?" she asked, looking at each of the other parents in turn.

"Yes, let me be blunt," Catherine Newsome broke in. "It's this new young teacher, Miss Shelby."

"Isn't it Mrs. Shelby?" Jill Helman asked.

"Well, I certainly don't know," Catherine answered. "I've tried to find out if she has a partner, but I must tell you I don't know if she's Miss or Mrs." Under her breath she snickered to Tom Helman, sitting next to her, "Or if her partner is a him or a her."

"Whether Miss or Mrs., she's Eddie's algebra teacher," Fred Anderson said.

"And Aubrey had her last year for geometry," Adele added. "She's tough as nails, but Aubrey squeaked by."

"Well, now that's just the trouble," Catherine said. "Our children shouldn't have to 'squeak by.' She should be helping them learn and from what I can see, she's not doing it. Our Tommy is failing her class and he's always done well in math before this. He's a very bright boy. But she's not doing her job."

Each of the others, in turn, talked about the difficulties their children had had in Miss, or Mrs., Shelby's class. She had taught algebra, geometry, and pre-calculus. Adele began to realize that a consensus was building up: Ann Shelby was difficult. Some said she favored the boys over the girls and paid more attention to them in class. Others, especially Catherine Newsome, said that nobody was learning from her, and that no student should have to go to summer school to make up material that Miss, or Mrs., Shelby couldn't, or wouldn't, teach during the year. Jill Helman didn't express any view one way or the other, although her husband, Tom, agreed that their son, Eric, had complained more about Ann Shelby than any of his other teachers.

Adele noticed that her husband, Fred, was the only person in the room, other than herself, with a slightly divergent view. Fred suggested that maybe it wasn't terrible to have a tough teacher—maybe that's what some of the young people needed, and maybe the fact that it was a woman was all to the good. Not often, he noted, could you find a woman gifted at mathematics. Interrupting, Catherine Newsome took strong exception to those views and suggested that in no way should she be teaching the course if the students couldn't pass it. She wasn't even sure of Shelby's qualifications and thought perhaps the board should look into that. It would be helpful, of course, if she could speak for the whole group and not just for Tom and herself.

"Agreed, then," Catherine Newsome summarized. "If there are no objections, and I don't hear any, I'll bring this up at the next board meeting. I'll put it on the agenda for the fourteenth." Nobody spoke up.

"There's one other thing," Catherine started. "I'm not altogether sure I should bring it up here but I do believe it does have some important bearing. My son, Tommy, told me that one of his friends told him that he saw this Shelby teacher—to use Tommy's words—'smooching in the hall'."

"Is that really our business?" Adele Anderson asked.

"Why yes, certainly," Catherine assured her. "That would be a public display of affection, and our school bylaws are very explicit about teacher conduct of that sort. It's the sort of thing that calls for a severe reprimand, in my opinion. I assume you all think I should bring that up at the board meeting, as well." Nobody spoke up. "Very well, then."

On their way home, Adele and Fred Anderson questioned why they had been invited. "I'm not sure I agree with them. I'm afraid they're trying to railroad that poor teacher," Fred began.

"Well, why didn't you speak up?" Adele asked.

"Why didn't you? Do you agree with them?"

"I don't know. Either the rest of them know the lady better than we do, or they all have a chip on their shoulders," Adele answered.

"Well, you know the Helmans do. They're never happy with anything at the high school," Fred said.

"I just wish we had said something."

"I don't think Newsome gave us much of a chance."

"She's on the school board," Adele continued, "What does she need us for?"

"For ammunition, I'd say."

***

Two days after the meeting at the Newsomes' home, the school board met in what Catherine called an "emergency meeting." She had sent an email to Jeffrey Fisher, the chairman of the board, asking him to hold an extra meeting before the end of the school year to discuss three issues: the incompetence of a senior high school math teacher, public displays of affection by a teacher in the high school, and the district's rules concerning academic eligibility for varsity sports in the high school.

Fisher had assembled as many of the board as he could get on short notice. Five persons were necessary for a quorum, and he had gotten six of the nine board members, including himself and Catherine Newsome, who began the meeting by listing her grievances concerning Ann Shelby and Charlie Brannigan.

"I have documented evidence from several annoyed parents who have come to me complaining about the practices of this particular teacher," she began.

After listening to Catherine for about twenty minutes, the board decided to appoint a committee to look into the matter. They thought, however, that Catherine Newsome should not be on the committee. Tom Halliburton was the first to raise the possibility of the appearance of a conflict of interest, since Catherine's son, Tommy, was both in Ms. Shelby's class and on the basketball team. He made no mention of the fact that Tommy could lose his basketball eligibility if he failed to remedy his failing grade in math by going to summer school.

"But I thought we might handle this matter immediately," Catherine protested, shaking her head and putting both palms down on the table in front of her. "It's the sort of thing that needs to be nipped in the bud. We can't have teachers going around 'sucking face,' as Tommy calls it." She looked around the table at the others, as if to emphasize her point.

"If it's true," Fisher replied, "and we don't know that it is, Ms. Shelby will need to be confronted with evidence and have the opportunity to defend herself."

"But what about her incompetence as a math teacher? Are we just supposed to let that slide, too?" Catherine whined.

Fisher took a deep breath. "Catherine, I understand your concern. But we can't begin a witch hunt—"

"Well, I never!"

"We've appointed a committee, Catherine. Tom Halliburton will head it up, and we'll get a report before our first meeting in the fall. If there's no other business, I think we should call it a night."

***

Two weeks later, summer school was in full swing. Mr. Shibilski's algebra class had nine students. Three of them were transfer students, and the others had failed the course with Ms. Shelby in the spring term. Three disgruntled tenth grade boys sat in the back of the classroom, waiting for Mr. Shibilski to show up: Tommy Newsome and two of his buddies.

"Did you see bitch-lady down the hall?"

"Yeah, I think she's here to coach the girls' softball."

"My old lady's after the school board to get her ass kicked out of here. She can't teach worth shit, the bitch."

"Yeah, but she smells good." The three laughed.

"Better than Shibilski, anyhow."

"Yeah, I used to like it when she'd stand near the windows. Get the sun shining just right and I could almost see through her dress. I mean, you could damn near see through her panties."

"Jeezus, Tommy, you're a pervert."

"Yeah, like tell me you never noticed."

The room grew suddenly quiet. "Homework, please." Casimir Shibilski walked up and down the aisles, collecting papers. He was one of those older teachers who brooked no nonsense from anyone. He taught summer school because he needed the money. He had three children in college and another about to graduate from high school. Each of them had done well in school, thanks in no small measure to Shibilski's demanding manner.

Shibilski looked to the back of the room where Tommy Newsome and his friends were still whispering and giggling. "That'll be all back there. I'm ready to begin. Please open your books to page thirty-eight."

CHAPTER 22

It was only eight thirty, and already the police station was hot and muggy. It had been an unusually hot summer for northwestern Wisconsin, and the air conditioning in the police station was old and ineffective. The officers had begun to assemble in the conference room when Kohlberg came in and put his coffee and notes at the head of the long table. The place smelled.

Officer Akishembie was the first to speak up. "Chief, before you begin, I've got a request. Could we petition the city again for new air conditioning?" A couple of the older officers laughed.

"I'll see what I can do, George," Kohlberg laughed along with the others. Ordinarily, communication among the officers and with the chief took place at the changing of the shifts and in the morning when the chief came to work. It was a small force, only seven officers including Kohlberg, so a lot of information was conveyed at the counter, in the lunch room, or even over donuts and coffee at the Snack 'N' Yak. Once a month, though, Kohlberg insisted on a morning meeting at which he expected all the officers, except the two assigned to the graveyard shift, to show up. One of his deputies, Karl Clemens, was assigned half-time to his department and half-time to the plain-clothes investigative team in the sheriff's office. Kohlberg encouraged him to come to the meetings whenever he could, knowing that it wouldn't always be possible for Clemens to be present since he was often out of town working on a case. Today, though, Clemens was present with all the others.

After Kohlberg had dealt with routine business, asked for any news, complaints, or suggestions, he put his papers on the table and looked over his glasses at the deputies in front of him. "Probably the biggest news again this month is that the murder—I think that's what we can call it by now—at the casino back in mid-January is still unsolved. We had four muggings there in two months. In one of them, the victim froze to death. Holy God Almighty, I still think young Cartwright was just lucky he didn't freeze to death." He turned to Clemens, lowered his voice, and asked, "Anything new on the Cartwright case?"

Caught off guard, Clemens looked at his notes before answering.

"There were a number of smaller incidents at the casino in the early spring. The tribal force handled most of them, but we do get called in from time to time. There was another mugging over there three weeks ago, and a number of minor incidents before that. But things seem to have quieted down in the past month or so."

The other deputies at the table were shuffling their feet and loosening their ties.

"Did you ever follow up on the Feuermann lead?" Kohlberg asked.

"Frank Feuermann? Yeah, I know Cartwright thought he heard him the night he was beaten back in December, but there's no solid evidence linking him to any of these. We've been trying to get a hold of him for questioning, but he seems to have left town. The place he was renting on Fifth Street is vacant and the realtor doesn't know where he went. She said he came in and paid his last month's rent and said he and his family were moving. That's all she knew," Clemens reported, wiping his sweaty brow with the cuff of his shirt sleeve.

"You know, Karl, this is hard for me. I know Feuermann—in fact, played cards with him probably once or twice a month for a couple of years. Even at that, though, I never got to know him real well. Still, it's hard for me to imagine—"

"I know, chief, this stuff happens. Like I said, we got no proof one way or the other. But it's still on the table."

"Have you checked with Fleet Farm?" Kohlberg asked.

"Oh, yeah. Same thing. His boss over there said Frank came in, picked up his paycheck for April and said he was quitting. Claimed he had to find something that would pay him more. One of his men—I think his name was Swenson—said he thought he heard Feuermann talking about moving to Milwaukee."

"Milwaukee? Are you working on that?"

"We're trying." Clemens answered.

"Jesus. I hope so. If Feuermann is in any way connected to any of this, we should have him back here. I know he belongs to Rotary; I'm sure you've checked that." Kohlberg said

"Yep."

"He's got a buddy from Rotary named Marty O'Brien. Marty's a good guy. You might give him a call. He's a friend of Charlie Brannigan's from Our Lady of Sorrows ... both ushers over there, I think. That's how I got to know Feuermann. Marty introduced him to our poker crowd."

"O'Brien, you said? I'll check," Clemens answered.

The others in the room were loosening ties, shuffling feet, looking at their notes, and getting water from the cooler.

"Well, keep on it and let us know. Any of you others hear anything, be sure to bring it in. I've talked to Cartwright and his wife; they seem to be doing alright. Lou is finally in AA, thanks be to God, I'd say." Kolhberg wanted to move on to other business.

"You can say that again," Bjorn Olson, the oldest deputy on the force, spoke up. "If that guy is anything like his old man, he'll be a rip-roaring son-of-a-bitch before he's forty."

CHAPTER 23

"Charlie?"

"What's the matter?" Responding to the alarm in Katie's voice, Charlie Brannigan threw his newspaper down and turned toward his wife, who sat on the sofa with her legs stretched out.

"Charlie?"

"What's going on? What's the matter?" He jumped up and rushed over to Katie

"I think this is it, Charlie. Oww."

"Are you having pains?"

"Yes … a little … but I think … I think maybe my water broke."

Charlie helped her up from the sofa. They had both prepared for this moment with meticulous attention to detail, and yet somehow now that the time had arrived, they both stood there in the family room staring at the wet spot on the sofa and waiting for the other one to say something.

Charlie broke the silence. "Well, your overnight bag is packed. I'll go up and get it. You stay right here. Here, sit on the chair for a minute. I'll be right down. Is everything you need in the bag?"

"Yes, I have everything there. Would you bring my missal from the night stand, too? I want to look up more saints' names."

"OK, OK. Are you all right?" His voice strained with concern.

"Yes, I'm fine, Charles Brannigan. Just go. Do you know I love you ... Daddy?" She grinned at him but it looked more like a grimace.

Charlie kissed his wife and ran up the stairs. About thirty seconds later he returned with the small overnight bag and Katie's missal. He reached for his keys on the counter and grabbed his coat off the hook near the back door. "Oh, my God, we still haven't called the hospital."

On the way to the hospital, Katie took her missal and turning to the index, began to read out the names of the saints whose feasts were marked.

"I thought we had already decided on names," Charlie protested.

"Well, yes, but what if one of these is a boy? Ouch." Katie twisted in her seat and repositioned her swollen belly.

"Not likely," Charlie answered. "Berkside said it's almost a sure thing they're both girls."

"Yes, but even with the second ultrasound you can't be one-hundred percent certain. Anyway, I think we should be prepared with a boy's name just in case. How do you like Kevin Charles? The middle name should be your name, don't you think?" She stretched her legs out.

"Fine with me, but Kevin? Sounds ... I dunno. No, I don't think so," Charlie answered.

"Patrick Charles?" She grimaced

"Now there's a name a boy could live with. Yes."

"Then that's it, if either is a boy, that is."

"Yes, I think a girl might have a hard time getting through school with a name like Patrick Charles," Charlie laughed.

Four hours later, at 10:53 P.M., the quiet of the hospital nursery was broken with the insistent cries coming from two brand-new sets of lungs.

***

Charlie woke up the next morning in the hospital recliner, across from his wife who was awake and watching him. He had kicked his shoes off but was otherwise still dressed. He reached in his pants pocket and handed her a crumpled piece of paper.

Flash Announcement
New Delivery — Just in
Date of Arrival — August 13, 2012
Time of Arrival — 10:53 PM Central time
Sent From: Heaven
Port of Entry: St. Luke's Hospital, Waumeka
Description: Two baby girls
Names: Mary Elizabeth and Kathleen Marie
Weight: 5 lbs. 3 oz. - and 5 lbs. 8 oz.
Condition on arrival: Excellent, mint, uncirculated
Receivers: Kathleen and Charles Brannigan
You may view this rare delivery by calling (715) 822-2233
Or by visiting
609 Crescent Circle
Waumeka, WI

He watched Katie, propped up on two pillows, read the paper.

"I wanted to make up our own announcements. How does this look? I printed it out on the computer in the lounge after you fell asleep."

Katie looked at the announcement and smiled weakly. Her red hair spread out on the pillow. The covers were pulled up around her neck. She was pale and drawn, but Charlie figured that was normal for somebody who had given birth to twins only nine hours earlier. She had had a relatively smooth labor. Dr. Janet Berkside had assisted in the delivery.

Katie set the announcement on the tray-table in front of her. "It looks fine," she said, "only …"

"What is it?"

"Well, you say, 'Condition on arrival: excellent.' That's not entirely—"

"I know, I know, but its close enough. They're both going to do just fine." Charlie leaned over to kiss his wife. Then he reached for the bassinet next to her, where one of the babies slept.

The other infant, Kathleen Marie, was in the pediatric intensive care unit. When she was born—the second child to be delivered—her Apgar scores were so low that Dr. Berkside had insisted on running tests right away. Kathleen's cry was weak and her muscle tone flaccid. Her sister, Mary Elizabeth, on the other hand, was healthy and screaming from the first moment of life.

"Do you still like the names?" Katie asked.

"I love them. Who wouldn't love the name Kathleen, just like her mother? And I think my mother will be pleased, too." Charlie's mother was Mary Elizabeth Hurley until she married Ed Brannigan.

As they were talking, Dr. Berkside knocked on the open door and came into the room.

"Hi, Charles, did you get any sleep at all last night?"

"Oh, I guess I was able to get in a couple of hours. Not much more than that, though. What do you think of our two baby girls?"

"They're beautiful. And Kathleen Marie is doing a little bit better. But we do need to talk." She pulled a chair up closer to the bed and sat down.

"What is it?" Katie asked, sitting up straight now. "She's going to be all right, isn't she?"

"Well, I had the pediatric cardiologist see her first thing this morning. He's convinced that Kathleen will need surgery. Very soon." She stopped to let her words sink in.

"There's no chance that she'll ..." Katie tried to pull a pillow up behind her so she could lean back.

"Katie, we've got some of the best surgeons in the country within easy reach," the doctor reassured her. "We could take her to the clinic at Marshfield, or over to Mayo. The cardiologist will be here in a few minutes to help you make that decision, but the decision needs to be made this morning."

"Let me see if I understand," Charlie asked. "We'll see the heart doctor this morning and that's when we'll decide if, when, and where Kathleen should have heart surgery?"

"That's it," the doctor answered. "You'll like Dr. Carlson. He's an excellent pediatrician and a first-rate cardiologist. Katie, I think you may already know him. He did grand rounds a few months ago—actually it was on a similar case."

"Can you tell us how serious this is?" Katie asked, staring at the doctor.

"It might be better to wait for Dr. Carlson to explain the problem and how we need to respond. He is certain from the tests we've done that Kathleen has what's known as hypoplastic left heart syndrome, HLHS for short. It means that the left side of her heart didn't develop properly. It can't pump enough blood out to the rest of her body. It's a congenital condition."

"How come we didn't learn about this while I was pregnant?" Katie asked.

"Well, sometimes the condition is diagnosed in pregnancy, but not always. Actually, it doesn't affect the fetus when it is in the womb, since it gets its oxygen from the mother and doesn't really need to pump blood to the lungs. The trouble comes after the baby is born. That's when intervention has to occur immediately."

"I still don't understand why we didn't know this earlier," Katie said in a tone that was both worried and demanding.

"Well, like I said, sometimes it isn't diagnosed until after the baby is born. I think in this case, we didn't see the underdeveloped heart in the second baby because the ultrasound was never entirely clear. Remember, we had a little trouble seeing Kathleen lying behind her sister. Even if we had gotten a good picture, there's no assurance we would have found this. In any case, Dr. Carlson will go over all the alternatives with you."

As they were talking, Dr. Ray Carlson came in to the room. Dr. Berkside stepped aside and stood near the head of the bed.

"Good morning, Mrs. Brannigan? I'm Ray Carlson." He drew closer and looked at Katie over the top of the glasses that had slid down his nose. "Say, didn't you used to work in Pediatrics?"

"Yes. Still do. Or, I would be if I weren't up here having babies of my own. How does Kathleen look to you? Is she going to be all right? Oh, Doctor Carlson, this is my husband, Charlie Brannigan."

"Nice to meet you, Charlie. Ray Carlson. Yes, I just now saw Kathleen briefly. I looked at the new X-rays and got some blood work back from the labs."

"How's she doing, doctor?"

"As I think Dr. Berkside explained, Kathleen—do you call her Kathleen? Kathleen has HLHS. Her heart isn't pumping the blood that the lungs need for her to survive. We need to get her on a drug called Prostaglandin, and she'll definitely need surgery within the next 48 hours." The physician went on to explain the Norwood surgical procedure, plus two additional operations in the baby's first year, each surgery having its own inherent risks.

"What's the bottom line, doctor?" Charlie stood next to his wife, holding her hand. "How likely is she to survive three cardiac surgeries as a baby?" he asked, clearing his throat.

"Before about 1980, her chances would have been zero. We didn't have these procedures. Now we can save almost seventy-five percent of the newborns like Kathleen. But we'll need to act quickly."

"Seventy-five percent?" Katie began to cry.

The doctor sat on the edge of the bed without saying anything while Katie took a tissue and wiped her eyes, and Charlie reached for a chair and pulled it up next to her.

Finally Dr. Carlson broke the silence. "If it's alright with you two, I'd like to set her up for surgery—if possible, the day after tomorrow. I'll call the Marshfield Clinic and see if Dr. Carrigan can fit her in. He's an excellent pediatric surgeon and he's done quite a few Norwoods. He'd be my first recommendation."

After the doctor left, Charlie and Katie talked together about their fears, their worries about the danger of surgery on their tiny infant, the impact of Kathleen's illness and possibly even death on her sister. They were able to talk about the odds that Kathleen might not survive, although Katie wanted to dismiss that possibility. "God will take care of her," she kept saying.

While they were talking, Cliff Smalley stuck his head in the doorway. "Good morning, neighbors," he called out. He wore a short grey lab coat and had a stethoscope sticking out of the right pocket. His cheerful manner clashed with their mood but was also a welcome relief. Katie attempted a smile.

"I just finished rounds, so I thought I'd come up and see how things are going."

"Cliff, my God, it's good to see you here," Charlie said. He got up and went over as if to hug his neighbor, but stuck his hand out instead. Cliff shook Charlie's hand and said, "I was just looking at Katie's chart. Katie, how are you feeling?"

"I'm doing fine. It's Kathleen we're worried about. Thanks for coming up."

"Yes, I saw that. A baby with HLHS is fairly rare, but I'm sure Berkside told you that Dr. Carlson is one of the best in the business."

"She did. We met him this morning. Seems like a good man. But he says Kathleen will need surgery," she reported in a soft quivering voice.

"Did he explain the Norwood procedure?"

Katie began to tear up again. "Yes, he did."

Cliff went over to take her hand. "She's going to be in good hands. And so will you, Katie. Sally and I are right next door. Please, don't forget that. Without children of our own, we've really been looking forward to this."

Charlie spoke up. "Thanks, Cliff. That means a lot."

"I'd better get back to the office," Cliff said as his beeper went off, "before Ms. Formby starts sending my patients back home. She's a great receptionist—keeps me on my toes."

"Thanks, Cliff."

When the two men reached the door, Cliff said, "By the way, Charlie, I saw Lou Cartwright last night at the AA meeting. He said I could tell you that he's doing fine. It'll be a fight, but I know he can make it."

Charlie shook Cliff's hand again. "Great. That's just great."

***

Charlie Brannigan went back to the school that afternoon to alert his office manager and the assistant principal that he would be out of the office for an indefinite period, and to gather some papers and books to take with him to Marshfield. Summer school was winding down, but still the hallways were buzzing with students going in and out of the classrooms; the sound of instruments warming up came from the band room at the far end of the hall. The bell rang, and quiet replaced the buzzing confusion. A slightly off-key rendition of "The Marquette University March," replaced the screeching warm-up noise. Suddenly, a laughing student bolted out of a classroom, almost bumping into the principal.

"Hey, hey," Charlie called. "Slow down."

"Mr. Shibilski wants me to measure the soccer field for a geometry problem. Says if I'm not back in ten minutes, I flunk. He doesn't think I can do it."

"Oh, he's just being cyclical, I'd guess," the principal noted.

"Don't you mean cynical, Mr. B? The word is 'cynical,' isn't it?" the student yelled back as he ran toward the side door near the girls' soccer field.

"I believe you're right," Charlie responded, shaking his head and smiling at the young man on a mission.

Back in his office, Charlie got a telephone call from the hospital.

"Mr. Brannigan, this is Dr. Carlson. I spoke with you this morning at the hospital. I've called over to Marshfield and set up the surgical appointment for Kathleen. I've already spoken with your wife, but I wanted to alert you, as well. Dr. Carrigan will do the surgery on Wednesday, the day after tomorrow. The transport team from the Marshfield Clinic will be here in an hour to pick up baby Kathleen from the hospital and airlift her to Marshfield. They'll begin her on Prostaglandin and intravenous feeding. We're going to want to have plenty of antibiotics on board before the surgery," the doctor explained. "You and your wife can leave tomorrow afternoon in your own car. If you would like to stay in Marshfield until the surgery on Wednesday and afterwards while the baby is recovering, you could stay at the Ronald McDonald House. It's directly across the street from the hospital. They provide temporary lodging for the families of patients in the children's hospital. That way, your wife can be near baby Kathleen and still nurse your other baby. Is it Mary Elizabeth? You need to have your baby's nurse call over and make a new family referral to the Ronald McDonald house for you. Then the house manager on duty will talk with you and do the preregistration and background checks, which won't take very long. Their office is open every day from 8:00 A.M. until 9:00 P.M., to check families in and out. Plan on being in Marshfield for at least three weeks."

"Thanks, Dr. Carlson. What about tonight and tomorrow morning? Will Katie stay at the hospital with Mary Elizabeth?" Charlie asked.

"Yes, I'd like her to stay here. It's better for her and better for your other baby. You can stay with her in her room, if you like. I'm sure Dr. Berkside mentioned that."

"Yes, thanks, Doc. This is all pretty scary."

"I know it seems that way, but these transport teams from Marshfield are excellent. And just like I mentioned this morning, once you're in Marshfield you'll be getting the best care imaginable."

"Thanks, Dr. Carlson. I'll be over there in ten minutes so Katie and I can say goodbye to Kathleen before they pick her up."

"Good luck, and let me know if you have any other questions. I'll be in the hospital for the rest of the day. Just have them page me."

"Thanks for all your help."

CHAPTER 24

———◆———

It was seven thirty when the door bell rang. Charlie Brannigan had finished dinner, cleared the plates off the table, gotten the cards and glasses out, and set four chairs around the card table in the family room. He got up slowly to answer the bell. He stretched from side to side and then, raising his hands high into the air, he straightened his full six-foot-six-inch frame. Tossing a phantom ball into the air with his right hand, he swatted it with the invisible racket in his left. *That one went right into the net. Guess I better practice that serve.*

Aaron Kohlberg was the first to arrive.

"Looks as if I'm the first one here. Seems funny getting here well before the sun goes down. Where is everybody?"

As if on cue, Cliff Smalley opened the door from the outside and let himself and Marty O'Brien in. "You guys ready to lose some money?" Marty announced. "Charlie, how're Katie and the girls? Any news on baby Kathleen yet?" He pulled a chair away from the card table and sat down facing Charlie.

"Katie's doing fine, thanks. She'll be staying in the hospital with Mary Elizabeth until we go to Marshfield tomorrow. Kathleen Marie has a serious heart defect and will have surgery there on Wednesday."

"Shouldn't you be with Katie now? We don't really need to play cards tonight."

"I'll get over there and stay with her tonight after our game. I told her we didn't have to play cards, but she insisted. Said I wasn't really needed at the hospital, anyhow. Guess there's not much I can do about the feeding, since she's nursing."

"Bet you wouldn't mind holding the bottle, though," Marty suggested. It was about as rough as the conversation ever got, and the men all laughed, including Charlie. He went into the kitchen and came back with three cans of beer, a soda and some chips.

"This has all happened so fast," Charlie said, setting the drinks and chips on the table. "Actually the operation on Wednesday will just be the first surgery; she'll need three of them over the next year or so. I'm sure Cliff could tell you more about it."

"That's about it," Cliff said, as he began shuffling the cards. "It's a stunning procedure. Personally, I think she'll be fine. She's gonna see Myles Carrigan, one of the best kid surgeons in all of Wisconsin—one of the best in the country, for that matter."

Charlie leaned back in his chair, stretched his back and shoulders and said, "Let's play some cards." After a few rounds, as he dealt the cards, Cliff said, "I miss taking Frank's money. Anybody heard from him, by the way?" They all looked at Aaron Kolhberg.

"It's hard," Aaron answered, shaking his head. "It's times like these you wish somebody else was police chief. You guys read the papers. Frank's on the lam. We don't know for sure that he's done anything at all; we're just looking for him so we can talk. I really can't say any more than that."

Later, after Cliff and Aaron said goodnight and left, Marty began putting on his jacket and turned to Charlie. "I dunno, Charlie. I hope I'm not in any trouble."

"What's the matter?" Charlie asked. "Come on over here and sit down. Would you like another drink?"

"No, no thanks." Marty sat on the comfortable chair in the corner of the room as Charlie sank onto the couch. "It's about this Feuermann thing. You know he was a friend of mine from Rotary?"

"Yeah, sure. What's up?" Charlie crossed his arms and leaned forward toward his friend.

"Well, the cops are looking for Frank. Something about robberies at the casino, and they think Frank is involved. There was this investigator guy from the police department called me and then came over to the house, asking about him. I think Kohlberg must have sent him."

"So?"

"I'm supposed to tell the cops if I hear anything. Well, I told him I didn't know anything and that I hadn't seen or heard from Feuermann since early May. That's when he moved out of the place he and Sophie were renting on Fifth Street."

"What's wrong with that? You haven't seen him, have you?"

"No, I ain't seen him, but well, you know, he's called a few times. He's in trouble. He and Sophie are living in Milwaukee ... renting some apartment from Sophie's uncle. I know where he is, but I couldn't rat on him. I like Frank. He's in trouble and he trusts me. I don't know what to do." Marty put his head down and clasped his hands together in his lap.

"Have you talked to Aaron?"

"No, that's the thing. I'm afraid they're going to put Frank in jail if they find out where he is and what he's done ..." Marty's voice shook.

Charlie stopped his friend in mid-sentence. "Marty, I don't know about you, but I need another drink." Charlie got up to get a beer. Marty called out, "I'll take one, too."

Charlie came back to the couch, gave Marty his beer, and set his own on the coffee table. "Marty, what do you think Frank's done, or has he told you?"

"Well, not exactly. There were a bunch of muggings at the casino. I know Frank was there and took some of the money, but he never hurt anyone. He knows the guys who did, though. That's the trouble. He can't turn them in, because he took some of the money."

"There was a murder over there in January, Marty."

"Yeah, I know. Again, Frank knows the guys, or thinks he does. He wasn't there that night, but he's pretty sure he knows who did it." O'Brien's voice began to clear and he began to look directly at Charlie.

"Was he there the night Cartwright got rolled?" Charlie asked.

"He was there, but he saw Lou later. He wasn't there when it happened. He saw Lou lying on the cement in the parking lot, and didn't do nothing about it. He had been drinking."

"Is he a big drinker? He never seemed to have a problem when he was here playing cards with us. I mean, he always had a beer or two with us, but what the hell, so did the rest of us."

"Well, Frank does have a problem with that sometimes. It's usually when he's at the casino. More than that, though, he can't seem to keep himself from gambling. Always needs more money. And once he's there he can't stop. I went with him a couple times. Holy shit, Charlie, we didn't get home until two thirty. I told him I just couldn't do that anymore. Maryann was pissed." Marty set his can of beer down and grabbed some chips that Charlie had brought from the card table.

"I can imagine."

"What am I gonna do, Charlie?"

"I don't know. I think you may have two choices. Either talk to Kohlberg, tell him what you've told me and take the consequences with Frank."

"Or?"

"Or call Frank—I assume you have his number—and tell him he ought to turn himself in for questioning. They're sure to go easier on him if he does that than if they have to hunt him down. Is there a warrant out for his arrest?"

"Geez. I dunno," O'Brien answered.

"You're his friend, Marty. Tell him that."

"To tell you the truth, Charlie, I'm scared. If Aaron finds out I lied to his detective, I could be in trouble … I mean, maybe it's obstructing justice, or something. Anyway, it's lying," Marty admitted, his voice shaking again. He took a gulp of beer.

"I still think your best bet is either to come clean or to get Feuermann to turn himself in. Tell him the predicament you're in, trying to cover for him."

The two men finished their drinks and Marty got up to leave. "Thanks, Charlie," he said, "I'll sleep on it. I'll think about what you said."

CHAPTER 25

Ann Shelby and Patrick Filey had been seeing one another off and on all summer. He took a summer graduate course in Modern European History at UW-Eau Claire and Ann coached the girls' softball team at the high school. Whenever they had a chance, usually on Fridays, they would either have lunch together—often a picnic at the park by the creek—or go out to dinner.

Patrick drove his Ford Bronco to the school to pick up Ann after the team's scrimmage late Friday afternoon.

"That's all, girls," she yelled to her team after they chanted the school yell and raised their hands in a team high five. "Don't forget to practice your pitching over the weekend, Carol. And the rest of you, do your exercises—sit-up, laps, stretches, you know the routine."

"Yes, Ms. S.," they groaned and then, laughing, headed back into the school.

Standing on the sideline, Patrick watched as she picked up the two bats and three balls that the students had forgotten to toss in their equipment bag. Smiling, she turned to him. "Hey you, give me a chance to shower. I'll be out in ten."

Patrick sat on an old wrought-iron bench with his back against the building. It looked as if birds had been the only occupants of the rusted seat for years.

Wearing a baseball cap over her wet blond ponytail and a Waumeka High T-shirt with a bumble-bee logo on the front, Ann pushed through the side door in less than the ten minutes she had requested and sat down next to Patrick on the old black bench.

"What's on the agenda for tonight?" Patrick asked. "Can we go to a movie? The new Tom Hanks?"

***

After the movie, they walked down North Main Street. As they passed by Sorenson's Jewelry, Patrick stopped at The Clock, took Ann by the arm, and kissed her on the cheek. "A little PDA beneath The Clock," he announced. Ann smiled, looked up at the clock, and then checked her watch. It was eight o'clock.

Patrick stopped the car in front of Ann's apartment, pushed his seat back, and turned toward her.

"I have to tell you, I was really impressed this afternoon. You're doing a great job with those kids. You can see they appreciate it."

"I wish their parents all thought so," she answered, leaning back against the door to face him.

Patrick knew that the school board had appointed a committee to investigate Ann's teaching credentials as well as one instance of alleged "conduct unbecoming a teacher."

"They're bastards. *I'm* the one who kissed *you*. Why aren't they examining my qualifications? Maybe I'm not fit to teach, either," Patrick said.

"Oh, Pat."

As he felt her hand slide up his arm and around his neck, he reached down to push his seat further away from the steering wheel. "Just a second." He pulled away from her embrace just long enough to lift the armrest that had been separating them, so that nothing stood between their bodies but thin air. As he pulled her to him, Ann fell onto his chest. He pulled her closer and put his hands around the small of her back, slid them down beneath the band of her panties, and was getting ready to take her right there in front of her apartment, when he realized what he was doing.

"Holy crap. We better go back to my place," he suggested.

They both sat up straight and Patrick reached down to pull his seat forward, then started the car.

"On the other hand," Ann said, "how about going for a drink instead? I'd love nothing more right now than to go to bed with you, but we haven't even talked about what we're doing."

"OK, I suppose you're right," he replied.

"You're not mad, are you?"

"No, not mad. Just a little disappointed, I guess. But maybe you're right. Where do you want to go?"

They couldn't very well go to the Snack 'N' Yak. Did he mind driving over to Eau Claire? They could go to Kelly's. "I'd just rather not stir up any more gossip in this town than we already have," Ann sighed.

"It's funny. We really haven't given them anything to gossip about. But Eau Claire's fine. Probably won't get back until after one o'clock, though. Is that OK with you?" he asked.

It was Friday night. She didn't mind.

They drove the back-country roads to Eau Claire, even though the interstate would have been faster. Farm houses and barns dotted the landscape. A half moon shone in the eastern sky, and the long drive gave them a chance to talk about school, their new classes, Charlie's new babies ... everything but each other.

They took a corner table at Kelly's and ordered drinks: scotch and water for Patrick and a glass of Chardonnay for Ann.

"Want to dance?" Patrick offered.

"Umm," Ann smiled and stood up. He held her close and smelled the soft fragrance of roses beneath her ear. He kissed her earlobe before she nestled into his neck. They danced for ten minutes until the band took a break. By the time they got back to their table, they noticed that the waitress had brought their drinks and a plate of nachos.

"I wonder if we're avoiding talking about us," Ann asked as she sipped on her Chardonnay.

"I'm not sure what there is to say," he answered.

"Patrick, we almost got between the sheets back there!"

"Well, so?" He took a huge gulp of scotch.

"Is that what you wanted to do?"

Darn right. Hadn't he said so? He reached for her hand, which she pulled away.

"But what does it mean to you?" She looked down at her glass and ran her fingers around the rim.

"Well, it means I like you," he replied. Another gulp of beer.

"That's it?" she asked, looking directly at him, her blue eyes examining his face, waiting for a more convincing answer.

"Well, I mean if you're asking if I love you, I mean, how does a person know that? I mean I just ... Oh, shit. Let's dance."

They danced again until Ann excused herself to go to the restroom. When she returned, Patrick had ordered another drink for each of them.

"Whoa. You're going to get me plastered," she laughed.

No. He just thought they could use a night cap.

"Are you going to be OK to drive?"

"No problem. I'm feeling fine. How about you?"

"Fine. But maybe we should go after this one. I'm afraid it's getting late."

They took the highway home and Ann broached the topic that had been on her mind since Patrick told her that he liked her.

"Pat, maybe we should cool it for a while, at least until this stuff with the school board blows over."

He didn't want to let the school board dictate how they were going to live their lives.

"It's not just that. I'm worried that we're moving too fast. In a few weeks we'll be back in school, seeing each other every day. It's hard not to want to be with you. But you know how the kids talk."

"Then what are you saying—I'm not supposed to call you?"

"Maybe just for a while. Like I said, until this business with the school district gets cleared up. Is that OK?"

"I guess it'll have to be." They reached Ann's apartment just after one o'clock, kissed, and said goodnight.

CHAPTER 26

———————

Dark clouds filled the sky and a late summer rain was drizzling on Waumeka when Charlie, Katie, and Mary Elizabeth left the hospital and headed to Marshfield. Charlie had preregistered online at the Ronald McDonald House, and the pediatric cardiac team had sent a referral.

In Marshfield, the Day Manager at the Ronald McDonald House greeted them at the door, as Charlie set their bags down.

"There are six other families here at the moment," the balding man explained. "Four of them have newborn babies at the hospital, just like you do."

After copying their photo ID's, reviewing the House guidelines, and giving them a House tour, he showed them to their room, a bright, cozy space on the second floor. The large, older home had been purchased ten years before for the purpose of housing out-of-town families of hospital patients. The place was large enough to house ten families in comfort. A small bouquet of daisies and carnations had been placed on the dresser with a card announcing, "Welcome to the Ronald McDonald House," and in smaller print, "Please let us know what we can do to make your stay less stressful."

It was a comfortable home where families could cook their own meals in the communal kitchen, using food and supplies that were provided, and eat with other families in a common dining room. In an adjoining sun room, a few chairs and a sofa were positioned in front of a gas fireplace. Between the sofa and fireplace sat a long coffee table with a half-done jigsaw puzzle of a Currier and Ives New England scene. After dinner, Katie nursed Mary Elizabeth and then she and Charlie joined another couple and an older woman in the sun room to watch the fire, have their coffee, and compare stories about their sick family members. Mary Elizabeth fell asleep on her mother's lap.

The other couple had driven down from Ashland. They were probably ten years younger than the Brannigans, Charlie thought. Their two-year-old son was in the hospital with meningitis. "It's the bacterial kind; that's the worst," the wife explained. "Heck, we just thought he had an ear infection, then what do you know, he comes down with this humungous fever. Geez peas, we didn't know what to do." Her husband, a salesman of farm equipment, explained that the baby was doing better now. "Heck, you just can't get better medical help, you know what I mean? Why, these doctors are the best in the world. And right here in central Wisconsin, yessir," he proclaimed.

The older woman sat quietly until Charlie asked her, "And what brings you to Marshfield?" A large Polish woman with grey hair high up on her head in a large bun, she told them how her sixteen-year-old grandson—she was his legal guardian—had been in an automobile accident and wasn't expected to live. She and her husband, a farmer from Wausau, had raised her daughter's boy since he was a baby. She didn't explain how she and her husband came to be legal guardians, nor how the accident occurred, and nobody appeared willing to invade her privacy.

"I'm sorry to hear that," was all Charlie could offer.

"Just say a prayer," the woman replied. "He's a good boy."

The group turned to watch the evening news on TV. Charlie and Katie excused themselves after the news and went to their room.

***

Since Kathleen Marie's surgery was scheduled for nine o'clock Wednesday morning, Charlie and Katie had an early breakfast of toast, eggs, and orange juice in the hospital cafeteria and arrived at the Newborn Intensive Care Unit by eight o'clock. Dr. Carrigan met them at the nurses' station.

Dr. Myles Carrigan was a small man who wore a checkered suit and a large bow tie. He had a broad, grinning smile and horn-rimmed glasses. Except for the glasses, he reminded Charlie of Howdy Doody. Charlie tried not to smile as he thought about the uncanny similarity. The doctor put his small hands together on the counter in front of him. He explained the surgical procedure, the risks involved, and his guarded expectation that Kathleen would survive after the three heart surgeries.

It was two hours before Howdy Doody emerged from the operating room.

"Well, I think Kathleen Marie is out of the woods, at least for now. She'll be in intensive care for at least forty-eight hours and, if all goes well, should be ready to go home in two to three weeks. I'll be here every morning at eight o'clock to check on her. The nurses have my number if you need to get a hold of me at any other time. Don't hesitate."

***

Within a week, Kathleen Marie began to thrive. She gained one pound, and pink began to return to her cheeks. Katie could nurse her again, and the doctors agreed that within a few more weeks the baby could go home with her parents.

The hours dragged into days and the days into weeks. It seemed that the rain would never let up. Charlie fixed breakfast every morning while Katie nursed Mary Elizabeth. After nursing and changing the baby, Katie came to the table but without much appetite. "Not cereal again," she complained. So Charlie fixed pancakes. Occasionally they went into town for a meal in a restaurant or across the street to the hospital cafeteria.

After two and a half weeks, Kathleen Marie was strong enough to travel. She would once again be transported, this time by ambulance, back to St. Luke's Hospital in Waumeka, where she was scheduled to stay overnight before Charlie and Katie could bring her home. Because of the care the baby might need in the ambulance, Katie was not allowed to travel with her; she and Charlie followed, with Mary Elizabeth, in their own car. Katie had pumped and refrigerated a bottle of milk and given it to the transport team in case Kathleen needed it during the trip.

The drive back to Waumeka from Marshfield took just under two hours. There was little traffic on the road, mostly a few trucks and an occasional tractor pulling a load of hay. Just as Charlie pulled into the hospital parking lot, the clouds separated and the sun finally shone. The tired parents stayed at the hospital overnight with the girls, then took them home the next morning. The two baby sisters slept on the way home, although Kathleen Marie coughed and spit up once. Her color had begun to return, but she still looked pale and weak compared to her twin sister, who lay beside her in the double infant car carrier.

Katie was exhausted when they arrived home and placed the babies in their cribs. "I'll need to wake them both and nurse them, and then I'll get us some lunch."

"Let me do that," Charlie offered.

"No, I said I'd do it. Just let me finish with the girls first, will you?" Katie turned and went up the stairs to the girls' bedroom. Since Mary Elizabeth was crying, she picked her up first and took her back down to the family room, turned on the TV, and began nursing. After twenty minutes, Mary Elizabeth appeared to be satisfied and began to fall asleep in her mother's arms. Charlie looked up from his paper and smiled as Katie laid the baby on her lap and closed her robe over her breast. She lifted Mary Elizabeth onto her shoulder and burped her for a few minutes before taking her back upstairs to her crib.

Suddenly Charlie heard Katie shriek from the babies' bedroom. "My God, no! Jesus, Mary and Joseph, no, no, no … Fuck it all, Jesus H. Christ! Oh, my Gooood …" Charlie grabbed the banister post, swung around, and raced up the stairs. When he got to the bedroom, Katie knelt on the floor, pounding her head into the crib. He tried to put his large hands under her armpits to lift her up but she pulled away and pounded her fists onto the floor, yelling, "Jesus Christ, look! No. No. No." The more he tried to calm her, the more frantic she became. After what seemed like several minutes, Katie fell back on her haunches and then fell into Charlie's lap, sobbing.

"I'll call 9-1-1. We don't know anything yet." Charlie tried to calm his wife, who continued to sob. Kathleen Marie lay listless and gray in her crib.

CHAPTER 27

———◆———

"*Dies irae, dies illa.*" The choir began to intone the traditional liturgy for the dead, as six tall candles flickered around the tiny casket draped in white. A small gold crucifix lay on top. Except for the choir, the church was hushed as congregants clutched one another's hands or wiped away tears. Sunlight coming through the windows on the south side of the church streamed onto the main altar but did little to brighten the grim atmosphere.

Katie and Charlie sat in the front row, flanked by Charlie's parents, his two brothers and their wives, and Katie's parents. Katie stared straight ahead, expressionless, until the priest walked down from the main altar to bless the casket. At that point, Katie's head dropped, almost hitting the pew in front of her. Despite her attempts to muffle her sobs, they could be heard throughout the church as her shoulders rose and fell in rhythm with her sobs. She moaned and began to curse until her mother put an arm around her and pulled Katie's head onto her breast.

Behind them sat aunts and uncles, cousins, and friends from all over Wisconsin, plus a few from as far away as Ontario, Canada and Omaha, Nebraska. The staff of Waumeka High School were there, some with their families, as well as many of the students. Most of the Waumeka police force, as well as Katie's co-workers, doctors and nurses and a number of nurses' aides from the hospital and several from the nursing staff of the Marshfield Clinic, helped to fill the church.

Police chief Aaron Kohlberg sat with his wife and Marty and Maryann O'Brien in the second row; Cliff and Sally Smalley sat behind them. At the back of the church, hunched over in the very last row, sat Frank Feuermann and his wife, Sophie. With the collar of his black tattered coat pulled up around his face, he looked like a turtle sticking its head partly out of its shell.

After the funeral Mass, the priest walked around the casket, sprinkling it with holy water and then incensing the space around the small box, according to the ancient rubrics of the Church. Then, following behind the casket, carried by four of Charlie's fellow ushers, Father O'Shaunessy led the procession down the main aisle and out to the parking lot, where the congregants returned to their cars, most of them to follow the procession to the cemetery. The priest's sermon at the gravesite was mercifully brief, as were the prayers. His vestments were white, he explained, rather than the traditional black because the Mass was the Mass of the Resurrection; a baptized infant, in the eyes of the Church, now celebrated eternal life with her Maker. The Brannigan's daughter was a saint in heaven. The brief homily, which was intended to be a comfort, drove into Katie's heart like a knife. The words made her curse under her breath and damn the very priest who had meant to provide her with some solace.

"May her soul and all the souls of the faithful departed, through the mercy of God, rest in peace," he prayed.

Again, moaning and sobs, not only from Katie but from two or three other groups as well. Charlie's mother had to be held up by Charlie's two brothers as she appeared to be sinking to her knees.

"Amen," came the response, and with that the service concluded. The priest removed his white surplice, put on his jacket, which one of the altar boys handed him, and began to offer condolences to his parishioners.

Cliff Smalley announced that he and Sally would like to invite anybody who cared to join them to come over to their house for a light lunch and to visit with the Brannigans. He explained where he lived and handed out several copies of the small map he had printed up for anyone who might not know the way.

162

***

The gathering at the Smalleys' house was larger than Cliff had expected, although he was well prepared for the group that came to offer their sympathy and support to his neighbors. Dr. Berkside was there, as was the heart specialist, Ray Carlson. Several of the staff from the high school had come: Patricia Cameron, Chet Magnuson (who was taking over as assistant principal while Charlie was gone), Coach Justice, and his assistant Jim Cartwright. Patrick Filey and Ann Shelby came together. Dan and Ruth Chickering, the elderly couple who lived on the other side of the Smalleys, helped Sally to make sandwiches and cut vegetables.

Cliff asked Charlie to sit down. Charlie's eyes were red, and his face looked drawn and exhausted. His white shirt was too big at the collar, making his Adam's apple appear to stick out. But Charlie insisted on helping Cliff serve drinks and snacks while Katie nursed Mary Elizabeth in a chaise lounge in the Smalleys' bedroom.

After Katie put the baby to rest in the bassinette they had brought with them, she came down the hall and into the kitchen. Cliff offered her a drink and some snacks.

"If there's anything Sally and I can do—"

"Yeah. We'll let you know." Katie interrupted him.

"You did everything you could, Katie, and so did the doctors. You've seen this before at the hospital, and so have I."

"Right. It's different when it's yours, though, ya know?"

Cliff looked away. He was sorry he had said something that might have seemed inane or heartless. "Yes, I'm sure it is."

Charlie was busy in the living room, thanking people for coming and offering them sandwiches and drinks. More than anything else, he wanted to go home and go to bed. He saw Marty and Maryann O'Brien standing alone and went over to talk to them.

"Marty, thanks for coming. Maryann, I hope you get a chance to see Mary Elizabeth. She's sleeping right now, but later."

"We really feel sorry, Charlie," Marty stammered.

"Thanks. We're going to come out of this. By the way, you know I'd swear I saw Frank Feuermann at the back of the church this morning. Is that possible?"

"That was him." Marty began to smile.

"What happened? Is he back in town? I didn't see him at the cemetery or I'd have talked to him."

CHAPTER 28

———◆———

The teacher's lounge was full and noisy. Chet Magnuson, Patrick Filey, Ann Shelby, and Casimir Shibilski talked about the upcoming board meeting. The fall semester was in full swing at Waumeka High School, and the school board prepared to bring up the topic of Ann Shelby's retention at their meeting on the first Tuesday of October. It was to be an open meeting, and a large number of parents were planning to attend, thanks to Catherine Newsome's spreading the word throughout the summer that there would definitely be a shake-up in the teachers' ranks in the fall.

Her son, Tommy, had managed to squeak through the algebra course with Shibilski during the summer term and was reinstated on the basketball team. He had decided to have a fall weekend party at his parents' summer cottage to celebrate.

"Ann, what do you think's going to happen at the board meeting?" Shibilski asked between bites of his pizza.

"I'm not sure. At this point I guess I don't really care. All I know is that Newsome woman has been gunning for me ever since I had her angel in my algebra class."

"Hell, Ann, they've got nothing on you. You gave the kid what he deserved," Shibilski said, gulping down his milk.

"Yeah, but 'bout those 'PDAs?" Magnuson asked.

"PDA? What the hell's a PDA?" Shibilski asked.

"Hey, man. Public display of affection. Gotta watch out for those things. They're catchy. Never know what might happen. People might start to enjoy themselves. Hey, maybe even crack a smile." Magnuson was on a roll.

"Listen, if Catherine Newsome ever cracked a smile, the best cosmetic surgeons in the world wouldn't be able to put that face back together," Shibilski replied. "Anyway, those PDAs, as you call them, were all Filey's fault, weren't they, Filey?"

Patrick Filey smiled and said he would gladly take full responsibility for the one and only PDA that had occurred within the school.

"Full responsibility and full pleasure, I assume," Magnuson joked. He turned to Ann, who said nothing now, and added, "If I were to do a PDA, Miss Shelby, well, let me just say I understand Patrick's ardor." Ann smiled and turned red for just a few seconds. Whether it was his age, or his awkward attempts at gentility, Magnuson could get away with comments that would get most men slapped—or at least reprimanded.

***

The board meeting began promptly at 7:00 P.M. Knowing that the attendance might exceed the seating capacity of the school boardroom, Jeffrey Fisher had the meeting moved to the Township hall, where the boardroom held up to one hundred people. At the center table were eight of the nine board members. Only Patti Frasier was absent. "Maternity leave," Fisher called it.

After the reading of the minutes and the treasurer's report, there was a lengthy discussion concerning the budget changes. Charlie Brannigan spoke to the board about the changes in the high school. The teacher/hall monitor program was going well, he noted, and would save the school several thousand dollars over the course of the year. The supplies and equipment budgets had been sliced to produce the rest of the allotted return. The board seemed satisfied, although Catherine Newsome wanted to know why more couldn't be taken from the art, music, and drama programs. These, she mentioned, did not have the state-wide recognition that the sports program, especially the basketball team, enjoyed.

At the end of the general meeting, the public were excused so the school board could go into an "executive session." Fisher asked Charlie to report on personnel decisions in the athletic program at the high school. Charlie noted that three teachers had offered to help as assistant coaches and that it would be within budget to keep James Cartwright in place helping Coach Justice. He pointed out that Cartwright's salary was a minimal stipend as long as he was still in school working toward a degree.

The final item on the agenda was "Teaching concerns at the high school: Ms. Ann Shelby."

"Tom, does your committee have a report?" Fisher asked Tom Halliburton, who was charged to look into the charges brought against the teacher by Catherine Newsome and two other members of the board.

"Yes, we do. Perhaps I should read it, and then you can all comment." Before Halliburton began reading his formal report, he explained that the committee had interviewed the principal, Charles Brannigan, the assistant principal, Chester Magnuson, and two other teachers, as well as Ann Shelby and Patrick Filey. At the end of his report, Halliburton summarized, "In other words, the committee found that Ms. Shelby is a demanding teacher. She is probably best suited to teach the honors students and the upper-division math courses. We found no evidence, though, that she was unfair or showed favoritism to any of her students. She came from Eau Claire three years ago, where she graduated *cum laude*, in the top ten percent of her university class. In other words, we don't believe that any action should be taken at this time."

Catherine Newsome sat up straight, drew a long audible breath to fill her ample chest with air, and asked permission from the chair to speak.

"Yes, of course," Fisher replied.

"I don't believe that the committee has addressed itself to the other very serious issue that was raised," Catherine objected.

"And that was?" Halliburton asked.

"Miss, or Ms.—whatever—Shelby's inappropriate sexual conduct in the hallways of our school."

"Oh, you're right," Halliburton replied. "The report did fail to include our consideration of that issue. In brief, we again found no justification for any action. The one alleged incident took place last spring. It appeared to be an innocent peck on the cheek, admitted by both parties—Ms. Shelby and her friend, the other teacher. They both regretted their action as well as the stir that it created. Both have spoken to the principal about the incident. Mr. Brannigan tells me he has been assured that their personal behavior will be kept strictly outside the school building and grounds in the future. Is that correct, Charlie?"

"Essentially, that's what they told me," Charlie replied.

Catherine Newsome wasn't satisfied. "If our teachers are allowed to get away with that sort of behavior in our school buildings, what's next? What sort of a message does that send to our students?"

"Actually, their behavior was observed by only two students and neither one of them seemed particularly shocked," Halliburton answered. "The unfortunate thing was that they couldn't wait to tell their friends, and once the word swept through the school halls, the story got rather embellished, to say the least."

"This is not a satisfactory resolution," Catherine Newsome countered. "I'm going to want to gather more information and come back to the board on this one. For now, I suppose things will just have to stand."

***

"Honey, I'm home." Charlie put his brief case on the table, hung his jacket in the closet, and called again up the stairs to his wife. "Katie, I'm back."

"I heard you the first time," came the sharp reply.

"Oops. What's the matter?"

"Nothing, I'm just tired." Katie sat in the easy chair in their bedroom, her red terry-cloth robe opened at the top, exposing her full, bare breast. Mary Elizabeth lay asleep in her lap.

"Here. Let me take the baby and put her in her crib. Would you like to hear about the board meeting?" Charlie asked.

"Not really."

"You really are tired. Let's get to bed. How was your day?"

"It was OK. I'm still having a little pain and I get exhausted too easily. And I don't enjoy Mary Elizabeth as much as I ought to."

"Sweetheart, we're both still grieving …"

"Oh, shit, Brannigan."

Charlie Brannigan fell asleep with the hope that his wife would get a good night's sleep and feel rested in the morning.

***

As soon as the alarm went off the next morning, Mary Elizabeth began to cry. Charlie realized that he must have slept through the two o'clock feeding.

His wife rolled over and kissed him on the cheek. "Honey, I'm sorry I was so grumpy last night."

"You were tired."

"I know, but I can't get out of it sometimes."

"Sweetheart, it's only been four weeks."

"FOUR WEEKS? Jesus Christ, Charles Brannigan, I lost my child forever. Don't you get it?"

"Katie, don't yell at me. It was our child, not your child. I lost a child too."

"Oh, right. Like you walked around for nine months with that child growing in your belly. Like you have tits that are losing their shape from getting sucked and pulled on. Like you get up every night to feed and … oh, shit, Brannigan, you just don't get it."

As Charlie got up from bed and took his pajamas off to take a shower, he looked back at his wife, who had picked up Mary Elizabeth to nurse her. "Katie, I'm wondering if you should check with Dr. Berkside, or one of the others."

"Why? I think she's doing fine. Anyway, she's scheduled to see Dr. Silver on the third."

"I'm not talking about Mary. I'm talking about you."

"What's wrong with me? You think I need help? Is that it?" She separated her index and middle fingers and put one on either side of her nipple to extend it for the nursing baby.

"You haven't been yourself. That's all I'm saying. And if there's something they could give you to make you feel better …"

"Jesus. What? Like Prozac? Or maybe I should start drinking, like your card playing buddies?" She leaned back in the chair and pulled her robe up around the nursing baby.

"That's what I mean, Sweetheart. You never used to talk like this. I'm getting scared."

"Well, get used to it, because this is the way life is." Katie began to cry. "Life sucks."

CHAPTER 29

———◆———

Patrick Filey hadn't been to Ann Shelby's apartment in several months, so when he asked if he could come over, Ann figured he must have something important to tell her. She vacuumed and dusted, put a vase of mums on the coffee table, set the dining-room table, and prepared a chicken and dumpling dinner for the two of them. He rang the doorbell just as she took the cork out of a bottle of white wine. She wore a short skirt with an apron and a loose fitting blouse and had her long hair pulled back and coiled in a bun at the back of her head.

"Hey, good to see you. Come in."

"Thanks," Patrick replied. He handed her a bottle of Chardonnay. She laughed and said, "I just opened one. Thank you. Mind if I save this one?" She took his coat, and when she turned back he stood directly in front of her, waiting to kiss her. She responded. As she put her arms around him, he held her even closer. Their tongues met briefly, and then Ann put her head on his shoulder. Finally she loosened the embrace and backed away.

"Well," she said with a grin, "is that what you wanted to tell me?" She walked toward the kitchen.

"That's part of it, I guess," he replied, following her into the kitchen. The aroma of chicken and dumplings filled the air. Patrick closed his eyes and took in a deep breath through his nostrils. "Mmm. Smells wonderful. Anyway, we can do a PDA if we're not in school. Remember?" He sat down at the kitchen table.

Ann smiled and then laughed. "That was the most ridiculous thing I've come across since I've been teaching. Sometimes I think the parents are worse than the kids," she said as she poured him a glass of wine. "We're almost ready here. I just have to finish the salad."

"Listen, I don't think we've heard the last of the Newsomes." Patrick informed her as he sniffed and then took a sip of the wine.

"What? Now what?" She took tomatoes, lettuce, carrots, a green pepper, and some spinach out of the refrigerator.

"I think their boy, Tommy, may be in trouble again. You know Jeremy Hastings? The skinny kid in my sophomore class?"

"Yeah, I heard he went out for the basketball team this year. I think Justice is going to use him. He's a sweet kid, but I'd be surprised if he's basketball material," Ann said as she mixed the salad into a large wooden bowl.

"Well, he may not want to play at all from what I've heard. In fact, he hasn't been in class for the last three days."

"What's the matter with him?" Ann held up a bottle of Italian dressing to get Patrick's approval.

"Yeah, that looks good," he said, nodding. "I talked to a couple of Jeremy's friends. They won't say much, but it seems there was a little initiation ceremony for the new basketball players over in Heckney Woods last weekend. I think Jeremy got the worst of it. Sounds like Tommy Newsome was one of the ringleaders."

"Good crap, Pat, does Coach Justice know about this? Have you talked to Brannigan?" Ann walked into the dining room with the salad and placed it on the table.

"No, not yet. I just found out about it this afternoon. I'm not sure what to do. The kids don't want me to say anything, and they won't say any more about Jeremy. Maybe I should call his parents."

"Tell Brannigan. That's his job," Ann suggested. With a pair of tongs, she put several pieces of chicken from a pot on the stove into a large bowl and then ladled chicken broth over it.

"He's just had so much on his plate lately," Patrick replied.

"Patrick, tell him!" she insisted, taking the bowl of chicken into the dining room.

"OK, OK. Anyway, I didn't come over to talk about Jeremy."

"Let's sit down. The chicken is going to get cold. Bring your wine with you."

They sat down across from one another, and Ann reached to light a single candle in the center of the table. She passed him the heavy bowl. "OK, then what did you want to talk about?"

"Well, here's the deal. There's an assistant principal slot opening up at West High in Stevens Point."

"And you've applied for it?" she asked, looking up from her plate.

"Actually, I applied and they offered me the job."

"Patrick, you jerk, you haven't told me anything about this. You mean you've interviewed and met with their board and I didn't even know it?" She put her fork down on her plate in a gesture of mock indignation.

"Well, it's not as if we've been seeing each other every day. I mean except for passing in the halls at school. I've sorta kept this to myself. The only one I've talked to is Charlie. I thought he had to know, given the timing."

"Are you going to take the job?" she asked hesitantly.

"Yeah, I thought and thought about it and I've finally decided to go for it."

"What did you mean a minute ago, when you said, 'given the timing'? You wouldn't start until next fall, would you?" She passed him a basket of rolls.

"Actually, they want me there in January. The assistant they have now has been out sick since last May and isn't expected to return. She's an older woman with a serious illness. I believe it's Alzheimer's by the way they were talking, but nobody told me exactly." Patrick broke a roll in half and buttered it, without looking up.

"Geez, Pat, what about your classes here?"

Patrick explained that his fall schedule was filled with one-term courses and that Charlie had offered to get substitutes for the classes he was scheduled to teach in the spring.

"I'm really going to miss you." That was an understatement, but she knew it had been her decision to cool their relationship. "Let's have our coffee in the living room," she suggested. "I hope you left room for apple pie and ice cream." She got up and took their plates into the kitchen.

After she poured the coffee and brought cream and sugar to the coffee table, Ann reached behind her, pulling out a hairpin to let her long, blond hair fall down around her shoulders. She sat next to Patrick on the old leather couch. He blew across his hot, black coffee, then set it down and leaned over to kiss her. They finished their desert as he talked about his plans for moving to Stevens Point, and she mentioned that the place wouldn't be the same without him. She wanted to say how much she would miss him, but couldn't bring herself to say the words.

Regardless, her grief at his parting and her sexual longing were communicated somehow. Patrick set his cup on the table and began to unbutton Ann's blouse as she undid the button on the waistband of her skirt. He put his hand on her knee. As if the hand had a mind of its own, it found its way up her leg and under her short skirt.

***

The next day, on the way to work, Ann stopped at McGriffith's Drug Store to get a greeting card. It was a plain card with a picture of a Northwoods lake, a single eagle flying over the pine trees. On the inside, she wrote a message:

> Soar, Patrick, to the heights you have imagined in your fondest dreams. Congratulations on your new appointment. I shall always remember our time together fondly.
> Love, Ann

***

Three days passed before Patrick caught up with Ann in the teachers' lounge. She sat alone at the table with coffee and a stack of papers in front of her when he leaned over and kissed her on the top of the head.

"Thanks for the card. I loved it."

She leaned up to see him looking straight down at her from behind. "You're welcome."

"It sounded as though it was all in the past tense, though. You didn't mean it that way, did you?" He looked around to make sure that nobody else was in the room.

She reached behind her and took his hand. "It's probably something we should talk about after school. Maybe we could take a walk down by the creek."

"Sounds good."

***

The path through Heckney Woods down to Bear Creek was quiet, except for the sounds of crickets and frogs and the crunching of new fallen leaves under foot. By late October, the leaves of the massive oak trees still clung to their branches, but the ash and maple leaves had begun to fall. As the sun peeked through the trees into the ancient woods, the two teachers kicked dead leaves from side to side. They spoke of the years they had worked together, of their feelings for one another, but also of the certainty of Patrick's leaving to a new teaching post and the uncertainty of his commitment to Ann.

"I had a wonderful time the other night, Patrick. I wished it could have gone on forever. But in the light of day, I realize it can't. You aren't sure of your feelings and besides that, you're headed to Stevens Point in another couple of months."

"Hey, Stevens Point isn't on the other side of the world. But I know what you mean and I have to admit that I agree with you. Now what do we do?" Patrick asked.

"I guess we do what the kids call 'just be friends'." She kissed her friend, whom she knew was no longer her lover. "Neither of us knows what the future will bring. Let's leave ourselves open to that."

"OK. But you have to come to Stevens Point now and then. And expect me to come here and visit you once in a while. Good friends can do that, can't they?"

"Of course."

The walk back through the woods to the school parking lot was bittersweet for Ann. She felt relieved, but she still wondered if she had just done the right thing.

CHAPTER 30

———◆———

The weekly card game moved to Cliff Smalley's house after Kathleen Marie died. Katie stayed home with Mary Elizabeth every day and almost every night. She had gotten a six-month leave from the hospital after Kathleen died, and she kept herself secluded. Her only nights out were the monthly nurses' meeting at the hospital. When Charlie asked her if she minded his going to the card games every week, she simply replied, "No, I don't mind being alone; just don't have them here."

Cliff looked around the table to make sure that everyone had drinks. The four men had decided that as long as the games were at the Smalleys' house, no alcohol would be served. They would get by with soft drinks and fruit juice. That way, nobody would need to put too much into the kitty for beverages and it would help Cliff keep his house alcohol-free. He had been sober for almost seventeen years but still went to AA meetings regularly, and he knew his limits. Having booze in his house for a few hours at the occasional party was fine but probably wasn't a good idea for a regular event like the card game.

"What's the news about Frank?" Cliff asked, as he shuffled the cards. "Has anybody been over to see him?"

"The judge gave him six months," Marty O'Brien said. "He wasn't involved in any of the muggings, but he was taking money to keep quiet. I don't suppose you can say anything more than that, can you Aaron?"

"Not really. Frank's been cooperative. It'll be good to have him out of jail and back at the card table … if it doesn't feed into his addiction, that is." He examined his cards.

"Do you think that's a problem?" Charlie asked.

"I'm sure, and as far as addictions go, he shouldn't be here for card games," Cliff added. "It's a shame, too. He's a nice guy."

"Maybe we could get together for breakfast now and then on a Saturday morning—you know, over at the Snack 'N' Yak, or something," Marty suggested.

"Sounds like a damn good idea," Aaron agreed. "I'm all for it. We don't need to support his addiction to support Frank. How 'bout you, Charlie? You been pretty quiet tonight."

Charlie looked at his cards, set them face down, put change in the pot, reexamined his cards—all without saying a word. "Yeah, I could do that."

When the game was over and everybody had said goodnight, Charlie stayed back to talk to Cliff. "I don't know how to ask you this, Cliff, but I'm afraid Katie needs some help."

"What's the matter? Is she getting run down with that new baby?" Cliff motioned for them to go into the living room

"It's not just that. She's not herself. She's either down in the dumps all the time or she's angry," Charlie replied.

"Well, everybody's entitled to a little rage, Charlie. Could be a touch of postpartum depression. It affects about half the women who have babies." Cliff studied his neighbor's face the way a doctor does when trying to gather more information.

"No, listen Cliff. It's more than just the baby blues. And it's been over six weeks since the twins were born and a month since Kathleen died. Surely by now …" Charlie dropped his huge frame onto the sofa, put his head in his hands, and began to cry.

Cliff sat down beside his friend, "Charlie, postpartum depression is not just 'baby blues.' It's serious, and if it's not treated it can go on for months, sometimes over a year."

"What can they do for her? It's getting bad. I mean, Cliff, she's yelling at me. You know Katie. That's not like her at all. I mean, she's not herself."

"I know. Tell her you talked to me. She'll be angry at first. But tell her I want her to call, either here or at the office."

***

"You told him what? Jesus Christ," Katie shouted, "do you go blabbing to the neighbors about every little thing that happens here? Now I suppose all your card-party buddies think I'm a mental case." Katie stood at the kitchen sink, scrubbing a pan.

"I talked to Cliff after everybody had gone home. It's a private matter. He's a doctor," Charlie tried to reassure her. He sat down at the kitchen table and looked up at his wife. Was Cliff right? Should he have told her that he had talked with his neighbor? Now he was more confused than ever.

"Right. Like he's not going to go and tell Sally. You asshole," she screamed as she slammed the pan into a drying rack on the sink.

"He won't say a word. He's a doctor."

Katie turned, threw her dish towel toward the counter, and left the kitchen. The towel fell to the floor. As Charlie got up and reached to pick it up, he heard the door to their bedroom slam.

CHAPTER 31

———

Charlie had scheduled a meeting with Coach Justice in his office first thing Thursday morning. "Thanks for coming in, Coach. Please sit down."

"What's up? I hope the board didn't decide to cut the basketball program," the coach said with a grin. He was a tall man—only a few inches shorter than the principal who sat across from him—with a five o'clock shadow that started at eight o'clock in the morning and got worse as the day went on. He always wore the same faded jeans and smelly sweatshirt. He lived alone and rarely bothered with laundry. He sat down on the couch and started to put his feet up on the coffee table in front of him but stopped himself and put them back on the floor.

"No, nothing like that," Charlie replied, "although it could potentially be worse. I want to know what your team was doing over in Heckney Woods a week ago last Saturday." He picked up a pencil from his desk and dropped it into a pencil holder.

"I dunno. I did hear some rumors," the coach replied offhandedly.

Charlie raised his voice. "You heard some rumors? What sort of rumors?"

"I don't like to say; they're just rumors at this point and I haven't checked them out."

"You've heard rumors and you haven't checked them out? I suggest you check them out starting tomorrow morning and report back to me in the afternoon. In the meantime, I'll be talking to the upper-division players this afternoon. I don't want you to say anything until after I've spoken to each of them. Is that understood?" He stared at the coach until Justice dropped the nonchalant attitude.

"Yes, sure. I'm sorry if ..."

"That'll be all, Coach. I'll see you tomorrow afternoon at three o'clock."

As Coach Justice got up to leave, Charlie picked up his telephone and pressed one button.

"Tricia, could you get all the varsity basketball players scheduled to see me this afternoon, one at a time, please, ten minutes each?" Charlie Brannigan spoke in fast, clipped, phrases that were sterner than usual. Patricia Cameron knew his usual moods, but this was different.

"What time should I start them?" his office manager asked.

"One o'clock. As soon as I get back from lunch. I want to be able to get them all in this afternoon."

"Yes sir."

***

By one o'clock, Tricia had managed to round up seven of the nine upper-division members on the boys' basketball team. Tommy Newsome and Jerry Abramson were absent from school that day. Each of the other boys was scheduled to see the principal for ten minutes. Speculation among the players at lunch ranged from the notion that he might want to offer them a word of encouragement at the start of a new season, to an admonition to keep their grades up. But why did he want to see them separately? Finally Jimmy Talbot suggested, "You don't think he's heard about our little trip to Heckney Woods, do you? Holy shit."

"Jesus, Talbot. How in the hell is he going to know about that? We know everybody who was there. Nobody's going to talk," Fred Finkle said.

"Yeah, but what if that is it?" Talbot asked. "What are we going to say?"

"Just tell him you don't know," Finkle replied.

The cafeteria began to empty out. Three students got up from the next table, threw empty lunch bags and milk containers in the trash, and headed out the side door.

Colin O'Rourke, the team's captain, spoke up, "That's stupid, Finkle. He'll know that we know. We'll have to tell the truth." The players were beginning to raise their voices. O'Rourke suggested they quiet down, as he looked around at the table behind them.

"O'Rourke, get real. He'll throw us all off the team."

"You don't know that. It was a simple initiation. That's all it was," O'Rourke replied. Just then the one o'clock bell rang for the start of fifth hour.

"Shit," Jimmy Talbot mumbled as he shuffled down toward the principal's office.

***

"Mr. Brannigan, you wanted to see me?"

"Yes, Jimmy, come in. Sit down. Do you know why you're here?"

"I'm not sure," Talbot stammered, sitting upright in a chair across from the principal.

"I want to know what happened a week ago last Saturday in Heckney Woods. I suggest you tell me the truth because, one way or the other, I will find out. Do you understand?"

"Yes, sir. Well, OK. We had a little initiation for the new players on the basketball team." Talbot looked away toward the books on the shelf to his left.

"And just what was involved in this 'little initiation,' Mr. Talbot?"

"Well, we paddled them, sir." He looked up at Charlie.

"You paddled them?" Charlie sat up straight and leaned forward toward the student, keeping his gaze on the boy's face.

"Yes, sir ... not hard ... with a canoe paddle. We just wanted to see if they could take it."

"And could they take it, Mr. Talbot?"

"Yes, sir. They done real good."

"Do you think you could take it?" Charlie began to raise his voice.

Not knowing what was coming next, Talbot stammered, "I … I don't know, sir. I don't know."

"Was there anything else besides this paddling?"

"No, that was all we done."

"Was anybody there besides the team?"

"A few other kids, maybe ten or fifteen, some of the seniors and some of the guys' girlfriends."

Charlie took a piece of paper from a stack and a pencil from his pencil holder. "Give me some names, Talbot."

"But, Mr. Brannigan, if I—"

"I said, give me some names."

"Ginny Burcham, Tom Ridgeway, Ellie Prescott, Maddy Tilleson … oh, and her cousin Jim Tilleson. I guess that's all I can remember. But they didn't do nothing. It was just us that done it."

"That'll be all, Talbot. I want you to say nothing to any of the other players about this until I've talked to each of them. Is that understood?"

"Yes, Mr. Brannigan."

"Now send the next boy in."

Charlie waited for Talbot to shuffle out, then reached for his telephone. "Tricia, have Ginny Burcham see me after I've talked to all the players."

The second player came into the office and sat across the desk from the principal. Charlie asked the same set of questions and got roughly the same set of answers, except that he could add to his list of observers. Each of the players in turn gave him the same story: Five boys were paddled in the woods by five of the upper-division boys. Four of the nine watched but refused to take part in the punishment. It appeared that Tommy Newsome was the one who suggested the initiation and planned the event. A paddle from the Newsome summer cottage was used to torture the younger boys.

After the last basketball player had been interviewed, Charlie called Ginny Burcham, a senior honors student and star cheerleader, into his office.

She already seemed to know what was on his agenda, so the principal wasted no time.

"Ginny, I'll get right to the point. Did you participate in the events in Heckney Woods a week ago last Saturday?"

"I was there. I saw what happened."

"What did happen? And let me urge you to be completely honest."

"Some of the senior basketball players initiated the new players."

"Yes, I know. How did that happen?" he asked

"Well, they took them one by one, and made them put their hands on a saw horse and bend over. They told them to drop their pants. Everyone was laughing at them." Ginny's eyes began to well up with tears.

"They had to drop their pants?" the principal asked.

"Yes. If they didn't do it right away, one of the seniors went over and pulled them down." She began to cry.

"Good God," Charlie mumbled under his breath.

"I don't know why we stood there. I don't know why we didn't do anything. We just watched. It was embarrassing."

"Jeremy Hastings is still not back in school. Do you know anything about that?" Charlie asked.

"I think he got it the worst," she answered. "Tommy Newsome was spanking him and he even started to cry, but Tommy didn't stop. He just called him a cry-baby."

After she told him the names of all the participants and a few of the on-lookers, Charlie dismissed Ginny, thanking her for her honesty. She wiped her eyes and got up slowly to leave his office. Charlie followed her out and went to his office manager's desk. "Tricia, if they're in school tomorrow, I want to see Tommy Newsome and Jerry Abramson first thing in the morning."

Charlie Brannigan stayed late at the office. He called Katie and told her he would be home by six, that he needed to make some telephone calls. He knew if he called at suppertime, he would be able to reach Jeremy Hastings' parents.

Jeremy's father answered the telephone. Charlie knew John Hastings by reputation: a fair but hard-hitting attorney with Sheldon, O'Rourke, and

Hastings, one of the largest law firms in the county. Charlie knew he was highly respected in the community and a man one did not want to mess with.

"Hi. This is Charlie Brannigan from the high school," he began. He explained the reason for his call and asked about Jeremy. He told Hastings that he was doing his best to get to the bottom of the problem and that the perpetrators would be dealt with.

Hastings responded, "I'm afraid it's rather too late for that. We are filing suits against those who assaulted my son and against their parents. By now they should have received their papers. We had initially intended to sue the school—you and the basketball coach, in particular—but we have been advised against it. My legal team believes we don't have so strong a case in that instance. Be assured, however, that we will do all that we can to bring these young men and their parents to justice."

Charlie then asked when Jeremy would be returning to school.

"Jeremy will not be returning to Waumeka High. We have enrolled him at the Christian Academy in Eau Claire; he will be safer there, and the education will be more in conformance with our values and beliefs. I shall, however, have a copy of his hospital records sent to the school for your information. If you are thinking of expelling those responsible, those records may be helpful to you."

"I didn't realize that Jeremy had gone to the hospital," Charlie replied.

"He was there for three days for treatment of contusions to his legs and buttocks, as well as a subcutaneous hematoma. You will find the details in the reports I shall have sent. Thank you for calling. I shall relay your concern to Jeremy. Good evening."

CHAPTER 32

———◆———

E arly the next morning, Charlie Brannigan put a call in to Henry
Derkheiser, the superintendent of schools.

"Hank, 'morning. I'm just calling to let you know about five suspensions
I'm imposing at the high school. Thought you should know." Charlie went on to
tell his boss about the assault in Heckney Woods, the hospitalization of one of the
victims, and his reasons for imposing suspensions on all five perpetrators.

"Well, thanks for keeping me posted, Charlie. Sounds like you've got things
under control, as usual. Let me know if you need any help from this end."

After his call to the superintendent, Charlie had Tricia Cameron's student assistant carry a typed message to each teacher in the building, including the librarian and her assistant and Coach Justice and his assistant, Jim
Cartwright:

> To: All teaching staff
> From: Principal Charles Brannigan
> Concerning: Urgent Meeting

Please meet in the conference room during the fifth hour
break this afternoon for an urgent twenty minute meeting. For

those people who don't get a break during that period, see if you can arrange for an in-class assignment. If a previously scheduled activity absolutely prevents you from attending, please see me sometime during the day. Do not discuss this with others in the building until after the meeting. As always, I appreciate your cooperation. Thank you.
CEB

Only two teachers—Ms. Finkbeiner, the librarian's assistant, and Betty Franklin, the home economics teacher, stopped during their morning breaks to tell Charlie that they wouldn't be able to attend the meeting. Both had commitments that took them away from the building before fifth period. After telling them what was on the agenda, he thanked them for coming in and asked them not to talk to anybody else in the building until after the meeting.

At one o'clock, Charlie Brannigan walked across the hall to the conference room with a stack of papers under his arm. "Hey, Mr. Brannigan. Hi," a short, Hispanic student called to him.

Looking at his watch, Charlie replied, "Buenas nachos, Carlos. Say, you better hurry. You're going to be late."

"No, no, Señor Brannigan," Carlos laughed. "It's buenas *noches*. But only at night. Now we say, 'Buenos días.'"

"Oh, yes, yes, of course, buenos días," Charlie replied with a smile. As the boy sped away, the principal added, "And no running in the hall, young man."

All the teachers except Casimir Shibilski were already sitting around the conference table when Charlie walked in. Shibilski opened the door behind him and took a place against the wall.

Charlie went to the head of the table and passed out a sheet to each of the teachers:

Dear Mr. and Mrs. _____,
    I am sending this letter home with your son, and will send another copy through the US mail, as is required by the policy established by the

Waumeka Board of Education. As you may be aware, your son was involved in an incident behind the school in Heckney Woods on Saturday, October 12, 2012. As I understand it, this incident was meant to be an "initiation" of the new members of the boys' basketball team. The younger boys were assaulted, and one was severely injured. I have spoken with each of the players who were involved in this cowardly act and each has admitted his role.

In light of the gravity of this offense, I have no recourse but to suspend your son from school for three days and expel him from the athletic program for the rest of this academic year. Your son will not be admitted to any noncurricular school functions, such as athletic and social events, including games and dances, proms, etc., for the remainder of the year.

The teachers around the table read the memo and, as they finished, began to mumble to one another. Coach Justice scanned the page several times and said, "What the hell? What the hell is this?"

"I believe you can read, Coach Justice," Charlie replied. "If your copy is not legible, here, please, let me give you another one."

"I can read it just fine, thank you. I just don't agree," Justice snapped.

"I didn't bring you in here to ask for your approval, Coach. I am simply informing you of the action I have taken. I wanted all of you to know how serious I consider this behavior and exactly how I have responded."

"It was a simple, childish prank," Justice countered.

Charlie drew in a deep breath and sat up straight, raising his head and shoulders so that everyone around the table could see his face. "One of our students—I should say, *former* students—ended up in the hospital for three days and will not be returning to Waumeka High. Four other students were assaulted. Do I have to say any more than that?"

"So maybe it got a little out of hand ..."

"Coach Justice, five young men were beaten behind our school. They were required to strip while their classmates assaulted them and their friends and girlfriends looked on. This is not the sort of behavior I will tolerate or excuse as a *childish prank*. I hope I have made myself clear. Are there any other questions?"

"That's our whole basketball team you've just disbanded. What do you think ... there's not going to be a basketball program at Waumeka High this year?" The coach coughed into his fist.

"Exactly right. Unless, of course, you can bring the second string up to the task."

"Fat chance. And besides my health classes, just what am I supposed to do if there's no basketball? Hall monitor?"

"As a matter of fact, I have thought about what you might do. You got my memo last week about Patrick Filey's resignation. As you all know, he's moving over to Stevens Point in an administrative position. Well deserved, in my opinion. The only problem is that we're really going to miss you here, Pat."

"Thank you," the young man replied from the other end of the table.

"It'll take us a while to find a permanent replacement for Patrick. In the meantime, Coach Justice, you are qualified in social science. I was thinking you could help us out in that area. You and I can work out the details."

"I just think this ain't gonna fly," the coach replied, pushing his chair back as if preparing to leave.

"I'm afraid it's already in the air. Are there any other questions?" Charlie asked.

"Have you spoken with the parents?" Casimir Shibilski asked.

"No, not the perpetrators' parents, but I assume they'll be calling once they get this memo."

Jaime Rodriguez, the Spanish and French teacher, scratched his mustache and rubbed his mouth. "Have you talked to each of the perpetrators? I mean, I'm a little surprised. I know three of these boys and I'm just surprised. I mean, Monsieur Thibault—sorry, André Thibault—seems like a decent fellow to me."

"He probably just got mixed up with a rotten crowd," Magnuson said. "Charlie, what do you want from us? Is there something we can do?"

"I don't think so. I just wanted to give you a heads up on how I've responded. We may be heading into another emergency meeting of the school board. If so, I'll let you know. They'd be required to make it an open meeting, so as many of you as wanted to could attend."

As the teachers left the room to go back to their classes, Coach Justice muttered, "You'll never get away with this, Brannigan." Jaime Rodriguez looked at him and said, "What are you saying? Somebody finally sewed cajones on our principal."

CHAPTER 33

———————

"I'm home, darling," Charlie called to his wife.

"I'm up here ... feeding the baby," she answered. Charlie walked through the hall and up the stairs to the bedroom, where Katie sat in the Boston rocker, nursing Mary Elizabeth.

"You look a lot better, sweetheart," Charlie said as he leaned over and kissed his wife on the top of the head. She looked up at him and he gave her another kiss, this time on the lips.

"I'm sorry I've been so miserable. Sometimes I just can't seem to pull myself out of it," she said as she stood up to put the baby, who had fallen asleep, back in the bassinet and then closed the front of her robe.

"Did you call Cliff?" Charlie asked.

"Yes, he wants me to come in tomorrow for some tests. Then he wants to refer me to a new internist, Hector Nastasio, for a complete physical before he makes any suggestions about therapy." She followed her husband back downstairs and into the kitchen.

"Don't think I've ever heard that name. Nastasio? He grabbed a bottle of Cutty Sark from the liquor cabinet and set it on the counter.

"Yes, he just finished his residency. He did his training at the Marshfield Clinic. Supposed to be pretty good."

"Good. When do you see Cliff?"

"Nine o'clock in the morning. He's going to try to set something up with Nastasio right after that, and I should get reports back by next week ... you know, the lab tests and that stuff. As soon as I'm done here, I'll fix us something to eat. You must be starved."

As Charlie went to the front closet to hang up his coat, the telephone rang. Heaving a deep sigh, he walked into the kitchen to answer it.

"Hello? Oh, hello Tom. Yes, I'm not surprised the board wants to meet, but you'll have to call me in the morning at the office. I really can't talk to you at the moment. Yes, I know she's on the school board. Tom, I said there's nothing I can do at the moment. I've just gotten home; I'm going to have my supper and I'll deal with that in the morning. Call me at the office or I'll call you."

"What was that all about?" Katie asked as Charlie hung up the telephone.

"Oh, I suspended five boys today. Remember the kids I told you about, the ones on the basketball team? Well I called them all into the office yesterday. No question about what they did. They all told me they did it. Same story from every one of them. And I didn't have any hesitation about what to do. Now let the board do whatever the hell they want."

"But who was that on the telephone?"

"Tom Newsome. I think he wanted to threaten me. I told him I didn't have time for him right now," he answered.

"Was Tommy one of the five?"

"The ringleader, apparently."

"But his mother is on the school board."

"Funny. Everybody is reminding me of that. What the fuck do I care if his mother is on the school board. I'm sorry. I've just ..."

"Charlie, pour us a drink and I'll put the spaghetti on."

***

Charlie Brannigan got into the office early the next day and was able to finish his paperwork before the first bell rang. He assumed he would have a busy day, trying to answer questions about the school suspensions, the fate of the basketball program, and everything else that hung in the balance of his decision. He looked out his office window, across the playing field to the woods beyond, and noticed that the sun was just coming up through the trees. From maples, ash, and weeping willows mixed with cedar and pine, the late-October colors splashed across the horizon. Sometimes, when he was exhausted from his daily grind, he told Tricia Cameron that he was going for a walk. He took the foot path through Heckney Woods down to the stream. The late summer and autumn flowers were just beginning to fade. *No time for that today*, he thought.

Going over to the other side of the room, he picked up a stack of papers on the coffee table and sat down on one end of the leather couch, putting his feet up on the coffee table. He began to examine the records of substitute teachers, when the telephone rang.

Charlie wasn't surprised that the first call of the day was from Tom Newsome.

"Look, Brannigan, I'm at the dealership and I don't have a lot of time. But you need to know that we're not going to stand for this grandstanding of yours. I've talked to the other parents and we're together on this. If I were you, I'd just send a written apology to the boys and get them back in school where they belong—and back on that team, Brannigan. We got a basketball season coming up."

"Well, I appreciate hearing your opinion, Tom. Is that all?" the principal asked.

"Like I said, it's not just my opinion, Brannigan. The parents are together on this one. Now are you and I on the same page on this one, or not?"

"I understand what you're saying, Tom, if that's what you want to know, and I appreciate the call. Now I also heard you say you were very busy this morning, so if you're finished, I'll just say goodbye."

"Hey, lemme remind you, Brannigan, you haven't heard the end of this, not by a long shot."

Charlie Brannigan hung up the telephone and leaned back in his chair. *Written apology? WRITTEN APOLOGY? What in the hell is that bastard thinking?* He slammed a pencil point down onto the blotter covering his desktop, breaking the point and leaving a hole in the blotter.

Within seconds, the phone rang again.

"Who is it this time, Tricia?" Charlie asked his office manager. "Oh, sure, have him come in. Thanks. Tricia? I mean it. Thanks."

The door opened and Chet Magnuson walked in.

"Come in, Chet," Charlie started. "Hey. You want some coffee?" He went to the outer office. Magnuson followed. The men got themselves coffee from a table that stood in the corner behind the counter, and returned to the principal's office.

"Charlie, I came in to see what I could do to help out."

"Yes, I've been meaning to talk to you. Things have been happening too fast. Chet, I really would value your private opinion on something. How're the teachers taking this?" Charlie sat back in his chair and motioned to Chet to sit on the couch. He blew across the top of his coffee cup, took a sip, and set the cup on the desk.

"Well, you know I'm behind you, Chief. One hundred percent. But I really can't speak for the rest very well. Some of them think it was just a prank, something that just got out of hand and maybe could have been handled with a slap on the wrist. If you want my opinion, I think they're just disappointed. You know, we were looking forward to a great season, at least going to regionals, maybe state. Who knows? Justice thinks we'd have a shot at the title this year."

"So you don't think I have their support?" Charlie asked.

"No, I really didn't mean to say that. I just think it depends on who you talk to," the assistant principal replied.

"Thanks, Chet." Charlie walked over to the coffee table, where he had left a stack of folders, and handed them to Magnuson. "I'm still trying to update our list of potential substitute teachers for the year. If you could help out, that would be great. If you need any help going over these records," he added, "just come in. I'll let Tricia know so she can make some time available for you."

For most of the rest of the day, Charlie answered telephone calls from parents, some of them irate, about the basketball team or about their suspended sons. He listened to their complaints and explained the procedures to each of them. By the end of the school day, he was weary and becoming more and more convinced that the parents intended to go to the school board with their complaints. Several had retained lawyers to defend against the lawsuit being brought by John Hastings, Jeremy's father. Most considered the lawsuit simply frivolous.

Just after the last bell, as Charlie went over the teaching schedule for the spring semester, his telephone rang once again.

"Yes, what is it, Tricia? Sure, send her in."

The door opened and Ann Shelby stuck her head through, looked around the room, then smiled at Charlie before entering and closing the door behind her.

"What's up, Ann?"

"Charlie, I just wanted to see how you're doing. You've got my support. You know that, don't you?"

CHAPTER 34

Charlie and Katie went to the ten fifteen Mass the next Sunday at Our Lady of Sorrows. Charlie was scheduled to usher, as was Marty O'Brien. Father Dan O'Shaunessy said the Mass. Afterwards, as they were stacking the collection baskets on a table in the ushers' room and hanging up their vests, Marty mentioned to Charlie that he and Maryann were going downstairs to the social hall for coffee and donuts.

"Why not join us?" he asked Charlie. "Ask Katie. Tell her Maryann and I hardly ever get to see her anymore and we want to see that baby."

"Well, she's got the baby with her, all right. She's over there in the pew in front of the side altar. She's been pretty tired lately; she may want to just go home and rest, but I'll ask." Charlie replied.

Katie agreed to have coffee and donuts with the O'Briens. "But just for a little while," she insisted. "I want to get Mary Elizabeth home so I can nurse her and get her to bed. I took her downstairs during Father O'Shaunessy's sermon so I could change her. She'll be ready for her nap before long."

After the O'Briens oohed and aahed over the baby, Maryann asked "When do you have to go back to work?"

"Well, I asked for six months after—after—well, after we lost Mary Elizabeth's sister," Katie explained. She coughed and then took a Kleenex from the open overnight bag that held the baby's supplies and wiped her eyes.

"I'm sorry, Katie. Marty and I were at the funeral and all, but I really didn't get a chance to talk to you. Not even at Cliff's house, afterwards; I guess you were busy with the baby, so I didn't really tell you how sorry we are." She touched Katie on the arm.

"It's OK, Maryann. We did get your card and the Mass intention; it meant a lot to us. We have a saint in the family now, you know," Katie said, trying to fake a smile.

Charlie decided to change the subject. "What do you hear from Frank Feuermann, Marty?"

"Well, you know he's in the slammer until next spring. I try to get over there to see him once a week if I can. I think he's doing OK. He's really embarrassed. I told him we'd all get together for breakfast now and then when he gets out. He's not sure he wants to do it. Just feeling uncomfortable and humiliated, I guess."

"Have you talked to Sophie?" Katie asked. The two couples had gotten coffee and were sitting around a long table in the basement of the church. It was musty and cool, and Katie had wrapped Mary Elizabeth in an extra blanket that she had in the overnight bag.

"Yeah, called her last week. They hired her on at Fleet Farm," Marty replied.

"No kidding? In Frank's old department?" Katie asked.

"Oh, no. She's in housewares. She says they're treating her real nice."

"Look, the next time you go over to the jail to see Frank, give me a call. I'd like to go along. Do you think he'd mind?" Charlie asked.

"Frank? No, I think he'd be glad to see you, but like I said, maybe embarrassed at first. You know Frank. He's pretty stubborn," Marty replied.

***

The county prison where Frank Feuermann was being held was a large sprawling farm on the outskirts of town. It was crowded to capacity so that four prisoners were housed in each cell, each man with his own bunk. Word had gotten out among the inmates that Frank had cooperated with the sheriff's office and had revealed the names of the men who had been robbing casino patrons. Their M.O. had been to spot someone who had both won a lot of money and had too much to drink. Late at night, when the patron went back to his car, the men would attack, taking his money and leaving him lying in the parking lot—either seriously injured, like Lou Cartwright, or as happened in one case, dead. Going to the dark corners of the parking lot and knowing the hours when they were least likely to be observed, the gang of three men had managed for two years to avoid detection. Sometimes they would threaten a bystander who had accidentally seen the assault. On more than one occasion, they needed to pay a witness part of their loot in exchange for a promise of silence.

One night Frank was one of those lucky—or so he thought— witnesses. They had given him $500 to keep his mouth shut. Twice after that, he made it his business to go to his car in the parking lot at just the right time; each time he collected his reward. It was a dangerous business. They could just as well have treated him the way they did their victims. The only trouble was that Frank was not drunk when he left the casino and would therefore be in a position to report who had attacked him. Now, because Frank had broken his promise of silence, two of the thugs were awaiting trial. While they were detained in another section of the prison, they had gotten word to their friends throughout the facility that Frank could not be trusted.

Frank sensed that trouble was brewing. Sometimes in the yard, he would walk up to two or three prisoners standing together. Suddenly their conversation would stop and they would just look at Frank, without talking, as if he were an unwelcome intruder. At other times, he felt that people were snickering behind his back or whispering about him. He tried to keep his back to the wall. It tired him out always to be on guard, on guard for what he didn't know. One night, waiting in line for his supper, he thought he heard the guy behind him grumble under his breath, something like, "Just you wait, snitch."

Frank tried to keep himself busy. He spent most of his free time in the recreation room where there was always a guard nearby. He would play pool by himself or watch the TV that hung from a wall in the corner of the room.

After a while, he rarely went outside. A few of the older men who had been in the jail for years were the only ones he could trust. He usually ate supper with a fellow called Froggie because of the way he garbled his words; Froggie had a low, gravelly voice, the sort of voice a person gets from years of smoking. In Froggie's case, the gravelly voice resulted from having his throat cut in a street brawl. Froggie and his friend, Blind Jimmie, were both in jail for armed robbery. Blind Jimmie had been legally blind for years, despite the thick glasses that he always wore. The two of them had held up the M&I Bank and were on the loose for a few months before they were caught, tried, and put in jail. The other men rarely had much to do with either of them.

One afternoon during free time, as Frank was all alone—except for the ever-present guard—shooting pool in the recreation room, Froggie grabbed a cue stick and walked over to the table.

"Set 'em up, Frankie," he grumbled. Frank pulled the balls together and began to rack them with the triangle. Froggie took a piece of resin that sat on the edge of the table and began to rub the tip of his cue very carefully, looking at it and blowing off the excess resin before putting the square back on the edge of the pool table. Frank hung the triangle on the hook at one end of the table. Froggie leaned over toward him and grumbled in his low growling voice, "Better watch your step. Word is you got yourself some enemies. Just keep your back to the wall."

As he lined his cue up on the table, ready to play, Frank tried to appear cool and nonchalant. "Hell, what could they do?"

"The way I hear it is ... well, let's just say you'd be better off wearing a steel jock strap."

***

Frank Feuermann shared a prison cell with three men only because the prison was overcrowded. Normally only two men, not four, would be assigned to such a small cell. There were two bunks on each side of the room and a sink at one end, next to a barred window that looked out onto the courtyard. It was considered a medium-security cell.

One of the men, the one who had been in prison the longest, was a forty-year-old man named Junior. He was completely bald and had a thick neck and a habit of pulling his head down into that neck and squinting whenever he looked at anybody. Junior had gone from one prison to another since he was fifteen years old. He had been convicted of a string of robberies, petty theft, and finally grand larceny. He had never known either of his parents and had been raised by a woman claiming to be his grandmother, although social services could find no proof of the relationship.

Q.X., another cellmate, had also been in prison for years after being caught on charges of drug peddling and money laundering. His nose had been smashed in so many fights that it was permanently crooked—bent to the left.

The third cellmate was a young black man named Rollins. He had been in jail for a year for the rape of a 15 year old girl and for pimping a number of minors in Milwaukee's inner city. Rollins read whenever he had a chance. He would devour whatever he could get his hands on: books from the prison library, magazines in the recreation room.

"Why the hell you always readin' that shit?" Junior would ask, pulling his head down and squinting at Rollins. "You're gonna ruin your goddamn eyes."

One night after supper, Frank's three cellmates waited until the guard had locked their door and left the area. Junior and Rollins sat on their bunks, each with a magazine they were pretending to read. Q.X. pulled out a dish towel that he had taken from the kitchen and hidden under his shirt. While Frank stood at the sink with his back turned, Q.X. walked up behind him, put the towel around his neck, and pulled back as hard as he could. Frank turned blue and began to gurgle. While he was held helpless in that position, Junior jumped up from his cot, approached Frank from the front, spat in his face, and called him "a fuckin' snitch." He then jabbed his knee upwards into Frank's groin. Frank slumped to the floor, writhing in pain. Rollins got up, walked slowly over to Frank, raised his booted foot, and brought it down as hard as he could on Frank's stomach. Frank continued to gurgle. Blood began to spew out of his mouth as the heavy boot came down again and again, first on his stomach, then his chest, and finally on his crotch.

Junior pulled his head down into his neck and peered at his victim, lying in vomit and blood on the floor. He reached under his mattress and pulled out an 8-inch blade. "Pull his pants down, Rollins. We're going to do a little surgery here."

"Jesus, man. Y'all do it."

"Just do what I said. Take his goddamn pants off or I'll do it myself."

"Leave the sniveling bastard there," Q.X. said, staring Junior down. "We better be sleepin' like babies before the freakin' guard comes by." Junior shoved the blade back under his mattress. Frank lay unconscious in a pool of blood on the floor as the three men got into their bunks and pretended to sleep. While other prisoners in that cellblock had cheered them on during the attack, it was now silent. One could hear Frank's intermittent gurgling and gasping. The only other sounds were an occasional cough from a nearby cell, and the loud snoring of one man directly across from Frank's cell.

It was two hours before the guard came to do a bed-check on the prisoners in cellblock D. When he came to Frank's cell, he turned his flashlight on the lower bunks first. Seeing that those bunks were occupied, he turned the light onto the upper bunks and noticed that Frank's bunk was empty. He focused the light onto the floor where Frank lay unconscious, perhaps dead, in his own blood, urine, and spit.

The guard ran down to the end of the corridor and switched the lights on over the entire cellblock.

"What the fuck ..."

"Jesus Christ, turn the fucking lights off."

"What the hell's goin' on?"

The prisoners in neighboring cells began to roll over and sit up as they realized what was happening. The guard called for reinforcements on the cellphone that was attached to his shoulder harness.

"What happened here?" he questioned Frank's three cellmates. Nobody answered. The guard repeated his question. "Did you hear me?" he yelled. "I asked what happened here!"

Finally Q.X. stood up from his bed. "Geez, I don't know. He must've fallen from his bunk."

"Shit, yeah. That'd be a nasty fall," Junior mumbled.

By that time, two other guards, both with guns at their sides, came into the block and down to the cell. When they saw Frank lying on the floor, they called for a stretcher.

***

The card game at Cliff Smalley's started right on time Wednesday night. As soon as everyone had a soda and the cards were dealt, the conversation turned to Frank Feuermann.

"Aaron, what's going to happen to Frank? I read that he got pretty banged up in the prison," Charlie asked.

"Well, yes. He's still in the hospital. The doctors don't think he'll ever fully recover. He had a lot of brain damage and still isn't talking or walking. As soon as they can get him in a wheelchair, they're going to transfer him to the Extended Care Facility out on Cornish Road. I'm afraid he may be there for the rest of his life."

"I saw him Friday night at the hospital," Marty added. "Sophie called and asked me if I'd go. The only sounds coming out of his mouth were gurgles, but I know he could understand me. He would nod and try to smile."

"What really happened to him?" Cliff asked.

"Not really sure," Kohlberg replied. "There were three other men in the cell, and it's clear that at least one of them beat him up, probably with their fists and feet, but nobody's talking. I'm sure the warden will get to the bottom of it. Somebody will be charged."

"By the way," Marty said, "I told Sophie that as soon as Frank gets transferred over to ECF, I'd try to go and see him, probably once a week. I'll go after work on Friday afternoons. Anybody wants to go with me, just give me a holler and we can go together. Even if Frank can't talk, I know he'd appreciate it."

"Count me in," Charlie said. "I'll be glad to go with you."

CHAPTER 35

———————

Chet Magnuson grabbed his lunch from his locker and headed to the teachers' lounge. He heard a wolf whistle in the hall, and just as he swung around to catch the culprit, he spotted Ann Shelby going into the lounge. Three boys ran out the front door, headed for the parking lot.

"Who the hell was that?" he asked Ann.

"Who knows? I've been getting that stuff ever since the Newsomes and company decided to use me for some sort of object lesson."

"How bad does it get?"

"That's about it. A whistle now and then and a few crude remarks behind my back."

"If you know who's doing it, we can deal with them."

"Nah. I'd just as soon not make an issue of it. It'll pass."

"Look, Ann. We can't tolerate harassment. Please let me know if you know who's doing this. I'd have chased them, but there's no way of knowing who was responsible, and you know their buddies will cover for them."

"That's the point. I don't bother with it," Ann said.

The two opened their lunches. Ann got up to pour coffee. "Anyone want coffee while I'm up?"

"No thanks."

"Doing fine."

As Chet watched Ann walk over to the counter and pour herself coffee, he realized how stunning she looked in her red sweater and paisley skirt. He focused on her long legs and let his thoughts wander, then stopped. He felt ashamed, as he thought he was beginning to identify with her adolescent admirers—or harassers.

While Ann, Chet, and Casimir Shibilski were having lunch, Charlie Brannigan walked in and joined them. After taking a soda out of the refrigerator, he sat down next to Chet and opened his lunch. Just as he unwrapped his sandwich, Tricia Cameron stuck her head in the door.

"Mr. Brannigan, sorry to interrupt, but your wife's on the phone. Sounds pretty urgent."

Charlie rewrapped his sandwich, put it back in the bag, grabbed his soda, and left the room behind his office manager.

"Thanks, Tricia," he said, as he walked by her into his office and grabbed the telephone. "Hi, darling. What's up? Oh, my God. When did that happen? You didn't pass out, did you? I'll get home as quickly as I can. Just lie down until I get there. We may have to take you into emergency."

He hung up the telephone and then picked it up and dialed the outer office. "Tricia, can you come in here?"

Hearing the urgency in his voice, the office manager jumped right up and burst into his office. "What is it?"

Explaining that he had to leave early, he asked Tricia to take all messages for him and to cancel his afternoon appointments: one with Jeremy's father John Hastings, and the other with Patti Frasier, the new member of the school board. She was to let the teachers know he would be back first thing in the morning and to call on Chet Magnuson if she needed help.

"Yes, sure," she answered.

"Good. Let Orlando know that I've left the building. I think he's all alone tonight, but anyway, he can close up when he leaves—probably around eight. Make sure he knows about the problem in the girls' east bathroom. Can you do all of that for me, Trish?"

"Yes, I hope everything is alright."

"Well, yes, it's Katie. She's having a problem and I may need to get her to the hospital right away. Thanks for covering for me. Mr. Magnuson is in his room until four thirty if you need him. Now I wonder if you could get Dr. Smalley on the telephone for me. Try his office first; otherwise he'll be at the hospital. Just page him if you have to."

As Patricia Cameron left his office, Charlie stuffed a fistful of papers into his old leather briefcase and pulled a large binder off the shelf: "Department of Education: Code of Wisconsin Regulations." He slid it into his case next to the stack of papers from his desk. As he went to the closet to get his jacket, the telephone rang.

"Oh, thanks, Trish. Hello, Cliff. Listen, I'm not sure how serious this is but ..." He explained as carefully as he could just what Katie had told him. "Yeah, I can get her there right away. I know you don't usually see patients in the emergency room, but it's just that ... well, could you be there with us? Thanks. It'll take me fifteen minutes to get home and another ten to get her to the hospital. We'll meet you in the ER then? Thanks, Cliff. Really appreciate this. It may be nothing, but I'm glad you'll be there."

Charlie grabbed his jacket and briefcase and closed the door behind him.

"Tricia, one last thing. Could you call Katie and tell her I'm on my way? She has a telephone next to her bed so she won't have to get up. Just tell her I'll be right there. Thanks."

***

Only two other people were in the emergency waiting room. Holding Mary Elizabeth in his arms, Charlie got up from his chair as he saw Cliff come through the swinging door.

"What's the verdict, Cliff? What caused the bleeding?" Charlie asked his friend.

"We won't know until we look at the lab results that I ordered last week. They should all be back by now. I'll also want an X-ray, and I would guess the gastroenterologist will want to do a scope."

"What sort of a scope?"

"A colonoscopy."

"What do you think's wrong with her colon? Is that what caused the bleeding?"

"It's hard to tell at this point. Even a little bit of blood mixed with the water in the toilet can look like an awful lot of blood. It could even be from polyps in the rectum, although the ER guy didn't see any."

"Do we schedule all those tests right now, or should we call in the morning?"

"No, they're going to have her admitted and get her to a room. Katie's going to have to stay here at least for the next few days. We'll want to keep an eye on her until we know what's going on. I'm going to run down and get her chart. As soon as they have her admitted they'll let you know what room she's going to be in. You can go up with her. I'll meet you upstairs."

"Cliff, there's one other thing." Charlie fastened Mary Elizabeth into her baby carrier.

"What's that?"

"Katie's depression. Do you think—"

"Charlie, I know what you're going to ask. But, look, until we know what we're dealing with here, it's almost impossible to predict. Let me just say that hormones can go whacky with a whole lot of medical disorders. Same goes for neurotransmitters, and they're all implicated in a lot of emotional turmoil."

"But ..." Charlie struggled to know more. Why was his wife despondent? And why was she bleeding?

"I know. I know." The doctor, adjusting the collar of his white lab coat, looked up into the eyes of his distraught friend. "Charlie, depression can do that."

CHAPTER 36

———◆———

It was about eight o'clock on a Friday night when cars began pulling into the Newsome's driveway. Catherine had called another one of her "emergency meetings," not of the school board this time, but of "concerned parents." A few of the parents—Nicole and Pierre Thibault, Pat and Tammy O'Rourke, and the Abramsons—had sons on the basketball team. A few others were from the school board: chairman Jeffrey Fisher and Patti Frasier, the newly elected member of the board. Others were people whom Catherine Newsome felt might share her desire to see Charlie Brannigan in trouble with the school board: Tom and Jill Hellman and Adele and Fred Anderson.

As they gathered in the Newsomes' large family room, Catherine greeted her guests. "Please help yourself to some coffee or tea. And there are plenty of cookies and brownies for those who would like them." She had asked her housekeeper to bake that afternoon and then to stay late to prepare a side table in the family room, setting out the coffee and cookies for the meeting. Almost all the guests knew one another either from basketball booster club events, parent-teacher conferences, or from previous meetings at the Newsomes'.

Earlier that evening at their dinner table, Catherine Newsome had insisted that her husband, Tom, begin the meeting. "Just get things started," she had told him, "I can take over after that."

Tom Newsome cleared his throat. "Well, I suppose we ought to begin. I think you all know one another, so let's get right down to the reason Catherine thought we ought to get together tonight." Sitting on the couch, he hunched his shoulders up so that it looked as if he had pulled his head down into his neck like a turtle. He looked directly at Jeffrey Fisher. "Once again it's about the high school and our so-called 'principal.' Some of us think he has gotten out of control. We thought some of you might agree. In any case, the situation needs immediate attention."

Tom Newsome began to lay out a case against Charlie Brannigan. He had exceeded his authority by punishing players on the basketball team. That should have been the prerogative of the coach. In any case, the punishment far exceeded the crime. It was a simple matter of a little hazing off school grounds. It had nothing to do with the principal. He had suspended players without first consulting the board. He had ruined any chance that Waumeka High had of a winning basketball team, or any team at all. He was changing teaching assignments willy-nilly.

With each charge that Newsome leveled against the principal, his wife interjected in an attempt to make the case stronger. After several such interruptions, Newsome turned to her.

"Darling, why don't you take over from here?"

Catherine was more than happy to oblige—and to give her opinion. Her son, she said, like a lot of others, was being treated unfairly. This was not the first instance of unfair treatment. Now his chance for a basketball scholarship to Madison would be in jeopardy. The community just couldn't stand for this sort of abuse.

After rattling off her own list of complaints, Catherine Newsome asked the others for their opinions. The Thibaults agreed that the basketball program should not be jeopardized, but they weren't sure about the legalities of the suspension punishment. Pat and Tammy O'Rourke simply wanted to see their son back on the team and agreed with Tom Newsome that a public apology from the principal was in order. The two members of the school board, Jeffrey Fisher and Patti Frasier were both quiet.

"Just listening and learning," Jeffrey replied when Catherine Newsome asked for his input.

The only couple who weren't at all sure that the principal had acted inappropriately was Adele and Fred Anderson. Their son Eddie was not on the basketball team, and although they could understand the frustration of those parents whose sons were on the team, they suggested that the principal had an obligation to insure the safety of the students.

"We heard that Jeremy Hastings ended up in the hospital after the hazing," Adele mentioned.

"That's crazy," Tom Newsome interrupted her. "That kid's a wimp—always has been. Probably had some sort of a little bruise and mommy had to take him in to see the doctor. His old lady's pampered him since he was in kindergarten."

Each of the parents in turn shared their opinion of Catherine Newsome's concern about the principal. After each one spoke, Mrs. Newsome turned to the next person, without commenting on their views or attempting to engage the group in a discussion. When they were all done speaking, Catherine sat up straight and set her tea cup and saucer down on the coffee table in front of her.

"Now then," she began, "As I see it, what we need to do first is to make sure that the total school board, and that includes the three of us here, knows of our most serious concern. Jeffrey, we'd like you to alert all the other members of the board, so that this issue can be raised at the next school board meeting, which just happens to be next Monday."

As nobody appeared willing to challenge Catherine Newsome's view of events or her plans for their remedy—even the Andersons sat quietly—her motion, such as it was, appeared to pass.

"I think I can make sure that this becomes a matter for the board," Jeffrey Fisher responded, "I believe it's better handled there than with an *ad hoc* group of parents, however well-intentioned." The innuendo appeared lost on Catherine Newsome, who replied, "Well, then, that settles it. More coffee, anyone?"

After the last guests, the Thibaults, had left the house, Catherine Newsome turned to her husband. "We finally have that son of a bitch where we want him. Did you notice that? Even the Andersons didn't disagree. I'll have a lot of telephone calls to make before Monday night. I don't want to leave a damn thing to chance."

"Just how are you going to bring it up?" Tom Newsome asked.

"You'll see. I'm going to prepare a nice little motion for the board's consideration. And I'll make certain that little Miss Patti Frasier will be happy to second it. You'll see."

"Just so you get Tommy back on the team. I don't care what happens to that bastard. He could rot in hell, for all I care," Tom said.

"He will. He will," his wife replied.

CHAPTER 37

───◆───

Charlie Brannigan got to the hospital by seven thirty the following morning. Katie had black rings under her puffy eyes and lay on her back, her red hair pulled over one shoulder and the sheet that covered her. He bent over to kiss his wife.

"How did you sleep, sweetie?"

"Pretty well. They gave me a sedative after dinner. How's Mary Elizabeth? Were you able to get someone to take care of her?"

Charlie reassured Katie that their daughter was in good hands with the Chickerings, their neighbors, who had raised four children of their own.

"Did Mary Elizabeth seem OK?" Katie asked. "It's a good thing we just started her on the formula, isn't it. Did she seem OK?"

"I'm sure she's wondering where her Mommy is. She cried a little when I changed her, but, yeah, she's fine," Charlie answered. "Tomorrow and Sunday I'll work on something more permanent. Even after you're discharged, you'll need some help. Has the doctor been in yet this morning?"

"Yes, they're supposed to do the colonoscopy at nine thirty. My lab results and the scope results should all be ready by tomorrow. The gastroenterologist wants to go over them with me in the morning. Can you be here?"

"Sure, it's Saturday. I'll just bring the baby along."

"You can leave her in the play room. They'll have a nurse there."

Charlie lay down on the bed and held his wife. They talked for another twenty minutes before the nurse came in. Charlie got up to leave. "Better get to work. I'll be here this afternoon, sweetie. I love you."

"I love you, too. Sorry I'm such a bother."

***

The day passed quickly for Charlie Brannigan. He met with a few of his teachers, walked the halls, sat in on the beginning of two class sessions and answered calls from parents. Jeffrey Fisher called just before Charlie got ready to pack up to leave for the hospital.

"Hi, Jeff, what's up? Yes, I know some of the parents are upset. I'm still putting out brush fires around here. Can't tell you how many calls I've had; not all negative, mind you. There are a few parents who seem to support the action we've taken."

"I wasn't sure if you were planning to attend the board meeting on Monday, but I know some of the parents want to bring this issue up. It would be important for you to be there," Fisher said. "It's an open meeting, so it'll be at seven thirty in the auditorium."

"Sure, I'll be there," Charlie replied.

Charlie had just hung up the telephone when Tricia rang him again. "Mr. Brannigan, it's the superintendent on line one. Can you talk with him?"

Henry Derkheiser had been in the school district for five years. He came from Milwaukee, where he had been assistant superintendent with a good track record of keeping parents and the community happy. Charlie knew that he was especially proud of the athletic programs in the city high schools. Ten years before, he had come to Wisconsin as a high-school history teacher and football coach from Nebraska. Charlie knew that his main claim to fame, however, was the fact that during his college years, Derkheiser had been an All-American halfback on the University of Nebraska football team. He kept a Cornhuskers pennant hanging in his office.

"Hank, hi. I'm sure I know what this call is about," Charlie began.

"Charlie, some of the parents are really incensed about this thing. You know we were looking forward to a really strong basketball season. I know I should have talked to you about this before, Charlie. But then I thought you had everything under control. You know, that you would probably have checked with all the relevant people before those dismissals. Charlie, if you could just ..."

"Hank, I didn't think I needed to get parents' permission before I suspended students. But let me get to the bottom line. You've seen my memo to the teachers. Do I have your support on my decision to suspend these students for three days and to expel them from the athletic program for the year? I did call to let you know."

"Yes, yes, I know, Charlie, but I didn't realize these fellows were the backbone of our basketball team. Didn't know the parents would be getting so upset." The superintendent's voice grew softer, as if he was holding the phone away from his face.

"Well?"

"Charlie, I just don't know," the superintendent answered. "It'll all depend on what I hear at the meeting on Monday night. I want to hear from the parents, of course. But hear me out, Charlie. If you could just reinstate those boys, we could avoid this whole thing."

"I couldn't do that in good conscience, Hank." Charlie began to sit up straight in his chair and squeeze the telephone. His face turned red and his throat went dry as he continued, trying to control his voice. "One of my students was severely injured, and several others were beaten." He couldn't believe what he was hearing from the superintendent. He knew the man was shallow, but this was too much.

"Charlie, I know, I know as well as you, but the press, Charlie. I mean some of these parents are already going to the newspaper with half-truths. Charlie, the *Gazette* would love to keep this story going. We could avoid all that."

"You know me better than that, Hank," Charlie replied, regaining his calm.

"Well, Charlie, I hope this meeting goes well for all of us."

"So do I, Hank, and thanks for the call."

CHAPTER 38

Charlie had always looked forward to Friday nights. He could come home, drop his briefcase, take off his jacket and tie, and help Katie get dinner ready while they both watched the six o'clock news on Wisconsin Public Television. Before Mary Elizabeth was born, they would often walk downtown to the video store after dinner to rent a movie and then spend the evening together on the couch in the family room, eating popcorn and watching a video … especially any Robin Williams movie. They had seen "Mrs. Doubtfire," "The Dead Poets Society," and "Good Morning, Vietnam" and had watched "Patch Adams" twice. Now Charlie dreaded Friday night. It had been raining all afternoon, a cold, wet, early-winter drizzle.

Holding Mary Elizabeth in one arm and an umbrella in the same hand, he set his briefcase on the step and unlocked the back door. The silence in the house was eerie. The hallway was damp and cold. He set Mary Elizabeth on the kitchen floor and took off his wet London fog trench coat, shaking it off on the landing floor before hanging it on a hook near the back door. Mary Elizabeth blinked as the apron hanging from a chair touched her face.

After putting Mary Elizabeth in her crib, Charlie called his neighbor, Cliff Smalley. Getting Cliff's answering machine, he left a message.

"Hey, Cliff, just calling to tell you I won't be able to play cards this week. As long as Katie's in the hospital, I better stay pretty close to home. You know, watching Mary Elizabeth and sort of taking care of things around the house. Say, if you get this after dinner, and it's not too late, why don't you come over for a while? If Sally doesn't mind, I could use the company. Anyway, got a few things I'd like to go over with you—you know, stuff about Katie's condition, and some things going on at school. Give me a call. Thanks."

Charlie fed and bathed Mary Elizabeth. After changing her and putting her to bed, he fixed a salad and an omelet for himself and settled down in front of the television. Cliff called at about eight o'clock.

"Sure, c'mon over," Charlie suggested. The men talked late into the evening. Charlie revealed his concern about Katie's condition, his worry that the doctors wouldn't be able to find what was wrong with her, and his even greater worry that her personality had changed dramatically in the few months since the twins were born.

"Usually I really look forward to Christmas. Probably my favorite time of the year." The previous year had been wonderful for them. Having just learned about the babies, it had been fun getting ready for them and visiting Cliff and Sally and their own family. This year, he wasn't even sure he'd put up a tree. Here it was, Christmas just weeks away, and they hadn't sent cards, gotten a tree, put up lights, nothing.

"What else is going on, Charlie?" The doctor, an excellent diagnostician, wanted to know what was bothering his friend. "Sounds like there's something we're not talking about. Is it this business with the basketball team?"

"You're right. Hold on, I'm going to get me another beer. Want another soda?" He came back to the couch with the beer and the soda, one in each hand. "You're right. I'm worried about what's going on at the school. I suspended a bunch of kids last week. You must have read about it. It's been all over the papers. The board's going to have a meeting next week to review my decision."

"So? Looks to me like you did the right thing. That one boy was badly beaten, according to the news accounts."

"I know. But we've been building up a great basketball team. Justice was pretty sure we had a shot at the state title this year. Now it looks as if I've single-handedly gone and dismantled the best basketball team that Waumeka High has had in 30 years."

"Are you kidding me? Your basketball players dismantled their own team. You did what you had to. You stand for something, Brannigan. You always have. And this town knows it. You're not going to let a bunch of bullies get away with assaulting their classmates just because they happen to be good basketball players, or have a mother on the board of education, or a rich daddy. To hell with them."

"You know that and I know that," Charlie said. But the superintendent didn't know it. And who knew what the community thought or believed or wanted. Charlie always thought he had a pretty good handle on public opinion in the town. Now he wasn't even sure that his teachers were behind him on this one. He had tried to get a reading from a few of the old guard, like Chet Magnuson, but it was a pretty mixed bag.

"What's the worst that could happen?" Cliff asked.

"They could fire me." Charlie's answer was fast and clipped.

"Right! And with about two more graduate courses and your dissertation, you'd have your PhD. UW-Eau Claire would snap you up in a heartbeat. Can you imagine their education department getting a faculty member with your experience?" Cliff reassured him.

"But, Cliff, I don't want to finish a PhD and I don't want to go to Eau Claire." He wanted to stay right here in Waumeka and be the principal of Waumeka High School.

"Then you will, Charlie. Then you will."

CHAPTER 39

A t nine thirty the following morning, Charlie arrived at the hospital. He left Mary Elizabeth with the nurse in the play room and ran up the stairs to the third floor rather than taking the elevator. Both the gastroenterologist and Dr. Janet Berkside were already in Katie's room when he got there.

"Charlie, oh my God, I'm glad you're here. It's not good news," his wife stammered and then began to cry, as he hugged her.

After a few minutes, Charlie let go of his wife and turned to Dr. Berkside.

"It's serious, but not terrible," the doctor said. "Dr. Resnick here is the gastroenterologist who did the colonoscopy yesterday."

"We found evidence of a malignancy in the colon," Dr. Resnick explained. "It's what we call an adenocarcinoma, a malignant tumor that is usually very slow growing. This one though, appears to be unusually aggressive. It covers a good portion of the transverse section of the colon and should come out as soon as possible. I've checked with the oncologist, who concurs."

"You're saying surgery?" Charlie asked.

"Yes."

"When?"

"I don't think we should wait. It's something we can do right here at St. Luke's. If the surgical team can schedule it, I'd say early next week." Resnick explained the need for surgery and probably follow-up chemotherapy, and the danger of the cancer spreading to other organs.

Frustrated, Charlie wanted to know the bottom line.

The gastroenterologist was wary. "You're asking about prognosis. Well, it's difficult. As I mentioned, ordinarily these are slow-growing tumors. I assume we're catching it in time. If we are, Katie should recover just fine."

"And if we're not catching it in time?"

Again the doctor was hedging. Like he had said, it was very hard to tell. They would need to make sure the tumor hadn't spread to other organs, as it did appear to be unusually aggressive for an adenocarcinoma.

"But why wouldn't they have found this four months ago when Katie was pregnant?" Charlie asked. He looked over at the OB-GYN doctor.

"It's hard to tell; symptoms might have been masked by the pregnancy itself." she replied.

"Is this rare? I mean, in a pregnant woman?" Charlie asked the gastro-enterologist.

"Yes, but it's not unheard of. But you shouldn't be too alarmed. We see these tumors routinely and can remove them successfully in the vast majority of cases. Perhaps the oncologist will want her to get some adjuvant chemo-therapy afterwards."

Not unheard of. See them routinely. The vast majority of cases. Charlie kept weighing the doctor's words. Was Katie in that vast majority?

After leaving his card on the night stand and encouraging Katie and Charlie to call him if they had any further questions, Dr. Resnick took his notes from the tray table and left the room.

Dr. Berkside explained who the surgeon would be and emphasized her desire to treat this condition aggressively and her commitment to win this battle. Charlie looked at Katie. She appeared to be reassured.

"One more battle, sweetheart," he said. "We've been through some others together and we'll get through this one." Katie leaned up from her pillow to return his kiss.

In the hallway, Janet Berkside caught up with Dr. Resnick. The doctor stopped her colleague, looked up at him and said, "Marvin, I should tell you that Katie did experience some rectal bleeding in the early months. We figured her hemorrhoids were responsible for that. She had some mild abdominal pain, nausea, vomiting, and some altered bowel movements. We assumed those were simply complications of the pregnancy. We prescribed bed rest. Now I'm wondering if they were indicators of the carcinoma."

"It would be easy to miss, Janet, especially in a pregnant woman."

CHAPTER 40

———

"Hey, you guys want a ride? I got my old lady's mustang. C'mon. Get in." As school let out and hundreds of students poured out of the building and headed toward the parking lot, André Thibault and Jimmy Talbot accepted Tommy Newsome's invitation. As they climbed into the red convertible, Tommy pulled a brown bag from under his seat and passed it to Thibault, who sat next to him.

"Mon dieu, so what the heck is that, anyway?" André gasped as he opened the bag. "That's not at all for me, Thomas, no sir. Not at all."

"C'mon. Have a swig. Or else pass it back to Talbot. I know he's thirsty, ain'tcha Jimmy boy?"

Talbot reached over the seat and snatched the bag out of Thibault's hand. Crouching down behind the seat, he unscrewed the top from a half-empty bottle of Seagram's Seven Crown and took a long gulp.

"Nice stuff, Tommy, my boy. Where did you get it?"

"From my old man's cupboard. He'll never miss it. He always drinks his gin."

Talbot took another gulp and passed the bottle back to Tommy, who put it under his seat—but not before taking a swig himself.

"Where we headed?" Thibault asked, as Newsome started the car.

"Hey, hey, I dunno. Who knows? Let's just take a little ride, OK, OK? Hey, isn't that Tits Shelby gettin' into her car? Yeah, yeah. God, wouldn't I like to help her out of them clothes ... oh, yeah, the bitch."

"Jeezus, Newsome. Cool it," Talbot warned his friend.

"OK, OK. Yeah, But let's just fellow, I mean, follow her just for the hell of it. You never know. She may be needing some help."

"Yeah? Like with what, Tommy?"

"I dunno. You never know. You never know."

Ann Shelby pulled out of the parking lot in her white Camaro. Tommy waited until she got to the corner and began to turn before he exited the parking lot, following her at a safe distance. With André Thibault next to him and Jimmy Talbot in the back seat of the red Mustang, he followed the white car for about three miles as it headed north out highway 68.

Suddenly the white Camaro began to shake and shimmy. Ann Shelby pulled off onto the shoulder of the road.

"Oh, no shit. She's got a flat. Now ain't that just too bad. Look at that. Guess the bitch'll be needing our help, just like I said. See there."

"Newsome, did you have something to do with this?" Talbot wanted to know.

"C'mon. How could you think such a silly little thing like that? Let's get our asses out of this car and give her a hand."

Tommy pulled his car up behind the white Camaro just as Ann Shelby got out on the driver's side. "Hey, Miss Shelby, can we help you?" Tommy called from his window.

"Looks like I got a flat. Darnit, anyway," the teacher said.

"That's OK. We can take care of that." The three boys got out of the Mustang, Tommy and Jimmy both a little wobbly.

"Pop your trunk open, Miss Shelby. Just open it up for me," Tommy called. "I'll get the jack out." As he tried to wiggle the jack loose from its holder, he scratched the back of his thumb on the retaining clip. "Shit," he mumbled, throwing the jack on the ground and then sticking his thumb in his mouth.

"Here, then, let me do that," Thibault offered, picking up the jack. He and Talbot began to change the left rear tire. There was almost no traffic on the highway at that hour; very few cars passed by.

"Hey, Miss Shelby," Tommy approached her and put his hand on the small of her back. "Why don't you just go in the car and sit down while we take care of this for you?"

Thibault and Talbot were busy trying to get the lug nuts off the blown tire. Tommy walked around the car with his teacher. Opening the right rear door he suggested, "Here, just sit here," and pushed her into the back of the car. She fell on her back, her legs dangling off the seat. In an instant, despite her wriggling and trying to hit him on his face and shoulders, Newsome put his hand on her chest, pulled her coat open, and whispered with boozy breath, "You're gonna enjoy this." He pushed her legs apart as he stood over her. Reaching up between her legs, he pulled at her panties until they came down around her knees and tore. He pulled them off and threw them away from the car. Ann struggled and cried out but had trouble righting herself from the back seat. When she tried to yell, her attacker took his hand off her breast and put it over her mouth.

"Hey, Newsome," Thibault yelled from behind the car, "we could use your help back here."

"Yeah, I could use yours too," Tommy replied.

Thibault looked through the rear window and saw what was happening. "Jeezus, Newsome, have you lost your mind? Sacré vache. Mon dieu. Holy shit."

Talbot walked to the side of the car to see what the commotion was about. "Hey, dude, you've really done it this time. I'm outta here. You're a stupid asshole, you know what."

"What're you talking about? You could get some of this when I'm done."

Newsome took his hand off Ann Shelby's mouth and in that instant she brought her knee up swiftly into his groin. Stunned, he pulled back just as she raised her knee as far as she could and gave him a kick in the same spot with her right leg. Newsome fell back into the ditch behind him.

The other two boys began to run back in the direction of town. Talbot turned back and yelled, "I'm sorry, Miss Shelby. I ain't got nothing to do with this. I'm really sorry."

Ann Shelby got up, pulled her skirt down, closed her coat around her, and went around the car to the highway, looking in both directions for any sign of another car. Tommy crawled up on his hands and knees and finally stood and stumbled to his car. He got in and fumbled with the keys. His thumb still bled from the scrape he got trying to loosen the car jack. Finally, spinning his car around so fast that it almost went off the road, he headed back towards town, hoping to catch up with his friends before they had a chance to tell anybody what had happened.

Within about three minutes, an elderly couple in an old Chevy Citation hatchback drove up on the other side of the road, going toward town.

"Can we help you, Ma'am?" The gentleman called out from across the road. "I see you got a flat tire. Would you like me to get help for you? We're headed into town."

Ann leaned on the side of their car, supporting herself, sobbing. She was out of breath but managed to gasp, "Could you please give me a lift? I'd like to go to the police station first."

***

The station was almost deserted except for a Hmong couple in Chief Kohlberg's office, who were complaining in loud voices about a series of break-ins at their fast food restaurant on the south side of town. Kohlberg got up to close the door when he saw Ann walk up to the counter.

Jimmy Ashblane, a young deputy police officer, sat on a high stool behind the counter. "What can I do for you, ma'am?" he asked.

"I'm here to report an attempted rape."

"And when did this alleged incident occur, ma'am?"

"It's not 'alleged.' Do you hear me? It *happened*! I was there. I'm the victim. And as for when it occurred … it just happened about twenty minutes ago," Ann shouted.

"Just a second. If you don't mind, Miss, I'm going to ask Deputy Colovassi to take your statement. It's much better to have a woman take the statement in cases like this."

He swung around on his stool and went down the hall behind the counter and into a door on the right. Within a minute he emerged, followed by a middle-aged woman in a freshly starched police uniform. She had her black hair pulled back in a bun. *She looks like my grandmother,* Ann thought.

"Uh, Angela, this is—I'm sorry, ma'am; I'm afraid I didn't catch your name."

"You didn't ask me. My name is Ann Shelby."

"Yes. Miss Shelby. This is Deputy Angela Colovassi. She's going to take your statement." The young man left quickly and went back to his stool behind the counter.

The policewoman picked up a note pad and a pencil from the counter and then ushered Ann back to the small conference room, where she asked her to recall the attack in as much detail as her "personal comfort allowed." Ann had no trouble going into detail, or in answering the probing questions that followed.

"Yes, he pushed me on my back … Yes, he pulled my panties off … No, I'm not wearing them right now … Where are they? Probably still on the road beside my car. At least that's where he threw them … No, there was no penetration. He hadn't even unzipped his pants when I gave him a knee and then a foot in the groin."

What surprised Ann even more than the graphic nature of the questions was her own complete candor in answering them. Considering herself a generally reserved person not given to discussions about private matters, here she was talking to a complete stranger about the most intimate topic possible. It was probably her anger that prompted the openness, she thought. Also, she felt a certain warm respect for the older woman. Her efficiency, self-confidence, and no-nonsense approach all appealed to Ann.

After about twenty-five minutes of questioning, the officer asked, "Is there anything else I should know, either about the incident or the young men involved?"

At least she didn't say alleged incident, Ann thought.

"If you'll excuse me for just a moment, then." Colovassi stood up and left the room. Ann looked down the hall and watched the deputy as she knocked on Chief Kohlberg's door. The door opened, and the Hmong couple exited. Kohlberg stood in the doorway.

"And let me know whenever there's a problem," Kohlberg called out to them as they left the station. He turned to his deputy. "What's up, Angela?"

"Chief, I have a young woman in the conference room who's alleging rape. One of the teachers from the high school. Her car's still out on highway 68, about three miles north of town. I'll need someone to get her to the hospital and someone else to check the crime scene."

Kohlberg walked back into his office, motioning to his deputy to follow him. "If you can take her to the hospital, Angela, I'll see if I can get Clemens to do the investigating. He's not scheduled to be here until the morning—"

"Chief, we can't wait for Karl Clemens; this really needs to be done now. This kid apparently ripped her underwear off and they're still there on the road. Now, if we don't—"

"OK, OK. I was going to say that I can call over to the sheriff's office and see if Clemens can go out right away. I may go with him, myself. What's the teacher's name?"

CHAPTER 41

———————

Charlie got to the school twenty minutes before the board meeting, which was scheduled for seven thirty. He went to his office, picked up a file folder from his desk, then headed down to the auditorium, where he sat in the front row. After spending about ten minutes going over his notes, he turned around to see that the auditorium was beginning to fill up with teachers, parents, and concerned citizens. His own teachers were sitting together at the back of the room, on the right side. Ann Shelby, seeing him look back, gave him a quick wave, raising her hand just high enough for him to see it, so that the wave would not be obvious to anyone else. Charlie managed a smile, waved back in the same way, then turned back to face the stage.

A few minutes later he turned around again to notice that the seats were filling up quickly. Patrick Filey sat next to Ann, and Chet Magnuson sat on her other side. Casimir Shibilski was next to Magnuson. In the row behind them sat six other high school teachers and staff: Patricia Cameron, Jaime Rodriguez, Sam Cohen, Betty Franklin, Ms. Finkbeiner, and James Cartwright. Sitting next to James were his brother and sister-in-law, Lou and Amber Cartwright. Amber held their baby, Rainbow, on her lap.

Across the aisle from the teachers, a group of parents and other community members had begun to gather. Among them, and sitting together, were many of the parents whom Charlie suspected were among those Catherine Newsome had invited to her "concerned parents" meetings: Adele and Fred Anderson, Tom and Jill Helman, Emily and Seth Frankel, and Terri Abramson.

As president of the board, Jeffrey Fisher rapped his gavel on the table and began the meeting of the Waumeka Board of Education by calling for a reading of the minutes of the last meeting. After the minutes were read and approved and the reports of the treasurer, the finance committee, and the curriculum committee were read and discussed, Frank reached across the table and pulled the microphone closer. He began to read from his notes:

"The only item on the agenda tonight under 'other business' concerns a recent action of Mr. Brannigan, the high school principal, namely his suspending of five students for three days and barring them from nonacademic events for the remainder of the year. This occurred after an incident last month in Heckney Woods—an initiation of some of the basketball players." Fisher went on to explain that the so-called initiation had been something of an annual tradition, although, admittedly, not a school-sponsored event. He acknowledged that there was some discrepancy concerning the seriousness of the infraction this year, some believing it to have gotten "a little out of hand" while others believed it was simply high-spirited fun.

"The question before the board now," he continued, "is whether the principal has acted within his jurisdiction in punishing the students for an infraction that took place off school grounds." He pointed out that several parents had expressed the desire to have the board look into the matter of having the suspended students reinstated, adding that several of them were valued members of the boys' basketball team.

"I'm sure I don't need to remind you that our team is on target for an exceptional season this year. Coach Justice is here, and I'm sure he could speak to that. Before that, though, Catherine Newsome has a motion she would like to present to the board. If that motion gets a second, we can begin our discussion of this urgent matter. Catherine?"

Catherine Newsome, who sat on the president's right side, straightened in her chair and passed her hand under her hair and along the back of her neck, adjusting her hair. She then pulled the microphone toward her and began speaking, glancing down from time to time to look at her notes through glasses that she slid far down her nose so that she could look at the audience over the top of the rims.

"Yes. I must say, not only as a board member mind you, but especially as a parent, that I am concerned, indeed, highly concerned, as I know a number of other parents are also, about what we consider an abuse of authority that is threatening our school district. In his failure to reprimand errant teachers last spring, or to dismiss incompetents," she looked down the aisle and over to her left, toward Ann Shelby, "and now in his excessive discipline of a few students, without consultation mind you, Mr. Brannigan, our high school principal, has shown an utter disregard for usual academic protocol and procedures. We therefore move that he be required to reinstate those basketball players he has suspended and apologize to them and their parents. If he is unwilling to do that, we believe the board should move to have him resign for the good of the whole district." A hush went through the audience. Catherine continued: "We surely want this school year to go down in history because of our great basketball team, the one that's going to win the state title. We don't want to be remembered because of some picayune little infraction or the behavior of an over-zealous principal."

"Are you stating that in the form of a motion, Catherine?" Jeffrey Fisher asked.

"Yes, I am. I so move," she replied.

"And I second that motion," Patti Frasier said in a small voice that was not much more than a whisper.

"Perhaps you'd like to comment, Charlie," Fisher suggested.

Without going to the microphone that had been placed in the aisle for members of the audience to use, Charlie Brannigan placed his hands on the arms of his seat and pushed himself up to a standing position. He towered over the seated audience.

He spoke in a loud, clear voice that made it obvious he did not need the microphone. "Thank you, Mr. Fisher, but I really have little to say. My views are common knowledge by now. Since my letter to the teachers about this issue was surreptitiously published in the local newspaper this morning, nobody here should have any doubts about my position.

"What has not yet hit the papers, however, is the fact that one of our former students was brutalized to the point that he had to be hospitalized. That boy's father is suing the perpetrators and their parents. I would only add that if young bullies are rewarded for their behavior, or are not stopped in time, they soon become adult bullies.

"Mrs. Newsome's remarks about how she would like this school year to be remembered reminded me of something I heard on the news this morning. It was fifty-eight years ago today, December 1, 1955, that Rosa Parks sparked a revolution in the south. We all know who she was, the brave woman who refused to give up her seat on a bus in Montgomery, Alabama. With that single act of courage she sparked a revolution that changed the face of this country forever. The meek shall inherit the earth. Now does anybody remember the name of the white man who tried to take her seat, or the name of the bus driver who insisted she move to the back of the bus? Of course not. The bullies of this world are quickly forgotten. That's all I have to say."

As Charlie sat back down the room again fell silent. Fisher looked over at the school superintendent, Henry Derkheiser. "Henry, would you like to address the board?"

"No," he replied. "I have spoken with Mr. Brannigan. He knows my views on this matter. Now I'd like to hear what the rest of our community has to say, the teachers and the parents."

"Thank you, Mr. Superintendent. Perhaps we can begin our open discussion then. If you would like to address the board, please use one of the microphones that are placed in the two aisles. Please address the board, not the audience, and please keep your comments brief so that as many people can be heard as want to be. We will need to adjourn at ten o'clock. Remember, this is only a fact-finding and opinion-sharing session. The board has already agreed not to vote on this motion this evening. Instead, we will vote in closed session, as has been our practice in dealing with personnel matters."

Several parents, who had been sitting together, each spoke in turn in support of the athletic program and of the hard work Coach Justice had done to bring the basketball team to a level where they now had a chance at the state title—except for the principal's unprecedented decision to suspend several players for what they considered a minor infraction.

Fred Anderson, who had been sitting with Adele two rows behind those parents, was next in line to speak. "I would like to address a question to Mrs. Newsome, whose motion we're considering. Have you or the superintendent given any consideration to who would replace Mr. Brannigan as principal of the high school should he be asked to resign?"

Catherine Newsome drew the microphone close to her and leaned forward. Looking out over the top of her glasses, she said, "Yes, certainly. We both believe, and I'm sure the community would agree, that at least for the time being—that is, until we could begin a proper search to identify and recruit a top-notch principal—until that time, I'm certain that the current assistant principal, Chester Magnuson, would be an excellent choice as principal pro-tem." Catherine pushed the microphone away from her and leaned back in her chair.

Chet Magnuson stood up and went to the line behind the microphone in the right aisle. There were two speakers in front of him; a line of high school teachers began to form behind him. Charlie Brannigan looked back to see his teachers, many with determined looks on their faces, approach the line forming in the aisle. A former wrestler, he thought of the times in his college days when he was pinned to the floor by a heavier opponent or by one who had used illegal moves that were never detected. He couldn't get the image out of his mind that it was happening again. Even worse than that, he feared what wrestlers called "the angle," the storyline of a feud between wrestlers that was fueled by fans and sometimes lasted for years.

CHAPTER 42

———————

George Akishembie sat behind the counter when Karl Clemens walked into the police station. The place was damp, cold—and quiet, for a Monday night.

"George, looks like you drew night duty again," the detective said.

"I don't mind, really. Marion tutors on Tuesday nights, so I'd be home alone anyways. But what brings you here?" Akishembie replied.

"I've got my preliminary report on the investigation on a rape case. Couple of kids apparently jumped one of the teachers from over at the high school. I wanted to leave this for Deputy Colovassi."

"I think she's still back there in her office. You can take it right back to her, yourself. Angela," the deputy called out.

"I'm here! You'll wake up the dead screaming like that," came the reply.

"You're working late, Angela," the detective said as he entered her small, dank office.

"Just catching up. Whatcha got?"

"My report on the Ann Shelby case. We were able to get some fingerprints from the spare tire and from the inside of the car. And we retrieved her underwear from the side of the road. By the way, did you say there was no penetration?" Clemens laid his folder of papers on Colovassi's desk.

"That's what she said," the deputy replied. "Why?"

"Well there was a spot of blood on her panties."

"Really, detective, there are other ways that might have gotten there. I'll talk with her." Colovassi reached for the file, opened the folder, and looked at the top page.

"Still, I'd like a blood sample. Can you arrange for that?" Clemens asked.

"Sure," she replied. "Have you talked to the boys?" She looked up from the papers in front of her.

"We've talked to Jimmy Talbot and the Thibault boy. Their stories match completely, and they also match what you got from the victim. I think you'll have enough to arrest Tommy Newsome." Clemens spoke with the assurance of someone who had plenty of experience with investigations.

"I'll ask Kohlberg to send someone over to the Newsomes' tomorrow after school. I don't think this should wait, and thanks for getting that over here right away," Colovassi replied

"Angela, I got to tell you, I don't get it. The kid's dad is one of the richest bastards in town and his old lady's on the school board. What was he thinking?"

"You don't get immunized from stupidity because your old man's rich," the deputy answered. "Besides, he's no kid. He's seventeen. If this goes to trial, he's an adult."

CHAPTER 43

———◆———

One by one, the parents who had assembled in the auditorium continued to give their opinions to the Board of Education. They knew
that within the next week, the board would meet in private to
decide the fate of the principal of the high school. Most of them mentioned
how important they thought the athletic program was to their community
and why the principal had overstepped his bounds when he suspended five
students. Others, clearly in the minority, expressed the view that the principal generally acted in good faith and reminded the audience that seven
times in the past ten years, Waumeka High School had sent a team to represent the district in the Wisconsin High School Quiz Bowl Tournament, and
had twice gone on to represent the state in the national Panasonic Academic
Challenge.

Although those statistics heartened Charlie Brannigan, he began to think
that this was one wrestling tournament he might not win. There were too
many heavyweights on the opposing team.

When the woman in front of Chet Magnuson had finished speaking, the
assistant principal cleared his throat and took the microphone in both hands.

"Good evening," he began. "My name is Chester Magnuson. I am the
high school assistant principal." Charlie swallowed and turned around to face

his friend and assistant principal. Was Chet about to pin him? The bright lights of the auditorium made Chet's bald spot stand out even more than usual. Chet held on to the microphone in such a way that it supported him like a crutch; he stood up straight, almost completely eliminating his usual stooped posture.

"A few moments ago," Magnuson continued, "Mrs. Newsome—I believe this was your position—suggested that I might assume the role of principal in the event that Mr. Brannigan was no longer available. Let me assure you, board, parents, and teachers alike, that neither any board member nor any administration official has discussed that option with me. If they had, I would have told them that I have absolutely no interest in serving as principal pro—whatever it is. Aside from being insulting, the suggestion is also ludicrous. Had the school board thought I was qualified to be principal, they might have offered me the job twenty-five years ago. No thank you; I am quite happy doing what I am doing, being assistant principal."

The aging assistant principal coughed and then, holding onto the microphone, pulled himself even straighter. He looked around the room, then up at Charlie, then he looked back at the table where the board sat. "I am also pleased to be doing my job with Mr. Brannigan as my boss. We don't always agree. Brannigan makes decisions every day that I'm glad I don't have to make and, as I said, I don't always agree with his decisions. But I can tell you this. Those decisions are always made with integrity and they are made for the good of the whole community, students, parents, and teachers. In my opinion, it would be foolish indeed to let go of an administrator with his reputation and track record over a stupid dispute about the suspension of five students. We should be debating, instead, how we're going to manage the enormous task of bringing these students into the twenty-first century—how we're going to prepare them for the tasks ahead, with competence, discipline, and above all, respect for one another."

Magnuson turned and handed the microphone to Sam Cohen, who stood behind him. Like Magnuson, Cohen spoke in support of the principal, recounting, as a few of the parents had already done, the academic successes the high school had enjoyed under Charlie's leadership. He was especially proud, he said, of the number of students who had gone on to distinguish themselves in the chemistry departments of some of the state's leading universities, in Madison, Stevens Point, and Eau Claire. He mentioned two students in particular who had become physicians after going to the UW Medical School in Madison.

Casimir Shibilski was next in line. Like the two teachers before him, he spoke in support of the principal and commented that he had had several of the basketball players in his class. For the most part, he said, they were solid students, and respectful. A few, however, were what he called "bad apples" that could spoil the whole bushel if not dealt with. He made it clear that it wasn't because they were athletes that they were delinquent. He himself had been on a college team, and he acknowledged that some of the finest men he knew had been members of that team. He wanted the board to understand that support of Charlie did not mean a lack of support for the sports program.

One by one, the teachers approached the microphones in each aisle to add their supportive comments. Charlie was shocked; maybe he wouldn't get pinned tonight after all.

Orlando DiFabrio, the school custodian, also took the microphone.

"My name is Orlando DiFabrio. I ain't … I mean to say, I'm not a teacher. Fact is, I'm just a janitor at the school, but I'm gonna tell you something … there ain't … I mean to say, there isn't no better boss than this here Mr. Brannigan. When a fellow needs help, Mr. Brannigan is there to help. You know what I mean, eh?" With that, DiFabrio turned and gave the mike to the next person in line.

The last person to speak was Coach Justice. He wore an old Harris Tweed jacket with leather patches on the elbows and cuffs, and a rumpled blue shirt with an oversize tie, probably from his own high school days. Charlie winced as Justice began.

"Good evening. My name is Justice and I'm here to see that we get some." A few people in the audience snickered at his attempt at humor. "I been doing a lot of—I'd guess you'd call it soul-searching— in the last few days. More than just about anything else, I want to be able to keep my team together this season. I know what a few of my boys done over there in Hickey

Woods—" again, a few snickers "—and I'm not sure to this day if it was a prank that got out of hand, or somethin' more serious. In any case, the principal has thought it right to suspend them from athletics for the rest of this year. I tried to talk him out of it, but he's a stubborn man. So am I. But I'm also a team player. Brannigan is the captain of this here team, like it or not, and by the way, sometimes I don't like it. So, like the other teachers you've heard from here tonight, I'm behind him. Anyway, besides, I decided I don't want any bullies on my team. I'm already looking at our junior varsity for some recruits. And I'm sure as hell going to be out there cheering for our girls' team. They're going to do what we had hoped to do—go for that state title. Go Bees."

With that, Coach Justice went back to his seat. Once again, there was a noticeable hush in the audience.

Charlie didn't turn around to look at his teachers. He hadn't gotten pinned, despite the fact that the wrestler's angle, his feud with Catherine Newsome, was apparent, given the diversity of opinions expressed. It wasn't a clear win, but the board would have a hard time firing him with all the faculty support he had received. He wondered whether they were simply moved by Katie's hospitalization—if that had anything to do with their support.

***

Charlie walked into his office early the next morning. After greeting Tricia and taking the mail from his mailbox, he settled in behind his desk and looked out the window, across the girls' soccer field, where early morning frost still tinted the grass. The fields would be quiet now until spring. Beyond the soccer field, the leaves were almost all gone from the trees in Heckney Woods, and Charlie could see all the way to Bear Creek.

It was good to have a moment of quiet. He had gotten up early to feed and change Mary Elizabeth and then to leave her once again with the Chickerings, two doors down. Ruth seemed to enjoy having the baby. Charlie asked if it wasn't getting to be too much for them, but they both insisted that they always looked forward to "little Beth's" visits. At least, he thought, it wouldn't be much longer—Katie should be able to come home by next Monday, if the surgery went as expected.

Charlie had just opened his briefcase when Chet Magnuson knocked and opened the door.

"You got a minute, Charlie? Just wanted to see how you're doing."

"Chet, come in. I was just about to get a note off to the teachers. I wanted to thank them for the support last night. I hope they weren't just feeling sorry for me because of Katie."

"Charlie, Charlie, nobody that I know feels sorry for you. The teachers in this building mostly say what's on their mind and call it like they see it. Anyway, what's up with Katie?"

"Well, you knew she was in the hospital scheduled for surgery later this week."

"Nope, I never heard a word. And I'm pretty sure nobody else has either, or they would have said something."

Charlie swiveled around in his chair to look out across the field. He changed the subject.

"Hey, it must've really gotten cold last night. That frost still hasn't melted off the grass."

"Yeah, winter's here, alright. But tell me more about Katie."

CHAPTER 44

———◆———

"Good afternoon, Mrs. Newsome. I'm Chief Kohlberg, Waumeka Police Department. This is Deputy Colovassi."

"I know who you are," Catherine Newsome replied. She pushed her hair back and took in a deep breath, raising her more than ample bosom. "Is there something wrong?"

"Ma'am, we're here to talk to your son, Tommy. We'd like him to come to the station with us. Is he home?"

"Yes, he just got home from school. But what's this all about, if you don't mind?" She stared back and forth from one officer to the other.

"There was an assault on one of the teachers from the high school last Friday, and I'm afraid your son has been implicated in that incident."

"Well now, then, you certainly have the wrong boy, I can assure you." Another deep breath, another raised bosom. "Not that some of those teachers have not been out to get him. But this just isn't going to wash, do you hear me? Do you realize I'm on the school board, Mr. Kohlberg?"

"Yes, ma'am. We are aware of your position on the school board. Now if we could just talk to your son?"

"I'm afraid you'll have to wait until his father comes home. He'll want our attorney present," Catherine insisted.

"Mrs. Newsome, we have a warrant for your son's arrest. We will certainly read his rights to him, and having an attorney present is one of them."

***

Tommy Newsome sat in the back of the police car as they drove to the station. He appeared too nervous even to question the police who were taking him into custody. By the time they arrived, Tom Newsome and his lawyer, Malcolm Clementford, were already there.

"We'll meet in the conference room," Kohlberg informed them.

Looking at a bandage on Tommy's thumb, the police chief inquired, "Son, what happened to your thumb?"

"Ah, nothing. I was just helping a friend change a tire and I smacked my hand with the tire iron," the boy answered.

"Sounds painful. Tell me, where were you last Friday afternoon?" Kohlberg questioned the boy in a tone that suggested both skill and delicacy.

"You mean after school?" the boy asked.

"Yes, after school."

"Well, I had the car, so I drove a couple friends home and then I went home. Why? What's this all about, anyway?"

"On the way home, would that be the time you helped change somebody's tire for them?"

"Yes, now that I remember it, it was Friday afternoon." the boy replied, gaining confidence.

"And whose tire did you change?"

"Just a friend's."

"Could it have been your teacher, Miss Shelby's?"

"Shelby's? Hey, dude, no way. No."

"That's strange, because the two boys you drove home both said you stopped to change Ann Shelby's flat tire."

"Oh, yeah. I guess maybe it was her. I just forgot."

"You had been drinking. Do you think that's why you forgot?" The chief was patient.

"No, I didn't have nothing to drink."

"Again, Thomas, let me remind you that there were two other boys with you who have both testified. Their independent testimonies corroborate one another. Now, let me ask you again. Were you drinking last Friday afternoon after school?"

"You don't have to answer anything more," the lawyer informed the boy. "They can take you to court if they think you've done something wrong."

"Hey, look, I was just trying to help her with her flat tire. I don't know what's wrong with that."

"Chief, can you tell me what my client is being accused of?" the attorney asked.

"Fourth-degree sexual assault," Kohlberg answered.

"What? What the hell's he talking about?" Tom Newsome blurted out.

"Yeah, what is this?" Tommy echoed.

"That's enough Tommy," his father said. "We'll have to get to the bottom of this."

"Before you leave, you should know that we have a warrant to get a blood test from your son, Mr. Newsome, and before we can release him, we'll need to get the judge to set bail."

Malcolm Clementford stood up and took his long black coat off the rack behind him. Before leaving the room he turned to the chief of police and said, "We'll see you in court, Kohlberg."

CHAPTER 45

———————

Katie Brannigan's surgery was scheduled for nine o'clock, but Charlie got up when his alarm went off at five. After changing Mary Elizabeth and giving her a morning bottle, he dressed her in a striped coverall and then bundled her into a one piece snowsuit with attached mittens and hood against the frosty December morning. He then drove her to her grandparents' across town before going to early Mass at Our Lady of Sorrows.

He got to the hospital by eight o'clock. Katie's room smelled like too much lemon-scented cleaner, or like wood varnish. Although Katie had just gotten her first sedative, she was alert enough that Charlie could talk to her for about fifteen minutes.

He sat on the edge of the bed and put his arms around his wife. "I love you, sweetheart. How do you feel?"

"Goofy right now," Katie giggled, responding to the sedative. "I'm glad they're going to get this thing out of me now, so we can have a good Christmas. We'll have to start writing cards and decorating the house as soon as I get home. How's Mary Elizabeth?"

"She's fine. She's getting spoiled by your parents at the moment. Sweetheart, when you get home, you'll rest on the couch. I can put up a tree and you can watch. If people don't get cards from us this Christmas, we'll send them Valentine's cards. As for cookies, I know a good bakery." They both laughed as the anesthesia took over and Katie slipped into unconsciousness.

Charlie kissed his wife on the cheek and went out of the room, down the hall and through the double doors to the elevator, and down to the cafeteria. He hadn't eaten anything all morning, but the smell of fresh coffee and bacon whetted his appetite. He got a Danish pastry and a glass of orange juice and headed back up to the waiting room on the third floor, where he grabbed a cup of coffee. He finished his Danish, had a few sips of coffee, and then fell asleep in his chair for about an hour. When he awoke, he looked at his watch and then noticed that Katie's friend, Nellie Fromager, was behind the charge nurse's desk. He asked how the surgery was going.

"I've been praying for her all morning," the nurse answered. "We should know in an hour or so. They don't usually tell us anything until it's over. But with Doctor Malone in charge, you can be sure he'll come out and tell us right away. You got the best, Charlie; you know that, don't you?" Malone was the chief surgeon at St. Luke's, a friend of Cliff Smalley, and a highly regarded surgeon throughout the state.

At ten minutes after eleven, Charlie saw the double doors leading to the operating room swing open. Malone, a tall muscular man, marched through the doors and down the hall, maintaining a stride that made it difficult for the two people with him to keep up. He wore blue scrubs. On his left was the head nurse of the surgical team, on his right a young male anesthetist, both wearing light grey scrubs and matching caps. All three had face masks that were untied from the back of their heads and hung down on their chests.

The next five minutes were all a blur for Charlie as he tried to comprehend what he was hearing.

"Transverse colon… serious liver damage … blood loss … complications … anesthesia … peaceful … I'm afraid she's gone, Charlie." As Charlie sank to the floor on his knees, Malone and the nurse knelt down next to him. The nurse and anesthetist tried to lift Charlie, but the surgeon shook his head. They stayed there with him for a few moments without saying anything, as

Charlie sobbed. When he began to hit the sides of his head, Malone put his arm around him and lifted Charlie to a chair. The two men sat together while the nurse and the anesthetist went back into the operating room.

***

After talking to the doctors and signing the necessary papers, Charlie spent the rest of the day and all day Saturday at Katie's parents. He tried to make arrangements for the funeral and care for Mary Elizabeth, but he kept falling asleep. He wanted to console Katie's mother and father, but they appeared to be more composed that he was. On Sunday, they watched Mary Elizabeth while Charlie went to Mass at Our Lady of Sorrows.

He got to church ten minutes early and slumped into a pew at the back of the church. He leaned forward and rested his elbows on the back of the pew in front of him, his head in his hands. The choir practiced the Gregorian chant for the Mass. "*Sobri estote et vigilate*," the choir director intoned. Charlie recognized the psalms and muttered. "Oh, right. The second Sunday of Advent, the time of waiting. *Sobri estote et vigilate*."

Charlie rapped his forehead on the pew. "Remain sober?" he thought. "Be watchful? Good God, what for? I've been sober and watchful for almost forty-five years. I've been waiting for you, and when you come, it's to take away my love. I thought you were a God of love. Is this the way you love people?" He began to cry.

Just then, Charlie felt a hand on his shoulder. He turned to Cliff Smalley kneeling next to him. Wiping his eyes on his overcoat sleeve, Charlie said, "Cliff, what are you doing here? You don't go to church."

"I know," Cliff responded. "But I figured I'd find you here. I heard about Katie on Friday at the hospital, but you haven't been home. And we haven't seen any lights at your place. I just wondered how you were doing."

"I've been over at Katie's parents," Charlie whispered.

"That's what we figured. Is there anything we can do? Sally's home all day now, if you need someone to look after Mary Elizabeth. Chickerings say the same thing. I talked to them last night and told them I was going to find you."

"The funeral's Tuesday morning, right here. Can you come?" Charlie asked.

"Yes, of course. And call me. Do you hear me, Brannigan? Call me if you need anything at all, or if you just want to talk."

"I will," Charlie answered.

***

The funeral Mass was at nine o'clock Tuesday morning. It was a clear, cold day with temperatures hovering near twenty degrees below zero. As people walked up to the church, hats pulled down and scarves wrapped around their necks, the snow squeaked under their feet. Charlie's parents had come up from Madison. They left Mary Elizabeth with the Chickerings. Dan Chickering apologized for not going to the church, but said that it wouldn't be safe for Ruth to go out in the cold and that they'd be happy to take care of the baby instead.

As Charlie looked out over the field across the street from the Church, he noticed a rainbow in the sky. He was puzzled; it was a clear, sunny day, although frigid. Ice crystals had formed on the trees and bushes, and he could see his own breath. He wanted to ask his father if he could see the rainbow, but he felt silly, so he kept it to himself. What if there was no rainbow? What if it was just his imagination playing tricks on him?

Our Lady of Sorrows began to fill up quickly as parishioners, friends, relatives, and neighbors hurried up the steps and poured in through the massive oak doors. Figuring there would be a large crowd, Father O'Shaunessy had instructed the altar boys to put up folding chairs in the two side aisles and instruct people that they could also go into the "cry" room at the back of the church, or upstairs in the choir loft. As it turned out, there was just enough room to accommodate everyone.

Charlie turned around and noticed Aaron Kohlberg and several of the police officers, as well as a good number of students and teachers from the high school. Chet Magnuson, who was acting principal at the high school while Charlie took bereavement leave, was in the back row. Chet had suspended classes for the morning, so that any student, teacher, or staff member who wanted to go to the funeral could do so. Charlie remembered that Chet's own wife had died ten years earlier and been buried from First Presbyterian.

In her heavy blue pea coat with the collar turned up, Ann Shelby sat next to Chet. Next to her was a whole row of teachers. When she saw Charlie, Ann left her seat and came up to shake his hand and express her sympathy.

Several members of the school board and a number of nurses and doctors had taken their places in the crowded church. Charlie lowered his head and thought about the fact that this was the second time in four months that his friends had gathered for a funeral—first for Kathleen Marie, and now for Kathleen Marie's mother, his dear wife. He began to cry.

CHAPTER 46

———◆———

harlie Brannigan took two days off from work after his wife's funeral. His in-laws came to stay with him for a week, to help out. He decided that by Thursday, he would go back to the office for at least a half day. When he got to the school early that morning, Tricia Cameron was already there.

"Trish, you're here early," Charlie said as he walked through the main office, taking off his heavy overcoat.

"Mr. Brannigan, I didn't realize you'd be coming back to school this soon. I've been trying to come in early to help Mr. Magnuson get the day started before he has to go teach his own classes. We've had a few calls for you. One was from an Amber Cartwright. I think she might be Jim Cartwright's sister?"

"Amber Cartwright? Oh, I know who that is. It's Lou's wife. Lou is Jim's brother. I'll call her right away. Then after I go through the mail, maybe you can come in and fill me in on what's happened in the last three days."

Charlie closed the door to his office behind him. On the coffee table to the right of his desk was a large bouquet of red roses with a card placed in front of the vase. On the envelope was printed in large letters, "FOR CHARLIE FROM YOUR STAFF."

He turned and looked out the window toward Heckney Woods. Leaves still clung to some of the oak trees, and snow clung to both leaves and branches. Charlie could see all the way to Bear Creek, which was covered with a sheet of ice. *Katie would have loved to go skating down there*, he thought. Just then, he heard a knock at the door.

"Come in," he called. It was Ann Shelby. She stood at the door for a moment, looking in at the principal as if to assess his emotional state.

"How are you doing?" she asked.

"Well, I won't say fine, but I'm here. Thanks for asking, and thanks for coming to the funeral. I really appreciated seeing so many of you."

"I just wanted to find out how you and Mary Elizabeth are doing, and I wanted to ask if there is anything I can do. Anything at all. "

"Thanks. Can you sit down for a few minutes? You don't have class first hour, do you?" Ann Shelby sat on the couch behind the coffee table. The two spoke for about five minutes, until the telephone rang. Tricia Cameron told Charlie that it was Mrs. Amber Cartwright on the line. Charlie put his hand over the telephone and turned to Ann.

"I'd better answer this. Thanks for coming in. I'll get back to you. And I promise I'll let you know whenever I need a helping hand. I appreciate the offer." He spoke into the phone. "Hi, Mrs. Cartwright. This is Charlie Brannigan. How have you been doing?"

"Mr. Brannigan, Jim told Lou and me about your wife dying. We were really sorry. We wanted to go to the funeral, but Lou had to work on Tuesday. So, the reason I'm calling is to let you know we can help out. If you need someone to cook a meal, or help with the baby, I'm pretty good with babies, and I could come over and everything."

"Well, that's a very nice offer, Mrs. Cartwright."

"No, just call me Amber. That's my first name, Amber. But you wouldn't have to pay us or nothing. We just wanna help. We remember last year at this time. Remember? Just before Christmas, how you and your missus came to help us out? Well, we're back on our feet again. We'll never forget that, Mr. Brannigan. It was you that suggested Lou get hisself into AA. Well, he done what you said. I don't know if I should tell you this, but Dr. Smalley is his sponsor over there at AA. And you know something—it's really helping. Oh, he's fallen once or twice, but not like before.

"And he's back at Fleet Farm, in hardware this time. He's done real good. Fact, they gave him a Christmas bonus this year. They only do that for the ones that's really done a good job. So we got you to thank, Mr. Brannigan. Now you just let us help you out. I could bring little Rainbow with me and just stay over at your place whenever you need, or you could bring Mary Elizabeth to us. You just let us know. By the way, Lou says hi. He's the one that wanted me to call after Jimmy told him about the funeral and all—"

"Well, that's very nice, Mrs., uh, Amber," Charlie broke in. "It's really good to know that I can ask you to babysit with Mary Elizabeth. I'll try to call you this weekend and maybe we can make some sort of arrangement. You're right, it really would be a big help. Be sure to say hello to Lou for me, and tell him to keep up the good work. You should both be really proud. Thanks again for the call."

Charlie stood up and went to the coffee table to smell the roses. He picked up the card and opened it. It was a sympathy card, with a blank inside so that all the teachers and staff could sign their names and a greeting:

Let us share your burden. —Chet
May you find comfort. —Tricia
Shalom, Charlie. May G-d comfort you and be with you in your time of need.
—Sam
God bless you. And thanks for steering this ship straight. —Justice
Peace and love. —Ann
Margaret and I will have a Mass said. Pax et bonum. —Casimir

***

While Katie's parents watched Mary Elizabeth, Charlie spent Saturday afternoon getting his oil changed, grocery shopping for the coming week, and shoveling the walk. Katie's mother, Karen, found the cleaning supplies in the laundry room and vacuumed and dusted, while Katie's father, Dave, watched the Green Bay Packers, Mary Elizabeth asleep on his lap.

Charlie finished shoveling the walk, set his shovel against the house, and went in the side door. He could smell a stew cooking on the stove, and his mother-in-law had been baking and left a plate of brownies on the kitchen counter. After he shook the snow off his coat and hung it up on the hook, he grabbed the plate of brownies and headed for the family room, where both baby and grandpa were dozing. Charlie set the brownies on the coffee table and went back into the kitchen to get two bottles of Point Amber beer and two glasses. When he came back, Katie's father had woken up and was repositioning Mary Elizabeth in his lap.

"How can the Packers play in this weather?" Charlie asked.

"Oh, they're playing in Indianapolis," Dave answered. "Anyway, they're losing to the Colts, big time." Charlie looked up at the TV screen just in time to see the Packers' running back grab a long pass, dodge every Colt in sight, and head forty-five yards downfield into the end zone.

"Looks like they haven't lost yet," he said.

"You're right. They might still have a chance. They just needed you in here watching."

"Where's Karen?" Charlie asked.

"Oh, she's upstairs napping. Got a lot of cleaning done this morning. Think she wore herself out."

The two men sat and watched the fourth quarter. The Packers almost pulled it out, but not quite. They ended up losing to the Indianapolis Colts, forty-one to thirty-eight.

As they watched the post game show, Charlie got up to answer the doorbell.

"Oh, I forgot to tell you. There's a couple called here a while back—said they were coming over with our dinner for tonight," Dave called out to Charlie.

"What about Karen's stew?"

"She said that'll be just as good tomorrow," Dave answered.

Lou and Amber Cartwright were at the door with a pot roast, carrots, and potatoes in a Crock Pot. Lou carried their baby, Rainbow.

"We just wanted to help out," Amber said as she walked into the kitchen and put the Crock Pot on the kitchen table. "And like I said, I can help out with Mary Elizabeth."

"Well, thank you. Can you come in and sit for a few minutes?" Charlie asked.

"Just for a bit, but we won't stay," Lou answered. "Rainbow is just about to fall asleep."

They went into the family room, where Dave had just turned off the TV and was getting up to leave. He stopped long enough for Charlie to introduce him to the Cartwrights. Then he excused himself to join his wife upstairs, carrying Mary Elizabeth with him.

Without taking off their coats, Amber and Lou sat on the couch and talked with Charlie about their desire to help with the baby. Lou held Rainbow on his lap.

"You know, I really would appreciate that," Charlie replied. "Katie's parents will be leaving on Monday, and our neighbors, the Chickerings, will take Mary Elizabeth on Tuesday and Thursday. Do you think I could bring her over to your place on Wednesday and Friday?"

"Sure, or if you like I could come over here to your place and bring Rainbow with me. Lou could bring me over on his way to work, couldn't you Lou? And if it works out OK for you, Mr. Brannigan, we could probably make that a regular schedule, couldn't we, Lou?"

"If we do that," Charlie insisted, "you'll have to let me pay you at least something. And by the way, call me Charlie." He was comfortable with the Cartwrights, knowing how careful Amber was with their own baby. With Sally next door and the Chickerings down the street, Mary Elizabeth would be well cared for, and Amber could turn to them if she needed to.

CHAPTER 47

It was six months before Tommy Newsome came to trial. The school year had ended without any further complications from irate parents. Catherine Newsome resigned her position on the school board in protest, and the basketball team had done an adequate job, considering that their best players had to sit out the season. Graduation had gone off smoothly, and Charlie's life was getting back to a semblance of normal. Mary Elizabeth spent her days with the Chickerings or the Cartwrights and her evenings with Charlie. Whenever Charlie went out in the evening or on a weekend, he called Katie's parents to babysit, either at Charlie's or at their place.

The June weather in Waumeka was pleasant but cool. Most people still wore spring jackets or sweaters, which wasn't really unusual for that part of Wisconsin. The morning of the trial was bright and sunny but still cool enough for a sweater.

"Order in the court. Will everyone please rise." The clerk turned toward the door behind him and waited for Judge Brammont Billsley to enter. "Hear ye! Hear ye! Hear ye! The Circuit Court for the County of Pinecone is now open. Silence is commanded."

Malcolm Clementford smiled when the judge took his place and said, "Please be seated." As defense attorney, Clementford was pleased that they were in Billsley's courtroom. The judge was known to be lenient with young offenders, unlike his counterpart down the hall, Alicia Cornwall, who would just as soon put sex offenders behind bars for the rest of their lives, regardless of their age. Billsley was a respected jurist who had been the circuit court judge in Waumeka for more than twenty-five years. He knew most of the families in town and hobnobbed with the wealthy at the North Pinecone Country Club.

"Let's begin. First of all, could somebody please explain to me why this case isn't being handled in juvenile court?"

The district attorney, Josiah Singleton, stood up. He was a short man whose stature was made even shorter by a congenital condition that left his lower spine so curved that his upper body leaned forward. From the waist up, his body leaned forward at a forty-five-degree angle from his lower body. As a result, he had to raise his head and keep his chin up in order to look straight ahead.

"Your honor, the defendant is seventeen years old, an adult in the eyes of the Wisconsin law."

"All right, all right, you can assume I know the law. I understand the defendant has waived his right to a jury trial. How does he plead?"

Malcolm Clementford stood up behind the defense table, adjusted his bow tie, and answered, "My client pleads guilty, Your Honor, but the defense intends to show that there are mitigating circumstances that lessen his culpability."

In a brief opening statement, Josiah Singleton stated that on the afternoon of December 8, while two of his classmates were changing a tire for one of their teachers, the defendant, Thomas Newsome, Jr., pushed her onto the back seat of her car, forcefully removed her underwear, and attempted sexual intercourse. The classmates in question were in the courtroom and would be called as witnesses. Ms. Shelby was also in the courtroom, although Singleton had no intention of calling her as a witness.

In the opening statement offered by the defense, Clementford acknowledged that his client had "touched his teacher inappropriately." But he stated that the defense would prove that the so-called victim, Ms. Shelby, was actually a perpetrator in that she was obviously and continuously seductive in the classroom and that the adolescent males whom she taught were tormented by her open display of sexuality. She had been seen by students, for example, in a sexual encounter with one of her colleagues in the school corridor. He added that the defendant's school record, his leadership in high school athletics, and the complete lack of any previous record of criminal or delinquent behavior would also be mitigating factors. He did not mention the lawsuit brought against his client by John Hastings, which had been settled out of court.

"I would like to call ..." The prosecution brought a parade of witnesses to the stand: the nurse practitioner who had examined the victim and found that no intromission had taken place; the police officer who had inspected the crime scene and found Ms. Shelby's panties beside the road near her car; the lab technician who had examined the blood on those panties and found that it matched the blood of the accused, Tommy Newsome. The defense insisted on only a few cross-examinations.

When it was the defense's turn to examine witnesses, Clementford began with the defendant. Tommy Newsome wore a blue blazer with a white shirt and a tie. His shoes were polished and his trousers pressed; his hair was combed and he looked for all the world like a male model for *Teen* magazine.

"Have you ever had Ms. Shelby as a teacher?" the attorney began.

"Yes, in tenth grade she was my algebra teacher."

"Was she a good teacher?"

"I didn't think so. Nobody knew what she wanted, and she couldn't explain things so you could understand them. Actually I don't think I learned anything from her that I didn't already know."

"And how did she treat the boys?"

"Well, she was kind of a flirt, always lifting her skirt up when she went to sit down. She always wore tight sweaters. It was kind of distracting, if you know what I mean."

On cross-examination, Singleton introduced himself to the boy and then asked, "You mention that you didn't learn much from Ms. Shelby during the term she taught you algebra. How many nights during the week would you say you studied algebra for at least thirty minutes that term?"

"I can't remember," Newsome said.

"In fact, can you recall ever bringing your algebra book home to study, even once?"

"I'm not sure," the boy mumbled.

"I'm sorry. I didn't hear you. Could you speak up, please?"

"No, I don't think I did bring my book home. But I didn't need to. I knew the stuff," Tommy Newsome answered

"And how did you do in your other courses that term? I mean, what grades did you get?"

"I got mostly Cs and two Ds," the boy replied

"I see. You also mentioned that Ms. Shelby dressed provocatively. Oh, by the way, when she sat down in class, where would that be?"

"What do you mean?" Newsome asked

"I mean, was there a chair for her to sit on?"

"Yes, behind her desk," the boy responded.

"Behind her desk. But you said you could see her hike her skirt up when she sat down. That would be quite impossible to see, wouldn't it, if she was behind her desk? But then, perhaps it was your imagination."

"Objection," Clementford yelled.

"Sustained," the judged responded.

"No further questions, Your Honor."

Next, the defense called Tommy's father, Tom Newsome, to the stand.

"Mr. Newsome, have you ever met the teacher in question?" Clementford began.

"Yes, I met her in the fall last year, at a parent-teacher conference," Newsome answered.

"And what was your impression of her?"

"Her classroom was a complete mess. She didn't seem to have a handle on what she was teaching."

"And how did she strike you personally? Would you say she was seductive?"

"Good God, yes. Tommy's absolutely right on that one. I'd say the way she dressed was definitely provocative. Tight sweater, short skirt, that sort of thing. Certainly not appropriate for a high school teacher with a roomful of adolescent boys."

"Thank you, no further questions, Your Honor."

Clementford sat down. Singleton rose and stood, stooped, behind the prosecutor's table. He turned around to face the courtroom. He raised his head so he could see to the back of the room and said, "Ms. Shelby." The teacher stood in her place at the back of the room.

"Could you please step to the aisle and stand there for a moment?" the prosecutor asked. Ann Shelby, dressed in a white blouse and a paisley pencil skirt, did as she was asked.

"Mr. Newsome," Singleton began, "Would you take a close look at Ms. Shelby and tell me if you think she is provocatively dressed today?"

"No, of course not," the witness answered. "She's in a courtroom. She knows how to dress to make the impression she wants."

"And what impression would that be?" Singleton asked.

"Of someone, a professional, who is modest and demure," Newsome answered.

"So you would say she is not provocatively dressed. Would you say she is actually modestly dressed today? Would you go that far?" the prosecutor asked.

"Yes, but like I said, that's not the way she usually dresses."

"So you would say she is modestly dressed. Would it surprise you, Mr. Newsome, to learn that the clothes Ms. Shelby is wearing today are exactly the same clothes she was wearing when she saw you and approximately twenty other parents at the parent-teacher conference? Thank you, Ms. Shelby. You may sit down. No further questions, Your Honor."

"Thank you, Mr. Newsome, you may take your place," the judge said. Newsome turned bright red, scowled at the prosecuting attorney, and mumbled something under his breath as he took his seat.

Finally, the defense called Charlie Brannigan, principal of Waumeka High School, to the stand.

"Before you begin, Mr. Clementford, I'd like to make a comment," the judge interjected. "Mr. Brannigan, before you begin your testimony, I want to express the sympathy of the court on your recent loss. Has it really been six months already?"

"Yes, Your Honor."

"Well, Mrs. Brannigan was an important member of the Waumeka community and she is sorely missed. I just want you to know that our thoughts and prayers have been with you."

"Thank you, Your Honor," Charlie answered.

The judge turned to Clementford and said, "You may continue, Councilor."

"Mr. Brannigan, how long has Ms. Shelby taught at Waumeka High?"

"Four years," Brannigan answered.

"Four years. And I understand she has been the center of a controversy during that time. Didn't a group of parents try to get the school board to have her dismissed?"

"Yes, but—"

"Please just answer the question, Mr. Brannigan. So she is a controversial teacher. And what were the reasons that the parents wanted her dismissed? Didn't the reasons deal with a lack of confidence in her ability as a teacher and rumors to the effect that she had been involved in inappropriate sexual conduct with a fellow teacher in the hallway?"

"Objection, Your Honor." Josiah Singleton raised his head and tried to sit up straight behind the prosecutor's table so that he could look up at the judge. "The councilor is answering his own question and putting words in the witness's mouth."

"Sustained."

"I'm done, Your Honor," Clementford concluded.

Singleton stood up and looked at Charlie for a few seconds before beginning. "I would like to add my personal condolences to those of the court, Mr. Brannigan," he began.

"Thank you, sir. I certainly appreciate that." Charlie appeared battered and confused after being questioned by the defense attorney.

"Mr. Brannigan, could you tell me something about Ms. Shelby? Is she a good teacher in your opinion?"

"One of the best."

"Then how do you reconcile that view with the observation made by the defense that parents wanted her dismissed?"

"It was a small group, including Tommy Newsome's parents and some mothers and fathers whose children were not doing well in Ann Shelby's class. I thought they had an axe to grind."

"An axe to grind. Well, is there any solid evidence that she is a good teacher? I think you said, 'one of the best'?" Singleton asked.

"Well, yes. I believe that the success of our students is the best indicator of the success of our teachers. Since Ann's been teaching our math courses, we've sent three students to the state competitions in mathematics. It's a highly prestigious honor even to be selected to compete, and last year one of our students came home with the state championship. Several of our students have gone to Madison, Stevens Point, and Oshkosh to major in mathematics. I understand that two of Ann's first students they were seniors when she first came to teach with us—have been accepted for graduate study in math, one to Yale and the other to UW-Madison. I'm not saying she should get all the credit for their success, but it is only fair to acknowledge that she helped to get them started on their way. She got them enthusiastic about math. They have written back and told us so." Charlie began to draw a letter out of his coat pocket.

"That won't be necessary, Mr. Brannigan. I'm sure the court takes the principal's word for that. Is there any other evidence of her ability?" asked the prosecutor.

"Yes, three years ago we instituted a teacher evaluation procedure, including peer reviews and student evaluations. Mr. Shibilski, her senior colleague in the mathematics department, sits in on her classes and evaluates her teaching. Students also have an opportunity to evaluate her performance. Ms. Shelby gets high marks on both fronts. Nobody, by the way, has ever mentioned inappropriate behavior," Charlie replied.

"Now about this so-called 'sexual encounter' with one of her colleagues in the hall. Could you explain that?"

Charlie explained that it was a one-time offense, if it could even be called an offence. Nobody had witnessed anything other than a simple kiss on the cheek. In addition, he had both teachers' assurance that such behavior would not take place in the school again, and to his knowledge, they had kept their word. And since then, he explained, the other teacher had been promoted to an assistant principal's position in Stevens Point.

"Thank you, Mr. Brannigan," the attorney concluded.

Since neither attorney had any more witnesses to call, Singleton gave a brief closing statement for the prosecution. He again explained to the court that Tommy Newsome was an adult, who knew what he was doing when he assaulted Ann Shelby and should be punished accordingly. There was no question of his guilt, since it had already been admitted, and nothing in the defense's case impressed him that the boy should get a lenient sentence.

Judge Billsley looked toward the back of the room, where Ann Shelby sat in the back row next to Charlie Brannigan. He looked around the room and then back at the defense attorney, who was about to begin his closing statement.

For the defense, Malcolm Clementford argued that the boy's age—he was only seventeen—should be a mitigating factor, as well as his good school record, and the fact that he had no previous court record. He pointed to the fact that Tommy came from a good, stable family. He did admit that the boys had been drinking that afternoon, "as boys will do on a Friday afternoon," but suggested that such behavior was not only age-appropriate but had impaired Tommy's judgment, which should also be seen as a mitigating circumstance. He again pressed the argument that, despite the principal's assertions to the contrary, Ms. Shelby had created an atmosphere in her class and in the school that was conducive to adolescent overreacting.

"Of course the principal will defend her," he said. "That's his role and, frankly, his duty. Parents, on the other hand, see a different Ms. Shelby, namely one who makes herself overly attractive to her male students. This, Your Honor, should be taken into account."

When he had finished, Judge Brammont Billsley leaned forward. Looking over the top of his glasses, he glared at the two attorneys, first one and then the other.

"Gentlemen," he began, "I'm frankly appalled. Rather than focusing on the accused, both of you have managed to turn this morning's proceedings into the trial of a teacher who has admittedly been assaulted." He looked to the back of the room. "Ms. Shelby, on behalf of the court, let me say that I am sorry this has happened."

He turned back to the attorneys, who stood behind their tables. "There is no question but that this young man is guilty of the crime he has already admitted. The only reason for these long proceedings is the determination of any mitigating circumstances.

"Mr. Clementford, I'm afraid that you haven't convinced me that there is anything in this boy's record or behavior that suggests I should be lenient. He is, as the prosecutor so quickly pointed out, legally an adult. Furthermore, the idea that alcohol abuse in a young adult should excuse other criminal behavior is ludicrous. You know perfectly well that voluntary intoxication is not a defense to general-intent crimes such as rape. Any notion that he has an exemplary record at school is equally silly. Aside from his lackluster grades, I seem to recall an item in the newspaper a while back about a beating that one of our high school boys sustained at the hands of his teammates. Wasn't Tommy Newsome one of those boys? Is this the exemplary behavior you're referring to? Finally, the fact that this young man comes from a prosperous and well-known family should in no way exonerate him or place him above the law. If anything, the opposite is true. More should be expected of him. Luckily for him, the law is blind and treats us all equally.

"I'll pass sentence once I have had a chance to read the sentencing report. Everyone here should be aware, however, that the maximum sentence for fourth-degree sexual assault is imprisonment in the county jail for not more than nine months and/or a fine not to exceed ten thousand dollars. This is a serious matter. You can expect to be back here within six weeks. This court is now adjourned."

As Malcolm Clementford began to gather the papers in front of him, he leaned over to his young client, who sat slumped in the chair next to him. "Don't worry, Tommy, we still have the sentencing phase. We get another chance to convince Judge Billsley."

Tommy's father, sitting behind the attorney, grabbed his shoulder and spat out, "Jesus, Malcolm, I thought you said you knew Billsley. Now what the hell do we do?"

***

At the back of the room, Ann Shelby tried to get into the jacket she had left on the back of her seat. Seeing her struggle, Charlie lifted the coat for her and helped her get it on. He left his hand on her shoulder for a second. As if out of the distant past, an old, familiar wave of pleasure and quiet satisfaction ran through him.

"Can we go for lunch?" he asked, as the teacher looked up at him with a smile.

"I'd like that," she replied. "I'd like that very much." She took his arm as she stood up from the wooden chair.

That evening Charlie called his neighbor. "Cliff, I'm ready to start playing cards again. Count me in for Wednesday night. Despite it all, Cliff, I'm feeling lucky."

Epilogue

———◆———

Waumeka High started the new school year with Charlie Brannigan once again clearly at the helm—and minus one of its more notorious students. Having been found guilty of fourth-degree sexual assault, Tommy Newsome was sentenced to nine months in the Ethan Allen School for Boys, a juvenile correctional institution in Wales, Wisconsin. Attempts by the defense to besmirch the reputation of Ann Shelby failed miserably.

As a result of her son's conviction and subsequent negative publicity, Catherine Newsome resigned her position on the school board. In the wake of her departure, two other board members resigned at the first meeting in the fall, and three new board members were elected. The new board vowed to work together with the vindicated Charlie Brannigan to develop the sort of school he had envisioned. Part of that vision was to have a college prep honor's math program headed by Ann Shelby, for whom his respect and affection continued to grow.

With the program just under way, Ann received the Edith Mae Sliffe award, a national recognition of her outstanding teaching in math, and then applied to UW-Eau Claire to pursue a graduate degree. Although Charlie couldn't grant her a leave of absence, he did promise that he would welcome her back when she finished her studies. He lost his favorite teacher for two years but gained the chance to visit her regularly—away from the glaring scrutiny of Waumeka students and parents. The back-country road between Waumeka and Eau Claire, with its rows of old oak trees, its farm houses and barns, was well travelled for those two years. By the time Ann returned to Waumeka High, she was wearing the engagement ring that Charlie had given her.

ABOUT THE AUTHOR

John Paul McKinney holds a PhD degree in developmental and clinical psychology from Ohio State University. He has taught at McGill, Smith College, and Michigan State University in Psychology and in Pediatrics and Human Development.

Author of over 75 articles, chapters, encyclopedia entries and widely used text books, and former North American book reviews editor for the international Journal of Adolescence, McKinney has also written short stories, one of which won an award (Writers-Editors Network International Competition – Honorable mention) and another of which was published in The Mountain Scribe Anthology. This is his first novel.

9345608R00161

Made in the USA
San Bernardino, CA
13 March 2014